THE
BOXER

THE BOXER

Nikesh Shukla

Hodder Children's Books
An imprint of Hachette Children's Group
Part of Hodder and Stoughton

An Hachette UK Company

Hodder
Children's
Books

HODDER CHILDREN'S BOOKS
First published in Great Britain in 2019 by Hodder Children's Books

1 3 5 7 9 10 8 6 4 2

Copyright © Nikesh Shukla, 2019

The moral right of the author has been asserted.

A CIP catalogue record for this book
is available from the British Library.

ISBN 978 1 44494 069 5

Typeset by Hewer Text UK Ltd, Edinburgh
Printed and bound by CPI Group (UK) Ltd, Croydon CR0 4YY

The paper and board used in this book are
made from wood from responsible sources.

For Sunnie and Coco

The fight is won or lost far away from witnesses –
behind the lines, in the gym and out there on the
road, long before I dance under those lights.

Muhammad Ali

Round 1

The bell rings and my paws are up. I'm on my toes, dancing under the lights, ball of foot to ball of foot, edging backwards, letting him come to me. I've seen him training – heck, I've even sparred with him a bit, so I know he's always on the front foot, no defence, so I figure I just have to let him come, absorb what blows I can and concentrate on the counterpunch. Here we are, in front of our witnesses, a long way from the gym, and the road and the shadow-boxing in front of the floor-length mirror. Under these lights, it's just Keir and me.

Neither of us thought it would come to this.

I wipe sweat off my forehead with both my gloves and bang them together, baring my teeth at my opponent. My mouthguard tastes stale and salty. It feels alien in my mouth.

He winks at me as he comes closer, moving with confidence.

It feels like an age ago that Shobu clasped my hands together, winked and told me I could do this. It's been less than ten minutes in reality, but all time has slowed

1

down. The lights whirring around us are so bright that I squint. I don't notice Keir stepping in quickly and snapping a jab in my face. I'm turning away as fast as I can so I manage to dodge the majority of the blow. But he's on me now. His gloves touch mine and he's driving his entire body into me, pushing me back towards the ropes. I can hear Shobu screaming for me to duck and weave, keep moving. I can hear the crowd crying out for Keir. It's my first proper match and I know he's more experienced than me. I just have to summon up the confidence from somewhere.

Shobu shouts, 'Sunny, just keep moving. Stop waiting for it to happen . . .'

I flick my eyes back towards her, in my corner.

My hesitation costs me, as Keir lands a cross on my cheek, knocking me off balance.

It's my fault.

1.1

It all started six months ago, when Mum told me she was going to teach me to cook.

She had agreed to take on a third night shift at a hotel in town, adding to her main job working at Tesco.

'I'm so worried about you eating properly,' she told me, 'but I don't have time to do anything.'

'I can make us food. I can clean too . . .' I told her.

'Beta, it is kind of you.'

'I know.' I smirked. 'Number one son, that's me.'

'Who can't cook.'

I laughed. 'How hard can it be? Look,' I said, grabbing her hand. 'I can keep things going here. You do what you need to do.'

'Listen, my number one son . . . my only son,' she said. 'Thank you, Sunny. But don't let it distract you from your studies . . .'

The next night she came home with a hundred frozen samosas and a big jar of tamarind sauce from Sweet Mart. She found room for the samosas in the icebox, while I put the jar in amongst the tins that had migrated with us from London. She showed me how to operate the oven so I could heat up enough samosas a day for snacks for us both and she wrote down a recipe for chana masala that, she said, was the

3

first thing she ever learned to cook. I wondered if Mum felt the same pang I did at that moment – the pang of passing along something precious. The moment came and went and she told me to stand up on a chair and reach for a plastic bag from the top of the kitchen cabinets. She had one foot on my chair to steady me and her hands up, ready to receive. I pulled the bag off the shelf. It was surprisingly heavy. And the inside was filled with dust. Like the bag hadn't been opened in years. I coughed as a sprinkle of tiny particles descended on the room like a mist. Mum told me to be careful. I thrust the bag at her and coughed into the crease of my elbow – the vampire cough – like I'd been taught by the Macmillan nurse. That way, I avoided spreading germs to Dad.

I got down off the chair and looked at Mum. I waited.

'What's in there?' I asked, wiping more dust off the surface of the bag with my index finger.

She smiled. 'On my wedding day, your ba decided to give me a rice cooker as a present. That was how I knew she did not like me.'

She pulled a white plastic machine out of the bag. It looked unused but a bit old-fashioned. She set it down on the table and stared at it.

'How do you mean?' I asked.

'Who the hell doesn't know how to cook rice? It was her way of telling me that I couldn't cook at all, and that I would never be good enough for your dad. Anyway, I'm glad I kept it. It finally has some use.'

'*I* don't know how to cook rice,' I said, shooting her a look.

'Darling,' Mum said, placing a hand on my cheek. 'Rice is very easy. This will just save you time. You're already doing a lot.'

'So . . . do you think it even still works?' I asked her as she placed the rice cooker between the kettle and the toaster. 'There's dust everywhere.'

She shook her head as if to say, *One thing at a time.*

'Let's get the chana masala right,' she said. 'Then we can negotiate rice.'

She threw me an onion and pointed to the handwritten recipe.

'What? Now?'

'Yes, baba,' she replied. 'Let's practise. I have thirty minutes before I need to go.'

'There aren't any measurements,' I said.

'You think I grew up with measuring cups and spoons? Everything I learned by hand and by taste. So will you . . .'

I looked at the onion. Suddenly it dawned on me – what I had suggested was ridiculous. I'd nearly burned the flat down a few weeks ago because I'd put buttered bread in the toaster. The toaster had shorted at the socket. The toast had smoked and caught alight. All the butter had leaked out of the bottom.

We hadn't replaced the toaster yet. Mum had left it there on the kitchen counter, plugged in, as a gentle warning to me to be careful. It still had ashy marks around the socket from the sparks. I hadn't had toast since. The kitchen still smelled, every now and then, of singed bread, even underneath the sizzling onions and garlic, cumin seeds and every other spice Mum used; a constant reminder of the time I'd tried to feed Dad breakfast and wanted to save time cos a World Cup match had been on.

Mum handed me a knife. It was black-handled and serrated. She'd had this knife for as long as I could

5

remember. The handle had worn away from overuse and it didn't look particularly sharp but I attacked the onion anyway. I cut it down the middle. My eyes watered. I rubbed at them with my fingertips. Mum stood over me, tutting and sighing as I struggled to keep my eyes open enough to chop everything up. Eventually, she took over and pointed at the hob.

'Heat up some oil,' she said. 'Then when you see bubbles, add a teaspoon of cumin seeds.'

I lit the hob and placed a saucepan on it, adding a dollop of sunflower oil from the bottle. When bubbles appeared, I opened Mum's spice tin and stared at the contents. Which ones were the cumin seeds? Were they the small black balls? The rugby-ball-shaped grey things with stripes?

Sensing my hesitation, Mum leant over and pointed at the right container. I spooned the cumin seeds into the bubbling oil and watched as they sizzled. A second later, Mum added the onions and the whole house was filled with that smell – the smell of Mum's cooking.

She pointed to a jar she'd taken out of the fridge.

'Lazy garlic, for the lazy cook,' she said.

She spooned half a teaspoon in and stirred everything.

We let it cook down for a bit before adding a tin of chopped tomatoes, garam masala, ground cumin and coriander, turmeric, chilli powder and ginger. I stirred until the curry had turned brown and was bubbling away. I was actually enjoying this. I was learning from a master. Mum's cooking was the best. She handed me an opened tin of drained chana and I added them and stirred.

Mum stood with her hand slightly raised, brushing my elbow. As I stirred, she pressed her cheek into my bicep.

With my free hand, I rubbed at the back of Mum's head. She yawned, then pointed to the rice cooker.

'Now we need to figure out how the damn thing works,' she said.

1·2

The following day, I was sitting on the train to college. I had woken up late.

There'd been shouting in the flat next to us last night, and a loud TV blaring out what sounded like one of the *Fast & Furious* films in the basement flat below, and, for no reason I could think of, a long fireworks display somewhere nearby. I'd been thinking about Dad, all alone in the hospice. He'd been in there for three weeks. Mum went every day on her way home, but I just couldn't bring myself to go see him. I imagined he was mad at me for staying away. But he was so out of it all the time, he probably hadn't even noticed. What a way to be alive – to not even really notice it.

Not that I cared.

Lying awake, with no one else around me, this was when all the things I tried to block out of my head crept in. Questions rolling and rolling around, like: *Why don't you want to see your dad? What's wrong with you? Don't you care? What if it's too late? Why are you so selfish?* I couldn't make them stop. So I'd lain in bed, staring at the ceiling, listening to explosions and gunfire peppered with bursts of happy reggaeton on the television below me. The more the questions had stayed in my head, the more I'd found them incomprehensible. Desperate, I'd tried whispering into the darkness. Was I talking to Dad? To myself? Either way, saying the words out loud, giving them breath, had been better than letting them all clog up my brain.

'Maybe I'm scared because I know he's gonna die and I just want to remember him in a way that feels real, not the him that's ill. Maybe it doesn't matter. We barely spoke anyway . . . even when we watched football and cricket. It's not like he was there for me, you know? Not when it counted. But he's my dad! He's my *dad* . . . I should go . . . Whatever our differences, I need to make my peace with them before it's too late. But how can I forget about the bad stuff? How can I forgive?'

I'd stopped talking when I'd heard Mum come in around 2 a.m. She didn't need to hear any of this.

At college, my mate Madhu sniffed at me as we waited to go into our History class.

'You smell nice,' she said, raising an eyebrow.

I sniffed at myself. I couldn't smell anything.

'Who stinks of curry?' someone said as they walked past.

I looked at Madhu. She had her Golden State Warriors cap pulled down so low it was touching her big red glasses.

'Oh, he's talking about you,' she said. 'I think you smell delicious. Good enough to eat, in fact.'

'Is it bad?' As I'd stumbled out of bed after only a few hours' sleep that morning, I hadn't been thinking and just put on the clothes I'd been wearing the day before. Big mistake.

'Depends on the nose. I can't vouch for these losers. It's fine though, come on,' she said, walking into the classroom.

'*Do* I stink of curry?' I asked, running after her.

'You smell of curry,' she replied. 'As I've said, whether you stink or not is a matter of perspective. I don't think you do.'

We both sat by the window and I pulled out my notebook. I kept my eyes on the desk because I knew if I looked up, Amanda, our teacher and my form tutor, would come over with sad eyes and ask if I was OK. She knew about Dad. She'd run into Mum at the hospice and Mum, being Mum, had told her. Turned out Amanda volunteered there, reading to people, like some sort of white saviour do-gooder. I didn't want anyone's fucking sympathy. I just wanted to finish my A levels, go to uni and live my life in peace and quiet.

Even with my eyes on the desk, I could feel a presence in front of me. Madhu tapped my upper arm and said, sunnily, 'Hey, Amanda!'

I looked up.

Amanda was looking down at me, doe-eyed, over the top of her glasses.

'Sunny,' she said. 'Just checking you're OK.'

'Yes, thanks, miss . . .'

'If you need any extra time with today's activity, please do let me know. I am here to help.'

'Thank you,' I replied, sensing my classmates around me. I didn't want any extra attention. I wanted to fade into the background as much as possible. I stared at a poster on Amanda's wall. It was a picture of the writer Toni Morrison, with an inspiring quote.

My skin itched with the feeling of being visible. Madhu rubbed my arm. She knew what was happening with Dad but never pressed me to talk about it. So far, I hadn't wanted to talk about any of it with her. Or Mum. Or anyone. And

Madhu respected that. We talked about comics, TV shows we both watched, Arsenal. I wished Amanda had the same level of respect. I just wanted her to teach me so I could get the grades I needed to go to uni. If I was going to talk about any of my stuff, it wouldn't be with her.

'God, Amanda is so annoying,' Madhu whispered to me.

'Innit,' I said, quietly.

I loved Madhu. Instantly, the second I met her.

Madhu was the one the college chose to show me around on the first day. She'd been waiting outside for me with Amanda when I arrived.

Amanda introduced us, saying, 'We all recognise how hard it is for students to start mid-term so Madhu is going to be your buddy and ease you in.'

Madhu smiled and said, 'It's cos we're both brown.' Which made me snort.

'Now, now,' Amanda scolded. 'That's not entirely true. We thought—'

Madhu interrupted. 'Literally cos we're both brown. It's fine. I ain't mad or anything. I get it. We are practically a hundred per cent of the BAME population of this college, innit. I need to show you the ropes . . .'

'It's not like that,' Amanda protested.

Madhu led me away from Amanda.

'I'm Sunny,' I offered.

'Well obviously,' she replied. 'I've been waiting for you, haven't I?'

She had shown me around the school and made me laugh at every turn, joking about different teachers, students and every peculiarity of the school: the staircase that got overtaken by goths at lunchtime, where to go if you wanted to listen to bad white-guy rappers, how to avoid getting roped into the school running club, which Madhu had said seemed like a weird wellness collective and, quite frankly, she preferred chips.

At the end of the day, when my head had been spinning with all the orientation, Madhu had taken me back out to the front steps.

'I'll meet you here every day for the next week, just till you get a feel for the place,' she'd told me.

I'd been at the school a month, and she still waited for me there every single morning.

'We need to think about your uni statements,' Amanda announced to the class, pulling me back into the room. I took out a pen. The prospect of uni seemed like a good way to distract myself from stuff at home. I knew I wouldn't be able to afford living away from home so I was only applying for unis in Bristol. And UWE had courses I was interested in. I just wasn't sure which one I wanted to do yet. And I didn't know how to decide.

I stayed late at college, trying to get some reading done. Dinner was already made for that night – leftovers. It was probably time to branch out to other dishes. I wasn't sure how many nights in a row I could tolerate chana curry. Also, I didn't want to go home to an empty house. The lounge was still set up for Dad even though he'd now been moved to the hospice. It felt almost like a shrine to him. And my bedroom was too small and draughty for me to want to spend any time in there. Staying in the college library was the only thing to do. I killed some more time going through uni prospectuses. I was trying to find the right subject. Maybe something science-y? Or History? But I couldn't see what that would be for. I'd need a job after uni. Would History give me that? It's not like I had a spare £100K or whatever to fart on figuring out what I wanted to do with my life. I had to be sure before committing myself to that level of debt. I added it to the list of worries swirling around in my head.

Madhu had left already. There was a youth arts collective in town she belonged to and they were all going to see some film tonight and then talk about it over expensive ice cream. It didn't sound like my kind of thing – not that I had the money to pay for a cinema ticket and a bus ride into the centre, let alone the ice cream. And anyway, it was nice, after a day of talking and being talked at, to be in an environment where there was enforced silence.

When I eventually headed out for the train, the college campus was pretty empty. Aside from a few people arriving for night classes and the security guy, I was the only one left in the building. I cut through the car park cos it was dead and there were no teachers around to tell me off, and I walked down the alleyway that led to the train station.

I didn't have a ticket but I knew there were no barriers. I'd pay if there was an inspector. But there never was at this time of night. Ever.

The platform was empty, so I sat down on a bench all the way up one end to wait. That way, I wouldn't have long to walk to get out of the station when I got off.

I'd just missed a train. Its lights glowed with a diminishing yellow as it disappeared in the direction of home. My brain was swimming with ways to attack my coursework. My feet felt like they'd been glued to my socks and trainers all day.

All I wanted to do was take them off and rub my toes into the carpet before lying down and going to sleep. My stomach rumbled.

I took a samosa out of my bag and bit into it. It had gone soggy. I'd put it in the plastic container while it was still hot and closed the lid, cos I'd been in a rush. While the pastry wasn't very crunchy, it still tasted delicious. The lamb, the peas, the garam masala. Bristol Sweet Mart did not mess about. It was legendary for its bitings.

I heard some loud chatter to my left and stole a look. I didn't want to make eye contact with anyone. I didn't know this area too well and I didn't know who lived here.

Three guys were stumbling down the platform, clutching beer cans, yelling at each other at the tops of their voices.

'And then, she basically let me kiss her cos I gave her a lift – what a stupid bitch . . .'

'Mate, that's nothing. There was this one girl who—'

'Shut up, you virgin.'

'Yeah whatever, mate . . .'

'I'm—'

'Virgin . . . virgin . . . virgin . . .'

I put my hood up and tried to make myself as small as possible. I carried on eating.

'Here, I'm starving – can I have a bite?'

I looked up to see one of the guys standing in front of me. He was pointing at my samosa.

'What is that shit anyway?'

'Stinks like curry, dunnit,' said one of his friends, sitting down on the bench next to me.

I felt the bench shudder for just a second with the impact of him. I kept my eyes on my samosa, not looking up.

I shifted in my seat, trying to make myself disappear. I stared at the half a samosa in my hand. I wanted to stand up and walk to the other end of the platform. That was all I needed to do. *Stand up. Walk down the platform. Stand up. Just stand up. Make your legs work. Why won't my legs work? Stand up! Walk away, for Christ's sake.*

But I couldn't move. I remained as quiet and as still as I could. I even held my breath. My stubble grazed my hood. The noise felt so loud.

'Oi, I'm talking to you,' the man in front of me said again. I could feel the third friend pacing behind me. It made my neck itchy knowing he was there, and I couldn't see his face, just heard him breathing and crushing a beer can incessantly. 'Give us a bite of your curry thing. What is it? A mimosa?'

His mates cracked up. The one behind me was creasing so much, he banged my shoulder hard as he laughed. I flinched.

'*Samosa*. Sam, you idiot. *Sam*-osa. Like you. Isn't that right, mate?'

'Can you even talk English?' the one called Sam asked. He suddenly stopped laughing. 'I want a bite. Now. I'm hungry.'

I didn't reply.

'Jesus fucking Christ,' the guy sitting next to me whispered, getting up. 'Not again . . .'

Without thinking, I took a bite of the samosa.

Sam smacked at my mouth.

I bit down on my tongue and my cheek stung with the smack. I cried out in pain. I bent forward, dropping the samosa and cupping my mouth. I'd never been hit before. I peered up at Sam. He looked angry.

14

Stand up! Walk away! Please, just stand up. Please . . . I thought. I whimpered.

'I said, I wanted. A. Bite,' I heard Sam say.

Something landed hard on my back. It felt like an entire body. It was so heavy it jerked me forward quickly. My nose whacked into my knee and I had the wind knocked out of me as I slumped off the bench. It was the man behind me. He'd jumped me. I fell into Sam, who kicked me away.

'Leave him, Sam,' I heard one of them say. Probably the one who'd been sitting on the bench. 'CCTV, innit.'

'This stupid immigrant needs to get a beating. When the vans come to take him back home, there won't be much left of him.'

'Forget it,' the other guy said. 'I'm walking home.'

'You shit-skin paki bastard,' the man who'd landed on me said, standing up.

The words hit me like I'd been doused in ice water. I forgot where I was, just for a split second, and rolled on to my back in shock.

I wish I'd looked harder now. I wish I'd seen their faces for more than a second. But then I remembered I wanted my body to be as small as possible and curled into a ball.

The first kick that landed crunched at my ribs. It was like running into a wall. The second, in my side, knocked all the air out of me. I forgot to breathe. Everything was burning. I wanted to die there and then. Just so it would end.

I didn't think it could get worse until Sam, the main guy, started kicking me in my stomach. With the full force of a Timberland boot. Cracking everything inside me. Sometimes he missed my stomach. He got my thigh, my privates, my ribs, my arms.

15

I was crying through it all.

I had never been in so much pain.

It was my fault.

They kicked me a bunch more times and called me every single racist name under the sun. Then the train came. And they both got on. Leaving me there on the platform, bleeding, coughing and crying. I had never been attacked before. I'd never even been hit. I just wasn't one of those kids you noticed or cared enough about to do damage to. I was the quietest person in the room. I hated being seen. I hated standing out.

It felt like hours, but was over in seconds. Scars that could last a lifetime, taking seconds to inflict.

I lay there on the platform crying in shame. Because I knew I'd have to explain this to Mum. And she didn't need another thing to worry about.

I sensed other people arrive on the platform at some point. Voices around me, concerned. But I just lay there, unable to move, unable to speak. I was like a stick insect, trying to blend into the platform in the hope that I'd be left alone. I didn't want anyone else to hurt me.

When the next train came, I tried to pull myself to the train door. I cried out when someone's hands went under my armpits, hoisting me up.

'You OK?'

'Can we call someone?'

'No . . .' I whimpered as they helped me up and on to the train. 'Don't touch me.'

I felt myself jolt down into a seat and lean forward. I thought I was going to be sick.

Everything in me was stinging, on fire. The doors beeped shut. The train carriage felt airless and there was a cold sweat all over the back of my neck and ears. I had three stops to travel, then a ten minute walk. I didn't know how I was going to do it.

But more than that, I felt a heaviness around me. Like my body was shutting down in order to manage the pain. It wanted me to sleep. I could feel my eyes closing. I could feel my hands going limp. My forearms were bruised, I could tell, from where I'd used them to shield my head from kicks. I wanted to cry.

Why had they done this to me? Over a samosa. Over a goddamn samosa. Why had they done this? Why hadn't I just given him a bite? Why hadn't I just got up and walked away? Why hadn't I stood up for myself? Would that have made it worse or made them realise I was a person and not a paki? My last thoughts before I fell asleep were to blame myself for everything that had happened on that train platform.

1.3

As I slept, I had sensations of people talking to me, shouting at me, being lifted and carried, before feeling the light change from murky and dimmed to intensely brighter.

I woke up to a blinding light. I flinched and gasped.

'Easy, easy,' someone said, softly.

The light went away and it took me a few seconds to focus my eyes. Smiling at me, a woman wearing green helped me sit up.

I whimpered. Everything was aching. Everywhere felt bruised.

'What's your name, young man?' she asked.

'Sunny . . . Shah. Sunil Shah. No, not Sunny . . . Sunil,' I said, confused. 'Where am I?'

'Bristol Temple Meads station. Someone noticed you slumped and bleeding on the train and pulled the passenger alarm. You look like you've taken quite a beating. Are you OK?'

I shook my head.

'No,' I managed to say, wincing.

'What's hurting?'

'Everything . . .' I said.

The paramedic smiled, kindly, and looked at her partner, who was talking to a police officer. The police officer turned his attention to me and leant down.

'Who did this?' he asked, softly. 'What did they look like?'

'Give him a second,' the paramedic said. 'He just woke up.'

She waved him away and put something white on my face. It stung. I tried to move away from her hand but she pressed whatever it was firmly on to me.

'Relax,' she said. 'We're going to sort you out. Is there anyone I can call?'

I shook my head. 'My mum's at work.'

'Dad?'

'No, he can't do anything.'

Slowly, I was regaining my voice. I talked the paramedic through everywhere that hurt and she assessed my injuries. She dressed a couple of cuts and applied pressure on sore points to see how serious they were. When she was done, she told me they were going to take me to A&E to get me checked out, make sure nothing more serious had happened. She asked if I could walk.

Commuters were looking at me with a mixture of bemusement and nosiness. I wanted to scream at them all to leave me alone. I hated that everyone could see me.

I nodded.

She placed her arm around me and helped me to my feet. I collapsed in her arms again. She steadied me, taking most of my weight. Her partner grabbed my other side and they walked me through the ticket barriers. On the other side, I felt like jelly, like my stomach was turning over and over, like I was going to be sick. Like I was floating. There was a rush of people coming and going and I could feel the heat emanating off their bodies, suffocating me.

'Put me down, I can't do this,' I said.

'Don't worry, we'll get the stretcher. Take it easy,' the paramedic said.

She helped me to sit on a bench while her partner disappeared, leaving the station.

'I'm Shanai,' she said, kindly.

'Pleased to meet you,' I replied. She laughed.

'That's very formal. Wanna tell me what happened?' she asked. She looked over at the police officer. 'I can be less, erm, direct maybe.'

I shook my head.

'That's fair. My advice would be to try to make some notes on what happened before you forget them. Sometimes trauma can make us sideline some details.'

'I will,' I told her.

Her partner arrived with a stretcher. I was forcing myself to ignore everyone around me. I felt too exposed.

Shanai lifted me on to the stretcher with her partner's help. They strapped me in and wheeled me out of the station.

Something about the motion and the heaviness of every single fibre in my body eventually made me fall asleep again before I even made it into the ambulance.

1·4

I woke up feeling something on my hand. It was warm and dry. I opened my eyes and looked down the bed. It was bright but the silhouette was unmistakeable.

Mum.

Sitting there, looking at me. She had her prayer beads in one hand so she could count them, something she did to calm herself down. The other hand covered mine.

'Mum,' I croaked, and she looked up at me.

It made me burst into tears. The crying hurt my insides and my tears stung at the cuts on my face.

'Sunny, beta,' she said. 'My baba. Are you OK?'

'Mum,' I repeated, unable to say anything else. All I wanted was for her to scoop me up and cuddle me and protect me from the outside world. I cried. 'Mummy, I'm sorry . . .'

'Sorry for what?' she interrupted. 'Why are you sorry?'

'They . . .' I said, but the lumps in the back of my throat and my dry mouth and my wanting to keep the memory of what happened out of my brain caused me to be quiet. I gave a quiet *hrrrrrr* noise that eased out some more crying. My shoulders shook.

'Sunny, darling, what happened?' she said.

I looked away, trying to steady my voice.

'Water,' I said. 'I need water.'

*   *   *

When we got home, she asked if I wanted to sleep in Dad's bed in the lounge. It hadn't been picked up yet. I shook my head. She smiled.

'You can watch television whenever you like,' she said.

'I just want to be in my own bed,' I replied.

She smiled again. I could tell by the way she kept looking at me, her mouth slightly open as if she was going to say something, that she wanted to understand what was going on and needed to ask me but was holding back. She helped me to my room and laid me down. We struggled to get my coat off. It got snagged on my elbow and no amount of wrenching could get it off. I was on a lot of painkillers so it didn't hurt too much. Mum kept asking if I was OK. I felt numb. Nothing in me. I said I was fine.

I lay on the bed and what usually felt so comfortable and familiar hurt. My body didn't feel right on this mattress. But I was too exhausted to complain. I shut my eyes as my way of telling Mum I didn't want to talk any more.

I felt her stand up and walk towards the door. I heard it creak open. I kept my eyes closed. I tried to focus on my breathing like Shanai had told me just before I was helped into the ambulance. Numb still. I wanted to feel something. I wanted to feel sad, angry, relieved to be home at the very least. But I felt nothing.

'Will you at least tell the police what happened?'

I opened my eyes. Mum was hovering in the doorway, her hand on the frame.

'I don't know yet,' I said.

'Who—' she started to say, but stopped herself and gave me a weary but reassuring smile instead. 'OK, get some rest.'

She closed the door.

I lay still, hoping for sleep to come. I wasn't used to sleeping on my back. I could only fall asleep on my side, facing the wall, one foot out of the covers. I stared at the walls, empty, hopelessly awake, desperate for sleep to take my body over.

I hadn't thought about what had happened the entire time I'd been attended to by Shanai in the station, in the hospital, in the taxi home.

It was my fault.

I looked at my lamp. I looked at the stack of unread *Spider-Man* comics on my bedside table. I'd had them for a few weeks and needed to give them back to Madhu. I looked at the mug of cold tea next to them. Mum had left it for me yesterday, but I had woken up late and not had time to drink it. It had scum on top. I looked at the street lamp outside the bedroom window above me. I looked at the bare walls. I looked around me at everything I could see, trying to distract myself from letting the thoughts in. I did not want to relive those moments.

Why had they called me a paki?

Why had they hit me?

Why hadn't I let him have a bite of my samosa?

It was my fault.

1.5

Two hours of sleeplessness later and I could feel the pain sneaking in. The pills were wearing off. My body still, lying on my back, and my mind doing everything it could not to think. It was my sides and my forearms that seemed to hurt the most. They had absorbed the majority of the blows.

Why hadn't I just got up and walked away?

Why hadn't I just given him a bite?

Was that all it had been about? A damn samosa?

It was my fault.

I wanted to remember every single detail about those attackers. Just in case I told the police. I also wanted to forget every single detail about them. I didn't want to tell the police. I didn't want any more fuss. Everything was at odds in my mind.

Why had they called me a paki?

Why had they hit me?

Why hadn't I let him have a bite of my samosa?

It was my fault.

Mum knocked lightly on the door and said she was going to her night shift at the hotel. She opened the door and stepped in. She put a steel cup of water down on the bedside table, on top of Madhu's *Spider-Man* comics.

And a steel plate of samosas.

Again, on top of Madhu's comics.

'Move. Them,' I said to her, hissing angrily. 'Now.'

'I beg your pardon?' Mum said.

I sat up, which caused my sides to burst with pain. I was breathing heavily and trying not to cry out. My entire body felt like it was on fire.

'Move them off those comics now. Respect people's property, Mum,' I shouted.

I'd never shouted at my mum before. Never ever. She was the only person in the world I wasn't afraid of talking to. I told her everything. I had never been angry with her, upset with her or annoyed with her. I trusted her. I came out to her when I was sixteen. She'd been quiet for an hour and then

23

told me she loved me and was glad I got to be who I was more openly. She'd then suggested we didn't tell Dad yet. She'd told me about his cancer even though he had wanted to keep it to himself. She held all our secrets. She was the person I trusted the most in the world.

And now I was shouting.

It was my fault.

Mum gave me a look that was a mixture of anger and sympathy and moved the plate and the cup off the comics. Without saying anything, she left the room. For work.

I sat there for a while in the same position, propped up on my elbows, disgusted with myself. What was happening to me?

I wasn't prepared for how terrifying the flat felt when I knew I was on my own.

I needed to sleep.

Mum had, in her rush to get out of my room after I'd yelled at her, left the door ajar. I could hear steps going past our front door, the occasional bang and voice in the distance. There was a quiet beeping somewhere in the flat, which I knew was Mum's Fitbit telling her to plug it in. The flat was entirely dark except for the street light outside my room making the curtains glow a deadened amber.

And I couldn't see people coming in the dark.

I needed to get myself to sleep. Urgently.

I started rocking myself from side to side. It hurt. It really, really hurt. Reshifting my lump of a body, the carcass that wore the skin that had made me the subject of an attack, was almost impossible. But, once I built up momentum, I was able to wrench myself on to one side, so I was facing the wall. It felt like everything was being pulled into the mattress. I adjusted my limbs until they stopped throbbing and I closed my eyes. It wasn't exactly comfortable, but it was familiar enough to try to convince sleep to rescue me.

A shout in the corridor woke me as I started to slip into sleep.

It was my fault.

I stared at bumps in the wall.

It was my fault.

I stared at the formation of old Blu Tack traces that had held up posters of Spider-Man, Wu-Tang Clan, Miles Davis and Mum and Dad on their wedding day.

It was my fault.

I'd taken everything down when Dad had become bedridden. I'd felt like I needed a change. I hadn't found what I wanted to replace those posters with yet. I didn't know who I wanted to be.

It was my fault.

My proximity to a samosa felt weird. Knowing it was there, this thing that had caused me such undue pain. The smell lingered in my nose, making me want to be sick. I had to do everything not to trigger the images in my head that would lead me back to that train platform.

I closed my eyes again.

Just as I felt sleep working its way up my body, towards my head, I saw him again, slapping my mouth. It was a quick flash. Blink and you'd miss it. *Bang.* But it jolted me awake.

I heard Mum come in around 4 a.m. I kept my eyes closed and my body still as I felt her shuffle about in the doorway.

She must have sensed I wasn't asleep. 'Would you like a cup of tea?' she whispered.

I waited till she'd left the room.

'No thanks,' I said to my wall.

It was my fault, wasn't it?

This wouldn't have happened if we'd stayed in London. If we'd not had to move cos of Dad's condition. I'd never wanted to come here. When Mum had told me there was a specialist in Bristol that Dad needed to see and we would be moving, she'd assured me it was temporary. I'd smiled and nodded, knowing that I had to support them, but as soon as I could, I'd run to the toilet and cried. I would be leaving everything I knew. My school. My home. My cousin. My precious life that had been so sorted and cemented and real to me. Everything had pointed towards a change that'd given me a dull burn in my stomach. I hadn't wanted to go. But I had. And look what'd happened to me.

It was my fault.

The endless refrain.

It. Was. My. Fault.

Mum came in twenty minutes or so later. Or was it five? I was so tired and in so much pain that my sense of time was askew.

'Medicine. Then sleep,' she said. 'Have you managed any sleep yet?'

'No,' I said, quietly. 'Mum, I'm . . . I'm sorry I shouted at you.'

'I understand,' she said, crouching over me. 'You can take your anger out on me today, but soon you will have to think about directing it towards the people who deserve it.'

I felt her put a hand under my neck and a hand under my

side. I tried to shift so she could pivot me where she needed me to be. I fell into her arms. The sense of weightlessness made my stomach ache from emptiness. The last thing I'd eaten was that goddamn samosa, yesterday.

She pulled me to the head of the bed and propped me up. She placed a pill inside my mouth and held a glass of water with a straw in it to my lips. I sucked down one pill then the other.

She stood up. 'You want me to lie you down again?' she asked.

'No,' I replied. 'I might as well catch up on work before college.'

Mum laughed then remembered herself. She looked at me over the top of her glasses.

'Darling, take a day off. Want me to move the television in here?'

'No, Mum,' I said, feeling my voice raise. 'You don't get reception in here. Only in that corner of the flat. For god's sake . . .'

'You're tired,' she said, loudly. 'I need to sleep before my next shift. You're not going to college.'

'Don't tell me what to do,' I shouted at her.

She sighed and left the room. I brought my fist down on the bedside table, slamming Madhu's comics and causing the empty steel cup to fall to the floor. It hurt, but it was nice to feel a pain that I had inflicted on myself.

I fall into the ropes. Keir pounces on me and links his arms in mine so I cannot free myself. I try to push against him. I can hear his name being chanted. There is sweat stinging my eyes. I can hear the referee shouting at us to break.

Keir stands on my feet so I can't move and he aims a punch to my kidney before the referee pulls him off me.

'You ain't even got a punch in,' he says, baring his mouthguard at me and grinning.

I tap my glove against where he hit me in the face. The referee brings us to the middle again.

He sets us to go and Keir stamps straight into me.

The bell rings. Keir pushes me as I turn away from him. I hear the referee scold him. The applause from the crowd breaks into murmurs. I bet they're all talking about how amazing Keir's doing, what a waste of space I am.

I walk back to my corner.

I look at Shobu, who is waiting with a bottle of water. She pulls out my mouthguard, thrusts the straw into my mouth and squeezes the bottle.

The water tastes incredible. Like I'm drinking it after a year of drought.

'What the *hell* was that?' Shobu asks.

'I'm trying. He's just more confident than me,' I tell her.

'So what? You both are fighting to win that ring. And from where I'm sitting, the ring belongs to you but you aren't even putting up a fight. Come on, Sunny.'

I nod.

I sit on the stool and face Keir. He winks at me.

'What are you scared of?' Shobu asks.

I shake my head. 'Nothing,' I say, looking out into the crowd. Hari's out there, in the stalls somewhere. I can't see him but I know he's there. He's watching me. He's judging me. He's gonna watch Keir give me the beatdown of my life and then I will never hear from him again.

'*Who* are you scared of, then?' Shobu asks.

I look at her. She gestures out to the crowd.

'N-no one,' I stammer.

'Exactly. The only person you should care about is the one in the ring with you.'

I immediately look away from her. She grabs my chin and forces me to face her.

'I heard you.'

'The only person,' she says again, stressing each word as if it were its own sentence, 'you should care about is *the one in the ring with you.*'

I don't tell her, but that's exactly what I'm afraid of.

Round 2

The referee stands between us. Keir is smiling. I know I have to land a shot early. Just to make him realise this won't be easy.

The referee looks at Keir and winks.

'No funny business,' he says.

He looks me up and down and winks at Keir again. Something about that wink unsettles me. It knocks my concentration. Like he's giving Keir the nod to go easy on me.

This pisses me off. So when he shouts for us to fight, I duck. Keir likes to look good, and for some fighters, landing the first punch is what they think does that. So I get out of the way of it by slipping to his right and I aim a left hook into his side. It catches him off guard and he grunts. He recovers quickly and lands a hook around the back of my head. I manage to block most of the punch with my free hand. He is wide open. I snap back my hook and jab him in his face.

Surprised, he falls back and I stand up tall, circling away from him.

I should get him on the ropes but something in me hesitates. I'm not an offensive boxer. Defend and counterpunch. That's what Shobu told me my type was. She had me pegged from the second I walked nervously into Easton Boxing Gym and asked if I could just watch.

2.1

By the third day of not moving from my bed, other than struggling to the toilet, the fear had been replaced with a numbness. I just could not be bothered to do anything. But I still needed to feel *something*. So while Mum was at work, I started to ball my fists and whack them against my bruises. The biggest ones were on my side, on my left forearm and on my thigh. I'd sit there and bang on my bruises with my knuckles until the pain was too much to bear. But at least I was feeling something. Anything.

My cheek stung where the cuts were healing. I imagined tiny men sowing skin cells into the cuts to repair them, like I'd seen in a kid's science book when I was young. It was the only book in our house and Dad had bought it for me from the library's for sale shelf when I'd complained that they never bought me any presents for Christmas.

'Here,' he had said. 'Here's a present. The gift of knowledge. Now go and learn about the heart and I will test you later.'

I'd read it cover to cover, hoping for him to test me, or at least give me more than five minutes of silence every evening before turning on the television and watching any news he could find. It was how I learned about the inner workings of the body, what white blood cells were, how spaceships worked and the different layers of the earth all the way down to its core.

I'd spent the next few nights reading the book at the dinner table, in front of Dad, who ate with half an eye still on the news.

The third day, he'd turned to me and I'd thought, *Finally, he's going to test me*. He'd picked the book up off the table, closed it and put it on an empty chair.

'You are getting haldi on the pages,' he'd said, turning back to the television.

A knock on the door stirred me from snoozing while listening to Kelela. I sat up, scared. Had they found out where I lived? Were they here to finish the job? Maybe they were gonna burn me alive. My heart was pounding, until I heard a familiar voice.

'Sunny, are you in there?'

Amanda.

I sat still. I didn't want to see her.

'Sunny,' she called. 'You're already an at-risk student, coming to us so late in the day. Please . . . Please don't do this to me. Are you OK?'

I sighed and shifted forward until I could put my feet on the ground. I was annoyed. She had come to my house, of all places. It felt like a violation.

I stood up and cried out in pain. A long stretch of stillness had made my back muscles seize up. One twinged as I tried to stand a bit too quickly.

'Sunny,' she said, banging the door again. 'Please. Let me in. I need to know you're OK . . .'

I hobbled to the door and opened it a crack, careful to hide my body and as much of my face as possible.

'Hi, Amanda,' I said. I was embarrassed for her to see me like this.

It was my fault.

'Sunny,' she replied. 'You've missed a few days of college and—'

'I've not been well,' I told her.

'You know the procedure for sickness. We ran through it on the first day. I'm just surprised. You . . .'

She stopped and slowly pushed the door open to reveal my face.

'Miss, it's not—'

'My god, Sunny, what happened?' she asked.

'I'm fine, miss. It's all good.'

Amanda sighed and put a hand on mine, where I was still clutching the door. I flinched and pulled away. Without thinking, I shut the door in a panic and stood with my back to it, leaning, panting, holding back tears.

'Will I see you tomorrow?' she asked, muffled by the door. 'I'm sorry.' She paused. 'Are you really OK? I'm sure I can just contact your mum. I . . .'

She stopped.

'Don't call my mum,' I said. Not that Mum would offer her any insight. I just didn't want any fuss. Why couldn't they understand I wanted to be left well alone?

'I'll . . . I'll be in tomorrow,' I sighed.

I hobbled to my bedroom and picked up my phone, deciding to reply to Madhu's many unreplied-to texts.

See u tomorrow, I wrote. **Been ill, innit.**

I didn't want to see Madhu, even. I would inevitably face questions about where I had been. She'd see from my face and the way I hobbled and couldn't straighten my arm that

35

something had happened. But she didn't need to know what.

I couldn't take the train. I knew that. The thought made my lungs feel like they were filled with hot air. I stood in front of the mirror and looked at myself. I didn't know what I was.

I couldn't get back on that train. What if I saw Sam? Or his friends.

Forget his name, my brain screamed. *Forget he existed.*

I had a tenner left in my wallet so I called a taxi. The tenner was supposed to be for travel, I figured. I didn't change my clothes because I didn't want to look at the bruises on my body. It was what I'd been wearing the night of the thing that'd happened. I'd only bled on my face.

I couldn't bend down and tie the laces of my kicks tightly, so I just slipped my feet into them and tucked the laces under my heel. Amanda would just have to deal with it. The hard ends of the laces were itchy against my soles but this irritant was the least of my worries.

I stood up and shuffled to the door. Standing had made me dizzy every time I'd needed the toilet the last few days, and this time was no different. I could feel a vibration in my left ear, like someone was patting it lightly, quickly. It pulsed and I stood still to let it pass. I checked I had my wallet, keys and phone. I looked at my backpack and weighed up not taking it. I wasn't sure I could support it on my back. I needed my books though.

I could hear the taxi guy beeping outside. I opened the flat door and stepped out into the corridor.

Something about the air outside my home was off. It made me feel almost light-headed. I took deep breaths and

36

stepped towards the taxi. The driver was beckoning me like he was running late. I thought, *Come on, in my own time*. But even so, I quickened my step.

Or at least I tried to.

But this was the longest I'd stood since the attack and I could only limp to the car. A neighbour nodded at me but I turned my eyes to the ground. I waved my hand to acknowledge him.

The taxi driver must have sensed my pain, because he got out of the car and opened the passenger side for me.

'You didn't shut your door,' he said.

I craned my neck round. He was right. I'd left our flat door open.

'Bloody hell,' I hissed. I could feel tears bubbling behind my eyes. The first time I would have cried since it'd happened. I looked at him.

'I can't. It hurts.'

'Is anybody inside?' he asked.

I shook my head.

He held his hand out. I looked at it. He mimed putting a key in a lock. I nodded. I pulled the keys out of my hoodie pocket and handed them to him. As I watched him take the keys I realised I wasn't scared. However, his kindness felt raw to me. Like when you'd itched something for so long it burned instead of stung.

'Just the Chubb lock,' I said.

He ran towards the flat. I looked around my street. Everything felt bright and oppressive. I squinted, trying to work out what the sky was doing. It was one of those white-but-still-cloudy days that gave England's climate such a bad rep.

A car beeped and a person shouted and I flinched as if it was about to crash into me. I looked around. There was no one there. No one except me and the taxi driver. I felt him put his arm over my shoulder to steady me towards the car. But the feeling of a stranger's arm around me freaked me out.

'No,' I said. 'I can do it.'

His arm felt heavy over my shoulder and when he lifted it off without a word, I felt lighter. I grabbed for the passenger door and used it to steady myself.

I took a deep breath and held it while I threw myself bum first on to the seat. The driver bent down and waited to see if I needed help moving my legs into the car. I didn't.

2.2

In the car, he played bhangra and spoke to his girlfriend on speakerphone and smiled at me occasionally in the rear-view mirror. When he hung up his phone, he lowered the volume on the bhangra.

'What happened, bro?' he asked, letting go of the gear stick and rubbing at his bald head.

'Nothing, man,' I said.

'You box?' he said.

I shook my head. I couldn't think of anything worse.

'No,' I said. 'I'm not into people hitting each other for fun.'

'Nah,' he said. 'That's not boxing.'

'OK,' I replied and stared out of the window as the car passed the Tesco where Mum worked. All I knew about boxing was Tyson biting that man's ear off. It was people being paid to punch each other and giving each other permission to punch back. Was sweat and swollen eyes and crowds baying for blood. Was not me.

'Bro,' he said. 'You gotta try it. Best way to learn about your body, innit. It teaches you to take up space. And be confident. Fighting isn't about going on the offensive, it's about defending yourself and ending the fight, innit. Boxing, it's all about the mind. It's mind games as well as punches. Bro, it gives you so much confidence.'

'Sure,' I said.

'Easton Boxing Gym, try it. Just by the library. I go there, innit.'

'OK.'

'If you go,' he said, turning round to face me at a red light, 'say Surinder sent you. I get a discount. Surinder. Want me to spell it?'

I shook my head.

'Fair play, bro. Here you go.'

I looked at the sign for college as he pulled in. I felt my chest heave in and out quickly and heavily. I could feel the itch of cold sweat up and down my neck.

I braced myself to greet Madhu, who was waiting for me in our usual spot.

2.3

Madhu ran towards us when she saw Surinder helping me out of the cab. 'Where have you been, Sunny? Wait, what the hell happened to you? Are you OK?'

After I'd texted Madhu to tell her I was coming in the next day I'd told her, whatever happens, don't make a fuss.

Surinder nodded at her, winked at me and got back into the car.

'I'm fine,' I said.

'Yeah,' she said, wincing. 'You really look fine. So super fine.'

'I don't want to talk about it,' I said.

'I know,' she replied. 'But you saying you're fine doesn't automatically mean all your bruises become invisible, you know. I still want to know if you're OK . . .'

'I am . . .'

I heard bhangra start up behind me and I turned. Surinder waved to me as he drove off.

Madhu touched my face, just by the deepest cut. She looked into my eyes, probably examining the black one, then she took her glasses off and pinched the bridge of her nose.

'Come on, man, we're gonna be late.'

She linked her arm in mine, like usual, and led me inside. Something about her touch felt different. Warm, comforting. Madhu liked to take the piss, but she really cared. And today, feeling her arm around me, something changed. It felt like it should have been there the whole time. Like, leaving London and everything I knew for this new city had been so jarring, but here was someone who effortlessly made me feel like I was at home. Sometimes I wished I wasn't an only child and I had someone – a brother, a sister – just someone else to take care of and to take care of me.

Madhu led me into the corridor. We passed Amanda's room. I flinched, thinking of her at my front door yesterday. Amanda came out.

'Hi, miss,' I said, looking at the floor. Luckily, Madhu kept us moving.

'Good to see you, Sunny,' Amanda replied. 'Don't be a statistic . . .'

Madhu looked at Amanda, like, *What the hell.* 'What statistic is that?' she asked.

'You know what I mean, Madhu—'

Madhu started to interrupt Amanda but I kept her moving now, desperate to sit down, everything inside me burning.

I knew I would have to take the train home after college. So I made sure I left with Madhu. I wanted to tell her why but I couldn't even think about it. How could I tell her I basically invited people to beat me up? Even though she was only going one stop, it still felt a comfort that she would be there on the platform with me.

As we approached the station I started to feel memories of that night creep in. It had been less than a week since it had happened but my brain was still doing everything in its power to fight the bad thoughts.

The platform was crowded. I couldn't see the bench up at the end of the platform where I'd been attacked. There was a comfort in people. It made me feel less like my head was spinning and I was able to listen to Madhu and her friend talk about some show they were both enjoying on Netflix. Something I'd never heard of. I managed to even look around and remind myself that one night couldn't steal away the everydayness of this train station for me. I used this place every single day I went to college, and there was no way I could let those men make me feel afraid in space that belonged to me. Maybe I could get through this after all. Bruises healed eventually. Maybe my heart could too.

Someone pushed past me on the platform. He turned to face me and apologised.

I froze.

It was one of *them*.

The one who had walked off and left his friends to kick the shit out of me. It was him.

Was it?

I was unsure. My cheeks felt flushed.

It was my fault.

My lungs suddenly felt airless. I doubled forward as he walked past and I needed to grip on to Madhu, interrupting her conversation, to steady myself.

'You OK, mate?' the man whispered and carried on walking.

Our eyes connected. His were dull, grey, passionless, with heavy bags underneath them. He wore a Raiders cap and a grey hoodie. He had a backpack on. He could easily be support staff at our college.

It wasn't *him*.

Just someone else wanting to go home, like me.

Was this what my life would be like now? Scared of everyone? Scared of being myself, in case I invited more trouble into my life?

2.4

Madhu sat in the seat opposite on the train, staring at me. When her friend took a phone call from his boyfriend, she raised her eyebrows in my direction.

'What?' I asked.

'You've painted me into a real corner,' she said.

'What do you mean?' I leant forward, hushing my voice.

'I want to ask. I'm not allowed to ask. But I cannot, for the life of me, think of anything else I want to talk about. So we're either sitting here in silence. Or we're talking about it . . .'

I edged back in my seat.

Madhu reached out and grabbed my hands.

'Just tell me!' she said, softly.

About a fortnight into our friendship, Madhu had decided she wanted to set me up with someone, having hounded out of me what sort of person I was into. I'd told her that I was shy and I didn't really like the idea of a date.

'Why?' she had said, shocked.

'I dunno. It just seems too intense. Like, maybe I could handle it if we went to see a film or something. But imagine sitting at dinner, just talking. It sounds terrifying . . .'

Madhu had giggled then said, calmly, 'I don't know why we're friends.'

'You're my friend cos you make me laugh,' I'd said, slinging my arm over her shoulder. 'Me? I have no idea. I'm so dull!'

'You're still figuring you out,' she'd replied. 'When you've managed it, I'll still be here, trying to set you up with all my single friends . . .'

It physically hurt me that I couldn't tell Madhu. I couldn't even tell her that she was my only friend. Up until I'd moved, the most important people in my life had been my cousin, and my mum, but I wasn't sure you could really call them 'friends'. And my dad. But he was Dad, you know? Out working all the time. Dad in name only.

When Madhu and her friend got off the train at their stop, I felt the panic rise in me again. I was surrounded by other students from college, but I felt alone and exposed. The lights seemed too bright. I shielded my eyes. I felt thirsty all of a sudden. My throat was dry and stinging like I'd been gargling salt. Each bump and jolt from the train reminded me of a different bruise on my skin.

My body didn't feel like mine any more. Everything about it seemed wrong. My shoes suddenly felt the wrong size. My T-shirt kept riding up my back. My fingers were so weak I couldn't make a fist. It felt like my body had been remoulded and reshaped for someone else. It felt like it belonged to a paki. It didn't feel like it belonged to Sunny. Because Sunny was not a paki. Sunny was a human being. Except Sunny now lived in a body that belonged to a paki. And Sunny wanted to do everything he could to leave it.

I am not a paki.

It was my fault.

I felt bile bubble in my stomach.

As we pulled into the next station – not mine, I didn't think – I rushed out on to the platform and doubled over, hands on knees, coughing and retching. No sick came. I turned and watched the train leave without me.

The sun was casting a golden shade over the nearby tower blocks and there was loud chatter from a pub garden that sounded joyous. But I just stood there on the platform, looking into the empty space where the train should have been.

Then I noticed there was a mural on the opposite side, done by a local graff artist called Sickness. His stuff was everywhere in town. It said 'Easton'. Easton . . . Shit! The taxi driver. The boxing gym. I squinted at the mural from my side of the station. It was of two boxers – one black, one brown.

44

They were circling each other. They looked solid, planted, their feet rooted to the floor. Their hands were up, ready to strike or defend.

They looked determined.

They looked like they were dancing.

I remembered what Surinder told me in the cab: *'Best way to learn about your body, innit. It teaches you to take up space. And be confident.'*

I'd never thought about boxing before. I'd never thought about self-defence, or a martial art, or anything involving fighting, or striking someone else. I didn't think it was for me. I had no interest in confrontation nor had I any inclination to hit anyone else.

But the way I was feeling, there was something appealing about learning to take up space. And learn about my body. Reclaim it from the paki.

I limped towards the station exit, clutching my bruised left arm. I didn't know what to expect. But it was better than being in my head.

Easton Boxing Gym looked like it used to be a primary school. It was a one-storey building in a horseshoe with a car park filled with vehicles and a basketball court outside. At some point, someone had painted the outside of the reception gold, like it was celebratory. The gold of the building was masked by brightly lit signs around the perimeter, each one with a different motivational phrase on it.

Easton Boxing Gym – Find Out Who You Are.
Give Yourself A Fighting Chance.
Bristol, Stand Tall.

Sure, I'd seen a couple of boxing films like *Rocky*. Maybe one Christmas with Dad. They punched meat or something. Had swollen eyes. Gruff trainers. Got beaten to within an inch of their lives before they even caught sight of winning. And I remembered that ear biting thing. I imagined boxing gyms to be dripping with men's sweat, stinking of vinegar and like stepping back into the eighties, with men everywhere cussing each other and watching to clock who they could beat down quickest. A boxing gym was not a place I imagined I would ever find myself. But here I was, standing outside the front door, curious, but hesitant.

The door opened in front of me.

A woman leant out.

'You coming in?'

'I don't know,' I said.

'Let me guess: you're curious about boxing. But you only know about gyms from films and think it's gonna be full of testosterone-fuelled men preening and fist-fighting?'

I nodded.

She smiled.

'Why don't you come in and have a look around? I can prove you wrong . . .'

'Can I just watch?'

'Yeah,' she said, shrugging. 'Of course you can.'

She kept the door open and beckoned me in.

It was like walking into a doctor's surgery, except all the posters were of people boxing instead of unhealthy body organs.

'I'm Shobu,' the woman said. 'I train some of the fighters here. What's your name?'

'Sunny.'

46

I felt her looking at me more closely.

'You caught quite a beating there, Sunny. You OK? You talked about it with anyone? How old are you?'

In the light, I saw that despite her serious face, she had laughter lines around her mouth and a scar on her neck. She moved her curly hair out of her eyes and I saw she had an aum tattooed on the inside of her arm.

'No to both,' I said, quietly. 'Eighteen,' I added.

'So what made you come to us?' she said, quickly.

'A guy called Surinder said I should,' I said, looking around at some of the posters. I caught sight of her, Shobu, on a poster dated five years ago. She had her hair tied into a thick topknot, her right shoulder dropped and her left fist up. She wore a Team GB 2012 kit. *Damn*, I thought. *I'm talking to an Olympian.* She was beaming in the photo, which was different from how she looked now, serious. Concerned, maybe? I knew I looked awful. It was hard for people to not wince when they saw the cuts on my cheek and my black-eyed squint.

'Oh, is it?' she replied, smiling. 'He's my flatmate. I guess I owe him commission if you sign up.'

'I just want to watch,' I repeated.

She nodded for me to follow her. I was led down a corridor to a set of double doors. I heard a bell, loud and short and unmissable.

'Watch out for skipping ropes. That's the main thing to remember. But everyone here is super friendly and focused. We all have a common goal: to give ourselves a fighting chance, whether that's in the ring or in life or in ourselves. You have a fighting chance.'

'OK,' I mumbled, looking around, in case I was about to be garrotted by a skipping rope.

'Honestly, it's the best place to be to learn about yourself . . .' she added.

'OK,' I said again. It was the most I could muster.

'I have a training session with someone. You're free to watch.'

She led me into the gym.

It was a surprisingly small room and it felt full, even though there were only four or five people in there. They were moving about quickly in an open space in front of some mirrors, shadow-boxing, watching their reflections while they threw and defended punches, eyes never leaving their mirror counterparts. The way they moved about – ducking and weaving, slipping left and right, rolling their shoulders back and forth, punching and deflecting, changing direction – meant they took up all the space.

The boxing ring ran from the back wall right into the middle of the room. It looked so big and imposing. I couldn't ever see myself in it. Shobu smiled at me and walked over to the ring. I watched everyone shadow-boxing. It looked weird. Watching all these people stare at themselves in a mirror and imagine a fight, acting it out in their own minds. I couldn't wrap my head around it. There was a trainer standing in front of the mirror watching them all. He nodded at me and wiped sweat off his bald head. I backed to the wall immediately, I didn't want to be noticed. I looked back at Shobu. She was talking to a girl standing on one of the steps up into the ring. Shobu smiled at me and waved me over.

Watching for the shadow-boxers and ensuring I avoided them, I skirted the outside of the gym. I passed a doorway through which I heard hard, flat slaps and gasps of air. Each thump reverberated around my head. I remembered when something similar had smashed into my body. I peered into the doorway down a long, thin corridor with heavy bags of all different shapes, sizes and colours suspended from a joist hanging across the ceiling. Two people stood in front of a bag, punching and breathing out with each shot, gasping for air and snapping their fists back to guard their faces. I stepped back into the gym. The stench of sweat and the thumping sounds were making me sick.

It was my fault.

I felt a compulsion to find a safe haven. Every pore in me was leaking fear and I couldn't be here any more. My stomach throbbed with anxiety.

I reached Shobu. She smiled and gestured to the girl standing on the step. I shuffled my feet, unsure.

'Sunny, this is Ruchi. Ruchi, this is Sunny. Ruchi, Sunny's thinking of joining us and just wants to observe a training session and see what all the fuss is about. You OK if he sits at the side and watches?'

'Sure, whatever,' Ruchi said. 'Just don't look too closely. I'm new to this.'

'You just remember to keep your guard up,' Shobu said.

Ruchi held out her hands and Shobu took a wrap of cotton out of her pocket. She placed a loop on the thumb and drew the wrap across the back of Ruchi's hand. She then pulled the wrap taut and wrapped it around her wrist three times, then around the middle of her hand three times. She drew the wrap up over the back of her hand between little and ring finger, across the back again and through the next set of fingers, before wrapping it once more over the back of the hand, between middle and index and then around Ruchi's thumb. She took the excess cotton, wrapped it around her wrist and sealed the Velcro.

'This is to protect your wrists and hands, and to lock your fingers in,' Shobu said, looking at me and smiling.

I glanced away.

'The trick to fighting is knowing when to fight and when not to fight,' Shobu said, to no one in particular, as she wrapped Ruchi. I liked the sentiment of what she was trying to say.

Ruchi flexed her fingers while Shobu wrapped the other hand. Shobu then held open a left glove for Ruchi to shove her hand into, followed by a right glove. She sealed them and ushered Ruchi into the ring.

By now, the people shadow-boxing had stopped and were practising combinations of punches in partners, with instructions shouted out by their trainer. They all tapped each other lightly and used their gloves to defend themselves. The point, I later found out, was less about practising the full force of the punch, but more the feel, ebb and flow of it. You had to perfect, by constantly correcting, the punch by focusing on every aspect of it, from how the power rose up from your feet, through your hips, into your shoulders and down through the arm to your fist, all the way to how the fist snapped back into a defensive pose. All this I still had to learn, but watching everyone in the class run through their techniques was mesmerising.

Shobu called out, 'JAB JAB CROSS HOOK HOOK,' and I heard a *slap-slap*. I turned my attention back to the ring. She held two pads up at head height and shouted something else. Ruchi, dancing about on the balls of her feet, responded with different kinds of punches. The *slap-slap* of Ruchi's fists against the pads was electric. So was the way she pumped her arms so quickly and thoroughly and connected with the pads, all while bobbing and dancing on the tips of her toes.

Shobu called out another command and Ruchi complied.

This time, however, Shobu slipped forward to the side of one of the punches and pushed Ruchi over. Ruchi fell and I gasped.

She looked up at Shobu, grinning.

'Stop dancing,' Shobu said. 'This isn't *Strictly . . .*'

'That was fair,' Ruchi said, accepting Shobu's hand and pulling herself up.

Shobu made Ruchi stand next to her and they worked on their feet.

'All your power comes from your feet – the power to defend and the power to strike, remember? The power of a punch rises out of the ground itself. My trainer told me that.'

The power of walking away rises up from the ground too, an unwelcome voice in my head said.

Ruchi pointed at me as they moved.

'Does he want to try this?'

'It's your lesson, Ruchi,' Shobu said. She looked over at me and smiled. 'If he wants his own lesson, boy needs to pay me, innit.'

The gym felt hot all of a sudden, and the music was throbbing loudly and quickly. I couldn't be here. I wouldn't stand in a ring and have everyone watch me.

I ran across the centre of the gym, without thinking, feeling the snap of a skipping rope sting against the back of my legs. Looking behind me, I saw Shobu was concentrating on Ruchi. I headed to the exit, dodging a man who edged backwards from a punch and stepped into me. I apologised as he muttered a swear word. I winced and pounded outside as quickly as my broken legs would let me.

I stood outside the gym catching my breath. My eyes stung with fatigue. I felt the churn of an empty stomach. Home was walkable. I was still hobbling but I wasn't going to wait for a train.

Hearing bhangra, I immediately looked up.

Surinder was sitting in his car, on the phone, with a door ajar so the inside light was on. He saw me and waved vigorously. He got out of the car and slammed the door shut. Still on the phone, listening, saying the occasional 'yes' and 'sure', he bounded over to me cheerfully. He didn't know how sick I felt. He dapped me and I obliged, reluctantly, and then he hugged me. He squeezed tight and I whimpered as I felt my chest nearly cave in on itself.

He said goodbye to whoever it was on the phone and let go.

'Sorry, bro, I was just so happy you came,' he said. 'What do you think? You OK? They get you in the ribs too?'

I nodded.

'What did you think of inside?' he asked again.

'It's not for me, bro, but thank you,' I replied.

Surinder looked at his watch and then back at me.

'I got some time, man,' he said, scratching at his ponytail and stepping backwards. 'Let me run you home. Take ten minutes and then I know you're back safely.'

'Thank y-you,' I stammered. I wanted to feel more wary talking to him, but he had that same thing that made me comfortable, that thing Madhu had and Shobu had. They were just, I dunno. Good people, I guess. Hearts in the right place. Never trying to get you to places at any speed other than your own.

It made me think about London. Usually I wished I was back there, but standing in front of Surinder made me feel like it was further away – in a good way.

It's easy to think kindly of a place you've known your entire life just because it feels familiar. Like, here I hadn't even unpacked my comics because I didn't see it as a permanent place to live. I'd grown up in our London flat. It just felt right. And to take all of our stuff and move it into a new place, it felt weird. Alienating.

Surinder reminded me of our neighbour in London, Asim, who was just some lovely guy you could count on. He once drove Dad to hospital. He helped us get rid of some furniture, taking it to a charity shop in his van. All for a stack of Mum's theplas. That kinda guy. And Surinder seemed just like that.

'No,' I finally said. 'I have no money.'

Surinder laughed.

'Bruv,' he said. 'I'm off the clock. I'm offering cos I want to. It'd be weird if you sat in the back though.'

I looked at him. He was already walking back to his car. I hesitated. I didn't want to talk to anyone about anything. And once I'd got into the car with him, he would be bound to ask. Especially if he was acting all friendly now. I heard the engine start. I stared at my shoes. I wanted to get in the car with him so I could go home and make chana curry and hope for these stings of anxiety to pass. I just didn't want to talk.

He beeped his horn and rolled down his window, shouting, 'Come on, bruv, I need to be back for training.'

I relented and walked to the car. Maybe I could just say, *I'm getting out if you ask about my cuts and bruises*. Or I could just answer in one word syllables or bombard him with questions. None of these options were my style.

53

I sat in the front seat and closed the door and Surinder was off, driving out of the gym car park and heading towards my home.

'Oakfield Estate, yeah?'

'Yeah,' I said.

'Man cool,' he replied.

We sat in silence. On the radio, two men argued about freedom of speech. One wanted everyone to be able to say what they wanted, even if it was an offensive opinion, so people could debate. The other one wanted there to be limits. The one who wanted limits called the other person a dickhead and the presenter jumped in to apologise and cut to commercials.

Both Surinder and I laughed. I stole a look at him.

He turned to me as he switched off the radio.

'You mention my name?'

'Yeah,' I said. 'Shobu—'

'You met Shobby Shobz?' he said excitedly, tapping the wheel with both his thumbs. 'She's the best, innit. Man, what a fighter she is. She moves with the quickness. Like, you can see her hands but you can't follow her movements. She's just unbelievable to watch. You shoulda seen her in 2012, man. My god, it was like watching water. Every movement was liquid, every punch the crest of a wave . . .'

'Yeah, she seemed nice.'

'Never does the washing up though,' Surinder said with a chuckle.

We fell into silence again. I could tell Surinder had something he wanted to ask me but was holding back.

The longer we drove in silence, the more I wanted to break it with something, anything. The radio was off, the engine was running quietly, Surinder's breathing slow and steady as he concentrated on the road.

'My dad's in a hospice,' I blurted out. What the hell, Sunny? Why *that*? 'He's been there for three weeks now, and I haven't been to see him. I know I should. I just haven't. Not for any reason. Just . . . I dunno why I told you that.'

I pinched at the flesh between thumb and index finger with my nails, till it stung too much and I stopped. Then I did it again.

'My granddad died last year,' he said, keeping his eyes on the road. 'I was going on holiday and my mum said, "Go see him, go say goodbye." Like she knew. But I was too excited about my holiday, man, so you know what I did with my only spare hour before I left, instead of going to see him? I went sunglasses shopping. I already owned sunglasses but part of me wanted something fresh for the hol, you know. And while I was on holiday, he died, like my mum sorta knew he would. And you know how I found out?'

'No,' I said.

'A cousin's Instagram.' He paused, like he was remembering. He coughed. I could hear a quiver in his breathing. 'I found out cos I was hungover and checking Insta, and my cousin put up a picture of my dada-ji, and all it said was "RIP". That's all he deserved, three letters. And I was, like, damn, I shoulda gone seen him and said my goodbye. I still think about that.'

'I hear what you're saying,' I said, quietly.

'And besides,' he added, jovially, 'you'll have a lot to talk about judging by how messed up your face is.'

I pulled down the mirror and tried to look at myself but it was too dark.

'How bad is it?'

'It's not bad – I'm joking, bruv. I'm joking. Sorry, sorry. Look, you got done in good, man. Report that shit. You want to talk about it?'

'No,' I said.

'When you do . . .' he said, then paused. 'Maybe talk to a mate or something. I'm still effectively a stranger.'

I laughed, and he laughed with me, as we pulled into my road.

2.5

It was midday on Saturday and I hadn't spoken to anyone in what felt like an entire day. I'd been cooking food for the week, trying to perfect chana masala, and also googling how to make something with a block of paneer I'd found in the freezer.

With the rest of the day looking empty, and feeling gassed by my conversation with Surinder last night, I decided to go back to the boxing gym. Mostly because there would be people there. Madhu hadn't replied to my text asking if she wanted to catch a film. Mum was sleeping off a double shift. The gym felt like the only place I could go for some human interaction. I didn't have any money to do anything else really. Even the cinema, come to think of it. So, the gym it was. If Shobu was there, I could talk to her. If Surinder was there, I could watch him train. Maybe I could try some stuff out myself.

The other option was going to see Dad.

I chose the gym.

I hobbled the twenty minutes to Easton, along the cycle path. I had to stop and rest a few times.

About three quarters of the way, I sat down on a bench and sipped at some water, looking up and down the path. There were no bicycles. There was a river next to this bit of the path and sometimes you saw brown and green tents down on the embankment where homeless people slept when it was hot.

I thought about the hot summer several years ago. Mum had been working. Dad had taken me to the shop and I'd spent most of the day sitting behind the counter, reading the same comic again and again and listening to a test match on the radio. Dad had then put me to work refilling the sweets. Which had been torture, because he wouldn't let me have any. On the way home, after we'd closed, we had walked through the park. I'd asked if I could go on the climbing frame. He'd shrugged. He'd had a paper under his arm and headed to a bench to sit down and read.

On the climbing frame, a couple of kids started yelling at me to get off. For no reason other than I'd got in their way. They were yelling and yelling and before long it turned to swearing. I argued back with them and went as far as to push one of them.

'Sunny,' I heard my father hiss. 'You leave those boys alone.'

'Dad,' I replied. 'They were calling me names . . .'

'Get down, now,' he said. 'We are going home.'

The two boys smirked at me, like, *Oh yeah, you're in trouble.*

I got down off the climbing frame and Dad grabbed my hand, pulling me home.

'Why are you pushing people and talking back?' he shouted, squeezing my hand tight till it hurt. I yelled out in pain. 'You are supposed to not make any noise, not make any fuss. And then I see you, making a fuss. How will you get through life being loud and making enemies?'

My dad, desperate to erase every inch of me in order for me to succeed.

I stood up from the bench on the cycle path and put my feet in the stance I'd seen Shobu direct Ruchi. My feet were shoulder width apart, both pointing to 2 p.m. I tried the shuffle Shobu did, the one that looked so effortless, where she moved around without her feet ever leaving the ground. I watched my feet move around and around, but I kept stumbling and twisting my legs in strange circles.

Ding-ding. A cyclist sped past me shouting that it was a cycle lane, and I felt my cheeks flush and my stomach churn. How much had he seen of me? How stupid had I looked? It was almost enough to send me straight home. But I could see the gym at this point. I closed my eyes, took a deep breath and hobbled towards it.

Outside the gym there was a kid about my age, chaining up his bike. He had a shaved head and an earring and for a second I thought it was one of my attackers. I approached slowly, squinting at him. He was hunched over a phone that was very close to his face.

As soon as I realised he wasn't one of them, I continued walking to the entrance.

'Hey,' he said to me, as I passed.

I swivelled around, ready to run if I needed to.

'Hi,' I replied, eventually, my eyes not meeting his.

'Did you win?' he asked, thrusting his phone into his hoodie pocket. I must have looked confused because he gestured to my face and smiled.

'Oh, it wasn't a match,' I said, realising he thought I was a fighter.

'*You shoulda seen the other guy*,' he replied in a New York accent and laughed to himself. He caught me looking confused again. 'Oh, mate, sorry, I wasn't taking the piss. I was just ... ah, never mind. Look, you here to train?' I nodded. 'Ah cool, me too. My name's Keir. You?'

I looked at the ground. He had brand-new crisp-white Air Force 1s on. I felt embarrassed that my beaten hand-me-downs from my cousin were so close to the bright sheen of his kicks. I noticed, on the toe of my left foot, a speck of red. Blood? I looked up immediately and crossed my left foot behind my right.

'S-Sunny,' I stammered.

I wanted to run but I could not for the life of me make my body move. It was like back on the train platform, but this time, something about Keir was making me *want* to stay.

He smiled, with his teeth. His hands were by his sides. He leant forward like he wanted me to hug him.

'Nice to meet you, Sunny. Have a good session.'

He entered the building and I watched him. He moved with a lightness that I missed. Like he wasn't even walking. His blond crew cut glowed and at the base of his neck he had a tattoo of two emoji eyes looking out. He was tall, wiry, and he had his boxing trainers draped over his shoulder, tied at the laces. He held his black boxing gloves in his armpit.

I knew I had to follow him but I was too embarrassed.

'You coming in?' I looked up.

He was standing at the door, next to Shobu, holding it open for me. I watched as they dapped then embraced, then she pinched his bicep while he tensed.

I nodded and shuffled towards the door, hesitating a little because I felt exposed.

'Welcome back,' Shobu said as I passed her. 'I sorta knew I'd see you again.'

I watched Keir disappear into the changing rooms and, this time, our eyes properly met as he opened the door with his shoulder. I felt magnetised, drawn to him. He wasn't my type or anything. Just, it felt like one of those pulls, where you know you have to get to know someone. Like you have to be in their glow. Cos maybe their glow would rub off on you.

'That's Keir,' Shobu said. 'One of my fighters. He's nearly ready. I'm very excited about him.'

'He seems nice . . .' I said, my voice trailing away.

I could feel Shobu looking at me expectantly.

'Sooo . . .?' she said. 'Saturday's kinda busy, Sunny. I need to know if I'm training you or not.'

I smiled at her nervously.

'I don't know,' I said. 'I haven't got any money.'

Her face changed. She went from stern to what I imagined was her *not-at-work* face. She smiled and pursed her eyebrows together.

'Look,' she said, stepping closer, her hand hovering by my elbow, like she wanted to offer comfort but didn't know if she had permission to touch me. 'Step into my office. Let me make you a cuppa. Let's have a chat.'

'You said Saturday's kinda busy thou—'

'It's fine,' she said, waving at me. 'Come with me.'

Slowly, I followed her.

Shobu lead me into a side room. It had a kitchenette and fridge, and a dining table. It looked like a staffroom, to be honest. There were health and safety notices and rotas and posters of previous fights across every wall except for one lined with lockers. Each one had a white label with a name on it. I looked for Shobu's as a distraction. Middle, to the left. There she was. As well as her name, there was a sticker of a lotus flower.

'OK. I lied,' she said. 'I don't have an office. I'm freelance here. The staffroom will have to do. Tea?'

I nodded.

We sat in silence for thirty seconds while the kettle boiled. Shobu then stood up and kept herself busy by preparing mugs, lifting up milk for me to nod at, sugar for me to shake my head at, flicking through a newspaper, checking the cabinets repeatedly, for what I didn't know. She clearly didn't like awkward silences. I was used to them. They didn't faze me.

'You're so quiet,' she said, finally. 'It's kinda unnerving.'

'Sorry,' I said, embarrassed. 'People have been telling me that since I was born.'

My nickname at school was Spook. Cos I was always there in groups, never speaking but just there. I didn't feel the need to speak as much as some people. With Madhu, conversation was easy because she talked a lot and I was a good listener. Also, we watched a lot of the same shows so we were both able to avoid any serious chat to talk about the new season of *The Good Place* or whatever. She knew about Dad and she knew not to ask. I respected that.

When I was younger and we lived closer to my cousin, Jags, he used to look after me while both our sets of parents worked. He was a bit older than I was and his elder brother was at uni somewhere else. I think he tolerated me. Basically, I was someone to play computer games against, so he could train up and get better and defeat his friends. We spent hours playing beat 'em ups. I was terrible. I never took the time to work out how to do certain moves. I didn't know that right-right-punch-punch in quick succession released a fireball or that up-down and the direction of travel plus kick resulted in a flying knee drop.

The night before we left London for Bristol, Mum had organised a gathering of all my aunties and uncles and cousins, to wish us well. I was leaving my childhood home and all I wanted to do was cry. I had barely left London the entire time I'd lived there. I knew nowhere else. I tried to keep my face neutral – Mum had filled the house with guests so I had to push everything down. Jags and his mum stayed late. Dad was sleeping. He'd sat in his chair and bossed us around the entire time we'd packed. Mum had done her best to not let it rub her up the wrong way. Meanwhile, I'd had to keep going into the bathroom to silently scream. God, he was annoying. So particular. *Pack it this way. Put that in there. Don't pack those together.*

While Mum and my auntie were cleaning up after the party, Jags sat on my bed while I did final checks that I had packed everything. I didn't own much. A few books, a hand-me-down laptop from him that took twenty minutes to load up, and some clothes – again, mostly his. My entire world fit into a suitcase with room to spare.

He was flicking through a football magazine he'd brought with him. He had dropped out of uni a few months ago to take a job with some YouTube gamers. He was earning a decent amount of money to play FIFA and chat shit with strangers on the Internet. He smiled at me.

'I guess this is goodbye for ever,' he said, laughing.

'You not going to visit?' I replied.

'Bristol? Nah, bruv. Long, innit. You'll be all right. You'll make some friends.'

He stood up, walked over to the window and looked out. I had written him a card, saying goodbye, telling him what an impact he'd made on my life, how appreciative I was that he had always been my big brother and how in a way he was my only real friend.

Silently I approached the window and handed it to him. He pretended to be startled by my appearance next to him.

'Spook!' he exclaimed. 'You are so good at haunting people. What's this?'

'Read it later,' I said, hurrying away from him, suddenly embarrassed. I made a show of checking all my drawers, even though I knew they were already empty. I heard him tear open the envelope and look at the card.

I heard him burst out laughing. He turned around and waved the card at me.

'Spook, what the fuck are you talking about?'

'I'm . . . I'm gonna miss you . . .' I said, quietly.

'Oh, bruv. It's sweet, I guess. But you know we're not friends, right? I mean, I like you, OK, but you're my little cousin. I babysat you for years. Not because I wanted to. But because I had to. You know how many times I had to turn down seeing my boys cos I had to look after the ghost who hates leaving the house?'

'No . . .'

'It was a lot. "Don't take him outside," my mum told me. "He's not good with people. He's a bit special. He's too shy. Your friends will make fun of him. Just keep him at home . . ."'

He laughed and put the card down on the bed.

'It's very, very sweet, Spook. But we're not friends. You're just too weird. Wow, it feels so good to be able to say this after all these years. This really *is* goodbye.'

He strode out of the room. I stared at the card. Yoda was staring back at me. I felt a fizz of tears in my eyes and I ran to the bathroom so he didn't see how much he had upset me.

When they said goodbye, an hour later, I pretended to be asleep. Maybe he felt guilty because he stood over me in bed and ruffled my hair, whispering goodbye. But I didn't care. He had let me down.

My so-called best friend.

'Don't apologise,' Shobu said, breaking my train of thought. 'It's my problem, not yours.'

Shobu placed a cup of tea in front of me and sat down opposite. She put her mug on the table then immediately picked it up again with two hands.

'What do you want to do?' she said.

I met her eyes and shrugged.

'I really don't know,' I told her.

We sat in silence. I noticed the faint tick of a clock, the occasional gleeful shout from the primary school adjacent to the gym, Shobu's fingers drumming on the table. Her knuckles were dry and she had a long cut on one of her fingers. I focused on it to avoid eye contact.

'You don't know?' she said.

'No,' I replied. 'I don't know why I'm here.'

'I asked what you want to do, not why you're here. You're here. So if you're up for it, all we need to work out is how to fill your time.'

I still wasn't sure. Maybe I just didn't want to feel scared any more. Maybe I wanted to know how to hit someone so they wouldn't hit me again. I smiled.

'What's funny?' she asked.

'I don't know,' I said, loosely. 'This is the most I've spoken since it happened.'

The last bit came out in an offhand way. Something about her relaxed me. And I was finding not telling anyone what happened tiring.

'Since what happened?' she asked.

I stopped smiling, realising I had said too much. I stared at the cut on her finger again.

'Sunny . . .' she said, softly.

'Since all this,' I said, pointing to my face.

'All . . . your bruises and scars?'

I nodded.

'How did they happen?'

'I don't want to talk about it,' I said.

'It might help to talk?'

I was sick of people asking. Sick of it. I just wanted to let it go. I could feel something erupting in me.

'I was attacked, OK?' I said, gabbling. 'Please stop asking me. I was sitting at a train station minding my own business and I got attacked. I don't want to say any more. I'm sorry. If I tell you more, then I'll remember and I don't want to remember.'

I put my hands in my pockets and bowed my head. It felt like a relief to say something. To a stranger. I felt lighter. But I was immediately on guard again.

'You don't want to remember?' she asked. 'How come?'

'Because I don't want to feel like I did again.'

'How did you feel?'

65

'Like I was less than human. Like I was a *paki* . . .' I spat out the last word and then stopped.

I picked up my mug and slurped.

'A paki? Who called you that?'

I slurped a bit longer than necessary.

'I know what you're doing,' I said.

'What am I doing?'

'You're getting me to tell you what happened in some nicey-nicey way instead of being bait.'

Shobu laughed. 'And what would be in that for me? I just need to know who I'm training and, most importantly, why they want training and what for . . .'

I gulped at my tea and slammed it down. I was ready to go. I didn't want to cause anyone any hassle. I stood up.

'I'm just being honest,' she said. 'Sit down, Sunny. Come on, mate. I think if you want me to dedicate time to training you, I should know who I'm training. Right?'

I hovered, pushing my chair back under the table slowly. Shobu stood up and put her palms in the air.

'Hit me,' she said.

'What? No,' I replied. I put my hands in my pockets for emphasis.

'Why not?'

'Cos . . . I'm . . . it's not me. I don't hit people.'

'You're not exactly gonna hurt me.' She laughed.

'No,' I said. 'It's not me.'

'How about now?' Shobu shoved at my shoulders.

I jerked backwards and caught myself from falling.

'Stop that,' I said.

She stepped forward till her right knee was between my legs. She shoved me again.

66

'What about now? Eh?'

She pushed me. Harder.

Without thinking, I balled my fist and thrust it in front of me weakly. I didn't want to be feeble again. I didn't want to be frozen. I didn't want to let fear make me still. She batted my hand away.

I cried out and thrust my fist wildly at where I thought her cheek would be. She slipped to her right and held up a palm to catch my fist.

She pushed me with her free hand and I fell to the floor.

I crashed down on to my tailbone. I folded my arms in front of me and looked up at her.

'How dare you?' I said. I wanted to cry.

'Do you know what you did wrong?'

'I don't give a shit,' I said, scrabbling and failing to get to my feet.

She offered me her hands. I grabbed them and pulled myself up.

'It's all about your feet. You forgot what I was showing Ruchi.'

'You hurt me,' I said.

'Sorry,' she replied. 'I know . . .'

She stood with her feet shoulder width apart, pointing to two o'clock. She put her fists up over her mouth. She ushered for me to do the same.

'When you hit me this time, swivel up from your foot and rotate your shoulders, yeah?'

I threw a punch. This time, thinking about the alignment of my body, I made sure the punch felt controlled. She slipped out of my punch and tapped me lightly on the side of my head.

'You lingered. Never linger. Back to defensive stance. Always. Protect yourself. Get in, do your business, get out . . .'

'Like a toilet,' I said, laughing.

'Like a toilet.'

She lowered her fists and sank back down into her seat at the table. She picked up her mug and sipped at her tea. I did the same. She sighed.

'You know, the only time I was called a paki, I let the guy get away with it. I was so disappointed with myself, I swore I would never let anyone do that to me again. The next day, Mum took me to my first self-defence lesson. Look at me now. No one is ever saying that word to me. Not even cos they think we're friends.'

'Did you see the person again?' I asked.

'We broke up the next day,' she replied, putting her fists up. 'My second biggest regret, after not knocking him out for saying it, was that I didn't end it there and then—'

There was a knock on the door behind me. It was so out of the blue, I jumped a little and swivelled round. It was Keir. He was gripping the door frame and leaning into the room. He smiled.

'Shobz,' he said. 'Chris is looking for you.'

'Oh crap,' Shobu said. 'Sorry, Sunny. The boss calls. Listen. Stick around, put some gloves on if you want. Wait for me after this lesson – I want to chat some more.'

She ran out of the room.

Keir entered the staffroom and picked up Shobu's mug, taking it to the sink and pouring the contents out. He put the mug down and turned around to face me. He smiled again. This time, I offered one back.

68

'You Shobu's next project?' he asked and chuckled to himself.

'What do you mean?' I said.

'Ah nothing, don't worry. Hey, shall I show you the equipment?' I nodded. 'You got wraps?' I shook my head. He opened a drawer and pulled some out. 'Here,' he said. 'They're a fiver normally, but there are usually so many just left in the gym every week, we wash 'em and give 'em to first timers. You OK with second-hand ones?'

I nodded.

He motioned for me to stretch my hand out. I did.

'You don't talk much, do you?' he said.

I shrugged and laughed.

'I'm sorry,' I said. 'It's . . . you know.'

I watched as Keir wrapped my right hand then my left hand. It felt strange having these bits of cloth insulating my hands and wrists from injury. I flexed each hand. Keir examined the wraps again and readjusted the Velcro on one of them. He clutched my wrists and grinned.

'You're ready,' he said.

'Thank you,' I replied, quietly.

He put his hand on my back and beckoned for me to go with him.

'Follow me,' he said, leading me into the gym.

The radio was playing 1Xtra loudly. It wasn't as busy as it had been the other night. Instead, people crowded around the ring as two fighters sparred. They shouted out encouragement. One of them had her name on her shorts: Maz. The other was dressed all in black.

'That's Maz,' Keir said. 'Commonwealth bantam champ, innit. She's so fast.'

The bell rang and the fighters broke off. There was applause from everyone watching. Keir handed me a skipping rope and took one for himself.

'When the bell rings, you skip. And you don't stop till the bell rings again. Ready?'

'No,' I said. 'I haven't skipped for years.'

'Then the next three minutes are going to be terrible for you,' he said, and laughed.

When the bell rang, I skipped. Once. Then I tripped and felt the rope lash against the back of my legs. I was lucky to be wearing my tracksuit bottoms. Also, I hadn't wanted Keir to know how much pain I was still in. I tried again but when I landed the stab in my ankle from where I'd been kicked was too much and I stopped. I watched Keir bounce up and down seamlessly instead. One foot, two foot, swap foot over and over.

He skipped fluidly. He was in constant motion but each movement was so small you could barely detect what he was doing. It was sort of beautiful. He looked at me as he skipped, moving instinctively.

'You OK?'

'My ankle . . .' I said. My voice trailed off as he doubled the speed of his skipping.

I stood there, dumbly waiting for the three minutes to end. It felt like an incredibly long time.

When the bell eventually rang, he grinned, grabbed my skipping rope and threw it into a bucket by the mirrors.

'It's always awkward the first time . . .' he said, smiling. 'Go get some gloves.'

* * *

As I slip his jab-cross, ducking and weaving right then left, I aim a hook into his side. He isn't expecting it and I hear him groan on impact. It gives me enough time to spring up and into him. I aim another hook on to the side of his head. He blocks it and his glove absorbs most of the impact but it's enough to get him off balance. I leap at him with both my gloves and push him backwards. He's on the ropes.

For a second, he looks up and our eyes connect. Just for a second.

It undoes me.

Everything floods back into my head. Everything that has happened since that first time in the gym, where he taught me all the basic punches and worked on my stance for an hour till Shobu was finished with her lesson.

In his eyes, I see all the time we have spent together, everything we've laughed about, everything we had between us. Like when he showed me kindness in those early days, like how he pushed me to be better than I was, like . . . It doesn't bear remembering. I scold myself for getting out of the match and into my head. I try to focus. I try to think about what happened the day it all came crashing down between us instead. I try to remember everything he said. I try to remember the look of abject hate in his eyes as he ran away from me.

I try to get my head back in the match.

It's too late. In those seconds where I opened the door to my memories, I lost this round.

He throws himself off the ropes and into me. And because my mind is elsewhere, my gloves, though up, are limp. They drop. He takes advantage and throws a triple jab – each time I step back, feeling his gloves on my cheek, making me stumble backwards.

He throws his powerful cross.

I am back in the match. I slip the punch and I swivel away from him, jabbing as we switch positions. We circle each other until the bell goes.

Keir immediately bumps his chest against mine as I drop my guard.

He throws his hands up as if to say, *What? What are you going to do about it?* The referee places a hand on his chest and pushes him back to his corner.

I stand there. My breathing is shallow. I taste something metallic in the inside of my mouth. I watch him sit down, eyeballing me the whole time.

This is not my friend, I have to remind myself. Not any more.

Round 3

Shobu massages my shoulders.

'You're tensing up,' she says.

'I know. He's in my face. All the time,' I say to her.

I spot Hari in the crowd. He's chatting to his friend. I can't believe he came back to watch this. Shobu taps my cheek.

'Stay in the ring,' she says. 'He's supposed to be in your face. The fight isn't just in those three minutes. You know this. The fight is happening all the time.'

'I can't do this.'

'Of course you can. I'm here watching you the whole time. You're frustrating him by making him miss a lot of his best punches.'

'It's not enough.'

'You got some good shots in.'

'Yeah, but—'

'Jesus, Sunny, what does success look like for you? You're wearing him down cos it's in his best interests to beat you quickly. He's the one people have been talking about. He doesn't want to look stupid. Or weak. You're

73

the underdog. You're supposed to go down easy. And you're still standing. And you're landing shots. To me, that's enough. Remember: you're in this match and you're in this round and you're in this ring and you're in this punch. Focus on the moment. The punch. You can do this.'

The bell rings.

I feel a panic rise up in me. I want to get out of the ring. I want to run away. I don't want Hari to watch me. I don't want to be defending myself from Keir. I don't want Shobu to know how disappointing I am. Everything is on top of me.

The referee is calling me towards him.

'Come on,' he's saying, urgently.

I stay seated.

3.1

The weeks went on and my body healed. Except it was now learning other forms of pain. While my bruises got better, my wrists and knuckles ached from flexing and striking. While my thighs felt less like a sack for broken bones, my knees bore the strain of every punch, every duck, every weave.

I kept boxing as my secret. I owned it. No one else. I was the only one with expectations of what it was and why I was doing it. And the more I kept it in my chest, the more I felt like it gave me power.

Mum cooked us both uttapam while I defrosted some dhal from the freezer. I liked Sunday mornings. It was the only day she definitely had the morning off. We were listening to Gagan Grewal on Asian Network. He had these themed shows where he played Bollywood from the sixties, seventies and eighties. Today he was focusing on songs in Hema Malini films.

Mum sang along, knowing all the words, and I hummed as best I could. I knew all the melodies and had an idea of what they were talking about. I had been listening to these same songs since I'd been born. Apparently I'd come into this world to the strains of the *Dil* soundtrack, which Mum had been listening to through Walkman headphones.

Mum made cooking uttapam look so simple. It was seamless, the way she ladled a dollop of the mixture on to the tawa and then spread it around the surface with the bottom of the ladle. She then grabbed a fistful of tomato, pepper and onion to sprinkle on the top. The way she was able to use tongs to pick it up and flip it without accidentally tearing through the savoury pancake was beautiful to watch.

She had made three uttapam. One more and we'd be ready. I was stirring the dhal robotically. The flat smelled amazing – like our home.

I caught her smiling at me.

'What?' I asked.

'I miss you, darling,' she said. 'I miss us.'

'Me too, Mum,' I said. 'How's work?'

'Why are you asking me about that?' She sighed. 'I was trying to have a good time with my baba. How's college?'

'Why you asking me about that? I'm trying to have a good time with my mum,' I said.

She laughed.

She thought about it.

'Any nice boys?'

I shook my head and tasted the dhal. It burned my tongue.

'I see,' Mum said. 'Be secretive. I see.'

I wiped at my brow with the sleeve of my hoodie and turned to sip my tea. She slipped her hand into my free one and squeezed.

'You been spending a lot of time with Madhu?' she asked. 'She is a good influence on you.'

Mum loved Madhu. She was glad we were friends, although I often thought Mum would prefer it if *they* were friends. The two of them had once spent an hour creasing at a sandwich I'd made. It was just a cheese and chilli-powder sandwich. I was coughing in the bathroom, trying to rinse my tongue and stop myself from crying. No big deal, but they both thought it was the funniest thing in the world.

'Just at college. No more than usual, why?'

'Because . . . I barely see you. You're hardly at home. I know I'm hardly at home. But neither are you. What have you been up to these last few weeks?'

I didn't want to tell Mum about what I was doing, but I knew what she'd say. *Why are you learning to be a thug? Why do you want to beat people up?* She wouldn't understand. And I didn't want to give her an opportunity to express her disapproval. I loved my new thing too much. She used to hate Dad and me watching wrestling. She said it was too violent. She'd *definitely* hate on boxing. I loathed keeping secrets from her though. It filled me with anxiety. We used to be transparent. I was already withholding information about what had happened at the train station.

'You know, studying . . . and stuff.'

'That's it?'

I nodded. Mum smiled at me, like, *Fine, fine, be like that.*

I massaged my left wrist.

Shobu had officially taken me on to train. She had paid the £50 membership for me and said I could pay her back a fiver a week for the ten weeks she thought it would take me to start seeing my potential. And then, after that, it would be up to me.

I asked about her hourly rate.

She asked about how much salary I earned.

'Exactly,' she said, breaking the silence that followed. 'Best not to ask. I'm not doing this to get rich, am I?'

77

We met three times a week – two evenings and one morning – and trained hard. We did technique in one session, fitness in another and pad work in the third. Each hour was intense.

I had travel routes in my head that were safe. Home to college and college to home was sorted in my mind. And home to Madhu's and home to the shops and home to the central library. I was able to tackle each one with a degree of confidence. I now took two buses to college. It added forty minutes on to my journey and I was sometimes late cos of traffic, but at least the bus felt safer than the train.

I had a new route to add to my list now. To the gym and from the gym. It was a little oasis on my journeys between home and college and it was starting to do good things for me.

I didn't hobble any more. My bruises had mostly healed. But something else was happening, I could tell. I was looking ahead of me as I walked, instead of down at the ground.

'You sure you don't want to tell me? Something is different about you,' Mum said and I put myself back in the room. 'Are you *sure* it's not a boy?'

'What?' I replied. 'Mum, no. I don't have time for dating. University, innit.'

'Have you decided what you want to do?'

I panicked, grabbed the ladle from her hand and rinsed it under the tap. I spooned some dhal into two bowls and smiled at her. I shrugged.

'Definitely something different. Like a weight has been lifted.'

She looked so relieved in that moment, it struck me that Mum had shown me the ultimate respect by not directly asking what had happened that night. And what was I thinking, choosing not to repay that respect by hiding the thing that was making me happy for the first time in ages . . .?

'I've been learning to box,' I said, carefully, while I filled up two glasses with water from the tap.

The atmosphere changed in the room. I heard Mum turn the hob off and sigh, before taking a seat, slowly. I turned around to face her. I put the glasses of water down on the small kitchen table and took a History book off my chair. I sat down. With nowhere else to put the book, I rested it on my lap, tearing off some uttapam, dipping it into my dhal and shovelling it into my mouth.

I bit down on a green chilli and it stung the back of my throat. I coughed. I took a sip of water even though that was never helpful.

Mum pushed the tub of yoghurt towards me. I opened the lid and dipped another piece of uttapam into it. I bit down. It made the sting go away slowly but I was still coughing hard.

We carried on eating.

'You're not saying anything,' I said after a while.

'What do you want me to say?'

'Nothing, I guess. You just didn't react to my news. You always have a reaction.'

'I'm used to silence and secrets now,' she said and looked up at me.

'Mum, that's not fair,' I said, knowing, instantly, it was the wrong thing to say.

'I cannot believe what I'm hearing,' Mum said, standing up. She lifted her plate and a cup of tea.

'Where are you going?' I asked.

'I'm going to watch television. I do not know why you want to learn how to beat up other people. This is not how you deal with your problems. You talk about them. You try to overpower them. You got attacked and scared? Your response should not be to learn how to do it back to people. This is not how we should be living our lives. I do not understand you. You are not a violent person.'

'Mum . . . It's not about violence—'

'No,' she said, definitively. 'I do not want to talk about it.'

She walked into the other room. I heard the television switch on and Andrew Marr start talking. I finished my uttapam as quickly as possible.

Thirty minutes later, Mum hadn't moved. I laced my beaten trainers ready for a run, while sitting next to her on the sofa. Her feet were practically under mine. I looked at her.

'I'm going out,' I said.

She nodded.

'To box?'

'No,' I said. 'To run.'

'OK,' she replied and turned back to the television. After a pause, she said, without looking at me, 'I know you won't talk about the attack, and I know in your heart you do not have the confidence to be a fighter.'

'You're wrong,' I told her. 'I *am* a fighter. I just never knew that about myself till I started this.'

I stood up and headed out.

3.2

Keir met me at the end of our road, like he did every other day, and we began jogging towards Eastville Park. There we could pick up a path that led us to Snuff Mills and back. It was a breezy, lukewarm day and I wanted to do anything other than run. I felt my uttapam sitting heavy in my stomach as I pounded the floor, more or less in sync with Keir, who was at the top of his physical game.

Keir had been the main reason I'd kept going back. We'd become close, quickly. I found him easy company, and he seemed to like mine too. He always asked me questions, like he was genuinely interested in me, and filled our silences with stories of fights he had seen, or brutal training regimes he had heard about, or basic Bristol local knowledge. He didn't mind that I longed to just listen most of the time. I finally had two best friends. If London Sunny could see me now . . .

After my very first session with Shobu, I'd been sitting on a bench in the changing room when Keir had come up to me.

'Hey,' he said. 'How was that?

He sat down on the bench opposite me and grabbed my hands. I flinched initially, still with the fragments of violence in my mind, but he was smiling and winked at me as he massaged my fingers individually.

'Sorry,' he said. 'It's good to keep the blood moving. How did you find that? I love Shobu. She's a great trainer. Doesn't talk down to us; doesn't get angry.'

'Are the other trainers angry?' I asked.

Keir thought about it. 'Some of them are,' he said. 'But Shobz is just really nice. Wants you and me to buddy up so you can get good enough to spar me. I can teach you some stuff. You can be a moving heavy bag for me.'

He laughed. I laughed too, but the thought of being struck made me feel sick. I just wanted to land shots myself.

'Hey, so what's up today?' he asked, as we ran through the gates to Eastville Park. 'You seem tense. All OK? Is it the attack?'

'No,' I said, my stomach burning. 'It's my mum. I told her about all this. She said I'm no fighter.'

Keir laughed.

'Sunny, you don't exactly have the fighter's spirit,' he said. 'Not yet, anyway.'

'You siding with my mum?' I asked, super pissed he was almost agreeing with her.

Keir got down on the ground and gestured to me to join him. We linked our ankles and feet and did full sit-ups, high-fiving as we came up. I was getting used to this routine now.

'A fighter has to have a clear mind, and know what they're fighting for.'

'I know what I'm fighting for,' I said. I paused. Did I though? Was I fighting so I was never attacked again or was I fighting myself? I didn't know. 'What about you? What are you fighting for?'

'My uncle was a boxer when he was a teenager. But the wrong shot to his head dislocated his retina and he was so shook he never fought again. The doctors said he'd end up blind in one eye. And that destroyed him. So much. But I can be the boxer he could have been.'

'So you're doing it for other people,' I said, laughing.

'Course I am. Do anything for the people who matter, innit. Family. It's all we have,' Keir said, seriously. 'Your turn. What makes you fight?'

'Well, I guess at first I was doing it for self-defence. But now . . . it's because it's helping me take up space.'

'What do you mean?'

'I dunno, man,' I said, collapsing on the floor for fifteen seconds of recovery. 'I spent so long not wanting to take up any space, have no one look at me. Now I'm starting to see how becoming a fighter can help me own my space.'

'I think I get you,' Keir said. 'Cos of what happened?'

'I'm not talking about it,' I said. 'Nice try.'

Keir laughed and jumped up. It was time to run again.

The first few runs with Keir had been hard because my fitness had been poor, especially compared to his. I was sure he'd been running slower than he would if I hadn't been there, just so I could keep up. I couldn't talk so he'd just talked at me – about college, about girls he fancied, about the best places in Bristol to go out and get food, and how to do stuff on a no-budget budget. I learned about him by listening, and liked him more and more every time we ran.

Today we were trying a slightly longer run. I was fitter now, and could manage a two-way chat without running out of breath.

'That used to be a chippie,' he said as we ran past a chicken shop.

'How do you know?'

'I used to live above it. It was my dad's. Martin's Legendary Fish.'

'What happened to it?'

'I dunno. The area changed. Dad thought it was better to sell up.'

'How did it change?'

'Let's just say, it's better suited to being a chicken shop . . .'

'Why's that?'

'I dunno. The area looks like it'll like fried chicken more than fish.'

'What do you mean?' I asked. Something had changed in his tone of voice, something that made me feel uncomfortable.

'Sorry, Sunny, listen, no offence. Sorry.' Keir was blushing now. 'It's just something my dad said. Shit. I didn't mean anything . . .'

'It's fine,' I said, quickening my pace a little.

'When did you move here?' he asked, after a few awkward minutes.

'Like, three months ago, just after half term.'

'Where from? London?'

'Yeah,' I said. 'There was a heart specialist here that we needed to see for my dad. It was too much for him to come and go on trains and my mum doesn't drive. So we relocated. I had the option of living with my cousin and auntie and uncle in London but thought it was better to be here for my mum, you know? It was supposed to be temporary but I guess we're staying.'

'Sorry to hear about your dad,' he said, veering off the path on to the grass. 'Glad you're not one of those normal London types though.'

We stopped under a tree. Keir looked at his watch and started shadow-boxing. I copied him, mimicking his every move. I still found shadow-boxing utterly bewildering to watch and terrifyingly embarrassing to do. So I followed his form and his line, trying to imagine a fight in my head and following it, from offence to defence, from moving to striking to slipping.

When his watch sounded, three excruciatingly long minutes later, we carried on running, a touch slower now, it felt like.

'What's a normal London type?' I asked.

'Huh?' he said, looking at me.

'You know, what you said – before we stopped.'

'Oh, right. All the people moving in from London and making everything expensive. Dad goes on about it all the time. He moans about it more than he does about immigrants.'

I stopped running.

'Oh yeah, man. Don't worry,' Keir added, smiling as he doubled back to where I was standing. 'Not you. You were born here, innit.'

'My mum's an immigrant,' I said.

'God, Sunny, listen, sorry,' Keir said. He was red-faced, but it might have been from the exercise. 'It's my dad that has the problem. Not me.'

'OK,' I said.

I felt uneasy but now Keir had his arm around me like it was all fine.

We ran in silence for a few minutes as I chewed over his words.

Quietly, he said, 'It's wicked you moved here. I love it here.'

'Yeah,' I said. I still wasn't sure.

Keir pointed to something as we passed.

'I used to come to this park all the time as a kid,' Keir said. 'Mum used to sit on that bench and read the paper cover to cover while I cycled up and down. This is where I feel most at home.'

He laughed and sped into a sprint. I followed him.

'Did you grow up in Bristol?' I asked.

He nodded. 'Born and bred, me,' he said, wiping droplets of sweat off his cheek. 'You can trace us back to the 1800s, according to my dad. My brother moved to Birmingham for work for like six months but came back and said he preferred it here.'

'Why?'

Keir lowered his voice, and spoke slowly, like he was being really careful what he said.

'Dunno. I just think he didn't like being away, you know?'

We carried on running, in silence this time. We circled back along the water before stopping at the bottom of a hill.

'OK,' Keir said, looking up the hill. 'See you at the top.'

He sprinted away. I followed. It was steep and, after about fifty metres, I slowed into a jog, into a walk, into standing still, crouched over, heaving air into my lungs. I could see Keir still running up as fast as when he'd started. At the top, he punched the air and swivelled round, dancing on the spot like he was Rocky at the top of the steps in Philly.

He sang the theme tune at me as I staggered towards him. Passers-by laughed and smiled supportively. I looked at the floor, away from them.

'Come on, Sunny,' he shouted. 'Hill sprints, build up those legs. Do it.'

I tried again and ran through the pain in my hamstrings. This was the longest I had ever run and the hill was brutal. Keir was clapping for me to keep going.

At the top, I fell down on the ground, heaving more shallow breaths into my lungs, letting the stings in my legs fade away.

'Nice one, man, we did it. It's nearly time for our reward.'

'What's that?'

Keir kicked at my leg and ushered for me to get up and follow as he carried on running.

We ran out of the park we had ended up in and out into a housing estate. Rows and rows of houses, long roads that all melded into each other. I felt disorientated. Away from the familiarity of the routes I considered safe, I was now in unknown territory. I was trying to control the panic. I knew I should trust Keir, but my brain was frantically retracing our route so I knew how to get home safely.

We stopped in front of a house.

He put a hand on the back of my head and brought us together till our sweaty brows touched.

'Wait here,' Keir said. He fished a key out of his tracksuit bottoms, ran up to the door and let himself in. I stared at the house and then up and down the street, wondering how anyone could distinguish one place from another.

A man with a terrier approached me. He stopped, right up in my space. He was wearing a white T-shirt and grey trackies. He turned his head to look at Keir's front door. He had a St George's flag tattoo on the back of his shaved head. He had grey eyes and a pursed brow. He spat on the floor. He looked at the house again and back at me.

'Can I help you?' he said.

I shook my head and stared at the floor. My heart was beating fast.

'What you doing here?'

'Waiting,' I mumbled, quietly.

'Oi,' he said. 'Look at me when I'm talking. Who you waiting for?'

'My friend,' I said.

'Right, right, OK. Your friend in there?' He pointed at the house Keir had gone into.

I nodded.

'What's his name?' he said, getting up in my face. 'Why won't you look at me? Is there a problem? Look at me.'

'Joe,' I heard, and looked up. 'What are you doing?'

Keir was leaving the house with two plastic shaker bottles, containing what looked like chocolate protein shakes. He gave the man a wide berth as he walked past him.

'Joe, this is my boy Sunny. He's just joined the boxing gym. Sunny, this is my brother, Joe.'

'Hi,' I said, offering my hand to shake his.

Joe looked at it and at me. He spat on the ground.

'All right, mate,' he said, rolling his eyes and walking into the house. Keir mouthed, *Sorry,* and thrust the protein shake at me before stepping back.

'We did it,' he said, staring at his front door.

'Keir, don't be hanging out with your mates all day, yeah? There's jobs here. Yeah?' Joe was standing on the front step, watching us.

Keir wiped his mouth and smiled at me. He looked at Joe, and for a second, I could see fear in his eyes. He rubbed his nose and cleared his throat.

'Yeah, Joe, OK,' he said.

Joe went inside and Keir gulped the rest of his protein shake.

'Sorry about that,' he said. 'Mum and Dad are coming back from this long trip to Australia and . . .' He stopped.

He cleared his throat again.

'Sorry,' he said again. 'Joe doesn't like strangers.'

'OK,' I said. I didn't know what else to say.

Keir looked at me. He stepped from foot to foot, nervously, like he was ready to go. I finished my shake and handed it back to him.

'I've given you a bad impression of my family,' he said, smiling. 'They're good people.'

'OK,' I said again.

'Look,' he said. 'We can train elsewhere. That's fine. I really like you, Sunny. You're committed and solid. All good, yeah?'

He held his fist out to me.

'Thank you,' I said. 'For the training session. And for the shake. See you at the gym?'

'Yeah, yeah, yeah,' Keir said, looking out at his street. 'For sure.'

I heard the door open again and Keir's brother's head appeared.

'Keir,' he shouted. 'I fucking said there's jobs that need doing.'

Keir flinched and shoved his fists in his pocket. I could see that hint of fear in his eyes again. I wanted to stand between him and the front door but I was stuck to the spot.

'You know your way back from here, right?' he said and turned and ran into the house. He hadn't even waited for my reply.

I stood on the street. The air felt light and shallow in my chest as I heard the door slam shut behind me.

I didn't know how to get back and I didn't have any data on my phone. I could see a main road up at the end of their street. Maybe there would be a familiar sight. I didn't want to move though. I didn't know where I was. I stood there. I was about to cry. I could feel it.

I managed to walk three doors down so at least Keir or his brother couldn't see me from the window or something.

3.3

'What's wrong with you?' Shobu said as I struck the pads the next day.

She dropped her arms and took a hand out of the pad, flexing her fist in pain.

'Nothing,' I said and put my guard up, ready to punch.

'No,' she said. 'There's something wrong. What is it?'

'There isn't, I swear,' I said.

I still had Keir on my mind. His brother was terrifying. And his dad had some funny opinions. I kept running through it all in my mind. Keir seemed so different from his brother. He was warm and inviting and kind and generous.

Should I be worried?

Shobu sat on the floor and ushered me to do the same.

'Sunny,' she said. 'I'm giving up my time and subsidising you. I know you have other things going on. But you keep them out of the ring. Or you tell me what's going on and we can deal with it. You understand?'

I nodded.

'I can't train you if your mind is elsewhere. And if you won't let me in, you need to leave whatever it is in the changing rooms. Do you understand?'

I nodded again, my eyes on the ground.

We sat in silence.

'How did you stop being afraid?' I asked, eventually. 'When that guy called you . . . that word? What did you do?'

'I came here. Right here. Not because I wanted to learn how to knock him out, but because boxing is about the mind, it's about self-defence. It's about being confident in yourself so you can stand tall. I'm not afraid because I know that he can't hurt me again. You're doing the same. You are learning how to take up space, unapologetically. Because it belongs to you. And there is no fear in that space. No way. Get up.'

'OK.'

I stood up and raised my fists. Shobu held out her hands, padded, and called out a combination. I threw two punches. The third one didn't land because she suddenly ducked and pushed me off my feet. I fell to my side, stopping myself from falling over.

'Did that hurt?' she said. I shook my head. 'You angry?' I shook my head. 'Exactly.'

I came out of the shower to find Keir sitting next to my things. He held his phone in his hand but he was looking expectantly at me when I approached the bench. He shuffled to one side to let me get to my bag. He smiled at me as I dried myself.

'Did you find your way home yesterday?' he asked.

He fiddled with the strap of his cycle helmet.

'Yes,' I replied.

'Good,' he said. 'My brother. He . . .'

'He did not want me there,' I said.

'Yeah, I'm sorry about that. He's . . . We're very different people. He just doesn't like people he doesn't know. Look, it's OK, we'll just find a route that ends at yours, yeah?' He paused. 'Also, I worry you think I believe all those things my dad does . . .'

I looked into Keir's eyes and backed away slightly.

'It crossed my mind, yeah,' I told him.

'It did?' he asked. Almost surprised.

'Why say it at all?' I said. 'My mum's an immigrant. Brown people like chicken. And what?' I could feel myself getting louder, talking in a voice I didn't recognise.

'Sunny,' Keir said. 'I am not my dad. I promise you. Or my uncle. I swear, sometimes the stuff they say, it just comes out, you know? I swear I'm not like them. I'm not . . . *a racist*.' He whispered the last bit.

'OK,' I said.

'I brought you something,' he said.

He reached into his bag and pulled out some boxing trainers. Thin, like high-tops.

'This is my old pair. But they're still in good nick, mind. Want them?'

'Thank you,' I said. 'That's very kind.'

'I'm really enjoying training with you, Sunny . . .'

Dylan, another trainer, poked his head into the changing room.

'Keir, come on, mate, Shobu says you're late. Three rounds, skipping. Now.'

'Sorry, mate,' Keir said to Dylan. He turned back to me. 'See you later?'

'I got college,' I replied.

3.4

I settled down at my favourite computer, away from everyone else in the library. The one sweet spot where no one could see your screen. I found it useful for googling articles about Dad's symptoms, trawling through Reddit forums on how to grieve appropriately when you dislike one of your parents – unspoken thoughts that I could never vocalise. I'd found this Facebook group for people whose parents were in hospices. I never participated but it was a good way of seeing that there were other people going through what I was. Not only that, it was a comfort that they all had different attitudes towards visits. Some went every day, some went once a week, some were building up to one perfect visit.

The day before Dad had gone into the hospice he had shouted at me for not making his tea milky enough. He liked to have a cup of tea that was half water, half whole milk, with two sugars. He was sitting up in his bed in our lounge, watching cricket. I handed him the mug and he slurped on it before throwing it to the floor, the hot liquid splashing across my feet.

He shouted at me that I was too stupid to get even a simple thing like tea correct.

In the kitchen, Mum had defended him, saying he wasn't well. But I knew then that I couldn't wait for him to not be around. It had always just been Mum and me anyway.

Today though, I was watching boxing training videos. And – bonus – the library was the furthest point away from Amanda's classroom, so she was unlikely to find me here.

Madhu dropped her bag on the table next to me and let out a long sigh. I pulled out my earbuds.

'Uni application done,' she said. 'You?'

I shook my head.

'Decided what you want to do?'

I shook my head again. Madhu tutted slowly.

'It's getting close,' she said.

'I know,' I replied.

Madhu got a stack of books out and I took the opportunity to close some tabs in case her natural nosiness took her over to my screen.

'You seen that guy Felix? New in my English class? He's so buff.'

'Is he?' I asked. 'I haven't seen him.'

'Don't pretend you ain't clocked him in the corridor,' Madhu said.

I had. He was cute. A little too clean-shaven-and-Oxford-shirt for me. But then, what did I know about my type? I'd never even been out on a date.

'So, what's new with you?' I said, hoping to instigate a change of subject at least.

'Oh, you know. This and that. Oh wait, listen, this Saturday, my dad's having a barbecue. He said to invite you and your mum. Come?'

'I'm training,' I said.

Madhu looked up at me.

'Training? For what?'

'Boxing . . .'

Madhu laughed. 'You box now? OK, Tyson, whatever . . .'

'It's true,' I said, throwing my guard up as proof.

'You couldn't box a flannel, Sunny. I saw the bruises . . .'

My face fell. So did my guard.

'Exactly,' I said.

3.5

Keir rubbed at the back of his head as we walked to the train station.

'Are you sure it's OK that I come?' he said.

We'd both showered at the gym and I'd put on a shirt Mum had ironed for me. Keir was wearing standard-issue Keir-wear – white T-shirt, grey tracksuit.

'Yeah, of course,' I said. 'Madhu's a great friend. She said bring someone. Mum can't come. There'll be loads of food.'

Mum was working. I was under strict orders to bring her a plastic container of Madhu's mum's world-famous chicken home.

'I just feel like I'm intruding,' he replied, quietly.

'Don't be. It's all good, man.'

'You're not gonna leave me sitting in the corner while you chat to all your mates?'

I smirked. 'Things get hairy, just tell everyone some of your favourite quotes from your dad.'

Keir stared at me. I laughed.

'Jokes.'

He punched me on the arm. 'Jesus,' he said. 'I said I was sorry . . .'

On the train, he and I did sprints up and down the empty carriage. We did pull-ups on the hanging bar and then squat jumps and lunges, alternating between the two.

By the time we arrived at our stop, I could feel a trickle of sweat down my back. I could also feel my glutes on fire. I felt strong. I loved the person Keir was helping me to become.

We walked along the train platform. I normally felt so big walking next to Keir. He was fearless. He would shove his hands in his pockets and roll his shoulders forward and back, jauntily, like he didn't have a care in the word. He usually had a smile on his face and would wink at anyone he knew.

Today, his head was slightly bowed. His fists were balled, at his side. He was shuffling. Was he nervous?

'So,' Keir said. 'What happens at an Indian barbecue?'

'We cook food and eat it and listen to music and talk . . .' I paused, cos I could see Keir was missing my sarcasm. 'And then we sacrifice a goat and recite the lines of every single Amitabh Bachchan film ever. Anyone who misses a line gets a stick to the back of their legs.'

Keir looked at me, shocked.

'I'm joking, man. God, you're ignorant.'

'Nah, man. I've just . . .' he said, hesitantly, like he was searching for the right words. 'I've never really been to one of these things before. I don't want to look like an idiot, you know?'

'It's just a barbecue,' I said, laughing.

'Do you like spicy food?' Madhu's dad asked Keir.

'Yes, sir,' he said.

It was strange to see Keir on edge. He entered the house with his fists still balled, his shoulders hunched, watching me carefully as I took my shoes off and flung them on a discarded mountain of sandals and chappals. He did the same. I watched as he bent down and stuffed the holey bits of his socks in between his toes. He looked up and shrugged.

Madhu's dad was standing in the hallway with his brother, rolling a cigarette. He winked at me and said, 'The silent assassin has come to murder my chicken.'

He laughed and patted me on the back.

'Hello, uncle,' I said quietly.

'Ravi,' he said to his brother. 'This is Sunny, Madhu's best friend. I have no idea why. I've never heard a full sentence from him.'

I laughed.

'Maybe that's why she loves you. You're the only one who laughs at her jokes.'

'Hello, uncle,' I said to Ravi.

'And you,' Madhu's dad said, pointing at Keir. 'Stay away from the chicken unless you want ring of fire tomorrow. Plenty of potato salad for you.'

They both burst out laughing as we squeezed past and into the lounge.

'Sunny, beta,' I heard Madhu's mum call. 'How are you, darling? Madhu is here somewhere. Have you eaten?'

I couldn't see her in the hubbub of guests. A large television in the corner was pumping songs on B4U. Then she appeared from nowhere, gave me a cuddle and pinched my cheek.

'I just arrived, auntie,' I said.

'Make sure you eat, OK? The chicken is delicious. Arvind has been marinating it for three days. Where is Mummy?'

'Working, auntie,' I said.

'Oh dear, she works too hard that mother of yours. She must take away some chicken. Make sure you don't leave without food for her.' She stopped to regard Keir. She smiled and tapped him on the arm. 'Is this your friend?'

'Yes,' I said. 'This is Keir. We—'

Madhu's mum held up a hand. 'Say no more,' she said.

She disappeared. I turned to Keir. He looked worried. 'That was strange,' I said. 'She must have thought you were my date.'

'Ha. As if.'

'Well, you're not my type.'

Keir exhaled nervously and looked around, putting his hands back in his pockets.

'I didn't know Madhu was your cousin,' Keir said. 'If I'd known I was going to see your whole family . . .'

'We're not related,' I told him.

'But you called her mum—'

'Oh yeah,' I said, interrupting. 'It's just a sign of respect for her. Like uncle, auntie. In front of them, cos Madhu is younger than me, she has to call me bhai, which means brother. It's a whole thing.'

I pushed us further into the house. It was heaving. There were kids playing volleyball with a balloon on the stairs, uncles watching cricket while downing cans of lager, a kitchen full of women preparing food.

We pushed past everyone. At the back door, Keir put his hand on my elbow.

'Are you sure it's OK for me to be here?' he said quietly, leaning down to talk to me.

'Of course, why?' I replied.

'I'm the only white guy,' he whispered.

'Really?' I said. 'I hadn't noticed.'

I laughed. It was funny. I preferred coming to Madhu's house than having her over at ours. Here, I was surrounded by a thriving brown community that looked and acted and played out roles exactly like our old one back in London. It had made me realise what it was that made me feel like I was at home. Even if I couldn't consider my cousin a friend, all it took was a wedding, some khandvi, the sound of a dhol and the laughter of family from the corner for me to feel like I was somewhere I belonged. Even if it wasn't *my* family.

Here I could be seen.

Here I didn't stand out.

I could understand Keir's panic. It was something I felt every single day. It was more pronounced these days after the attack. Especially in college, where Madhu and I were the only brown people in all our classes. There was a bunch of black kids who did English with Madhu, but the rest of the people of colour we saw worked in the cafe or in the cleaning team. We'd both joked about it incessantly. I remembered her cackle when I'd had a day off for illness and on my return, she'd said diversity at school had increased by thirty-three per cent

'I might go,' Keir said.

'No, Keir, stay. There's loads of delicious food. Come meet my friend.'

Deep down, I knew that part of the reason I'd decided to bring Keir into this space was because I wanted Madhu to see that my boxing gym wasn't full of toxic, masculine pricks. About a week after I'd told her about my new life, she'd been ribbing me about it and said, 'So, who are all these meatheads you hang out with? Can they still remember their names or have they all had every single letter knocked out of them?'

I'd told her that she was being unfair. I'd tried telling her about Keir and how he was giving up loads of his free time to let me be his training partner. We did runs and core strength and pad work together. I'd even told her about Shobu and she'd laughed and said Shobu sounded too good to be true.

I thought bringing Keir here would show her that my new mates were my mates for a reason. And Keir wasn't some meathead who could barely string a sentence together.

We walked out of the back door and on to remnants of carpet laid down on the patio so that you could roam around comfortably while barefoot. A team of boys was manning the barbecue like a production line: two were working the chicken skewers, two were on paneer skewers and another two were preparing sheekh kebabs on yet more skewers. The shop Madhu's dad ran used to be a kebab place and so when he ripped out the equipment he kept the barbecue pits and installed them in his garden under a cover. It was funny seeing a bunch of dads in the house, using it like a home – cooking, laughing, drinking. My dad had only come home to eat food prepared for him and sleep and get ready for work. This was what I'd always imagined a home would look like.

Madhu and two girls I assumed were her cousins were standing in the middle of the garden staring at their phones. Madhu looked up and saw me, smiling.

'Sunny, what's happening?'

She bounded over to say hello.

'Madhu, hey,' I said, returning her kiss on my cheek. 'This is my boy, Keir. Keir, this is Madhu. My . . .'

'Girl?' Madhu offered. 'Gal-pal, mate, friend. Bezzie? God, don't ever refer to me as a bezzie.'

'Or a BFF, right?' Keir said.

Madhu laughed. A bit too much. She brushed her fingers against her throat.

'Let's get some food,' I said to Keir.

'Thank you for letting me tag along,' he said.

'So,' Madhu asked, loudly, to stop us walking away. 'Where does my secretive friend Sunny know you from? London? I thought I was his only Bristol friend.'

'Sunny and I are training together at the moment,' Keir said.

Madhu's body language instantly flipped. Like, oh, boxing, seen. She pointed over to the barbecue.

'There's loads of food,' she said. 'Eat, be merry. Drink, I guess. We don't have any protein shakes but there are some eggs in the fridge.'

She turned back to her friends, who hadn't looked up from their phones the entire time.

'Let's get some food,' I said.

We walked towards the barbecue pits.

Keir wanted to leave after an hour.

We'd only really spoken to each other. Madhu had ignored us the whole time. Her dad had come over to give Keir a bit of chicken to try and when it'd burned his mouth, Madhu's dad had burst into hysterics. No amount of water or Coke could soothe the burning. He'd ended up drinking a beer and sitting on a chair, pouting. I ate some more food, did the rounds to say goodbye and then we headed back through the house to leave.

'Gotta run an extra two miles tomorrow,' he said. 'All that food is really bad for you, you know. You people eat like that every day?'

'No,' I said. 'Only special occasions. On the one day a year it's not raining so you can actually light a barbecue.'

Keir smiled as we walked back towards the bus stop.

'That was mean of Madhu's dad,' I offered. 'He knew the chicken was really spicy.'

'It's OK,' he said. 'He just wanted to humiliate the gora at the party. Don't worry. I know what gora means. You know, when I used to go school at Muller Road, I was the only white kid in the class and they all used to call me gora. Every day. And when I flipped out and told them to stop, they all started calling me "dudh". So racist, man.'

'It's not really—' I started to say, but Keir held his hand up to say, *Don't*. He was still angry. I didn't understand it. We made fun of each other all the time. I didn't get why this attempt at being light-hearted from Madhu's dad had rubbed him up the wrong way.

He apologised after a few minutes.

'Sorry,' he said. 'But it was really spicy and everyone was creasing, and I just . . .'

'I get it,' I said. I understood what it was like to feel the spotlight was on you when you didn't want it to be.

We sat at the bus stop.

'So, is your mate Madhu single or what?' Keir asked.

*　　*　　*

Keir lands an uppercut under my chin and immediately follows it with a hook to the other side of my face. I crash to the floor.

Madhu had texted me, just before the match.

I can't wait for you to beat his ass tonight. also you BETTER beat his ass.

I haven't really given him the fight he deserved. I can feel him shuffle towards me. He is closing up space so when I stand, he is on top of me.

The referee tries to push himself into the area between us.

I can hear Shobu yelling at me. 'Get up,' she shouts. 'Get up.'

The referee sends Keir to the neutral corner and begins his count with me. I wave him off. He looks like he thought he'd finished me and he smirks.

I spring to my feet and as soon as the referee gestures for us to continue, Keir bounds towards me. I jab at Keir, so quickly he's caught off guard.

Didn't see that coming, did you?

Round 4

Shobu is whispering tactics at me but I can't hear her. I'm not taking any of it in. I'm looking at Keir. Now I've surprised him twice, I know I can wear him down and beat him. Not sit back and let him tire himself out punching me as much as he wants, but let him think he's in control, doing his favourite manoeuvres – move quickly on the attack to the point where he's moving too fast to defend himself. It's all about absorbing blows and dodging the big hitters.

I know what he's like.

It took me a second or two to remember. But I know this man. I went to his parents' house. I ate dinner with them. I absorbed everything. I know where he came from. Who he wishes to be. I know him inside and out. And that is enough for me. I can feel danger appearing in my eyes. I can feel friction in my toes. Shobu taps me on the head to check I heard her. I nod.

The bell rings.

She pushes me up.

4.1

'Are you ready to spar?' Shobu asked. We were a month into our training. 'Pad work and heavy bag work will only take you so far. You need to put yourself in a real fight situation. Until you're dodging punches for real, it won't *feel* real. Sure you can hit a bag hard, but can you hit it hard while it's trying to knock you out too?'

Sparring was a big deal. I'd come a long way in a short time, but I wasn't sure I was ready. Not yet.

There was something about learning to box that was at odds with what I was trying to get out of it. I was trying to find the confidence to own my space and defend myself if I needed to. Boxing, everyone said, was about being quick and smart enough to know when *not* to hit as well as when to actually hit. And if you hit, you couldn't miss.

I knew I didn't want to be hit, but how the hell was I going to explain that to Shobu? The very idea of absorbing the full impact of punches terrified me. I knew it would take me right back to that train platform. But still, I couldn't get enough of boxing. It was intoxicating on every level. The power. The strength. The way it made me feel afterwards. The way I looked at myself. The way the bruises healed and my skin glowed. But it was all masking remembering what happened that day. *BANG* – those punches. That could be me on the floor. The very thought of it made me scared. I watched the Thursday evening sparring club every week. Everyone crowded around the ring, shouting out encouragement to both fighters, no one with any skin in the game, just friends who wanted to see their friends improve.

The way Shannon beat Anna into a corner and then let her out so they could carry on.

The way Derek bust open Alex's lip and ran to get him some ice.

The way Sidra and Fatima moved with the quickness, dancing around each other for five full minutes without anyone managing to land a punch.

All boxers under the age of eighteen would get free tickets to the proper matches the owner of the gym put on, but I never went. I could just about handle watching the sparring, but being close to a real fight would be too much. Everyone else went, and Keir ushered for the VIP section.

As much as I wanted to do that too, to spend more time with Keir, I couldn't. It wasn't me.

'What about all the technique simulations you make me do over and over with Keir?' I said to Shobu. 'That feels pretty real.'

'You think if you're in a fight with Keir, he's just going to lump for the combos I make you do? Nah, boss. He's trying to knock you out.'

'How is that not sparring already?' I said, stalling.

'No,' she replied. 'You two practise. Sparring is a live fight simulation. What do you say?'

'No,' I replied.

Shobu shrugged.

'We'll see,' she said.

Keir helped me wrap my hands. I still didn't have the hang of doing it with enough tautness that the wraps stayed firm after flexing my fists.

'I need someone to spar with,' he said. 'I trust you. I can't get any better without you.'

'Did Shobu put you up to this?'

'No,' he said. 'I need this though. Help me.'

'I can't,' I told him.

'What are you worried about?' Keir said.

The way he punched the samosa out of my hand.

The way he jumped on to me.

The way they both stood over me and kicked me.

That word.

I scratched under my arm till it hurt, trying to push the thoughts out of my brain. I tapped the side of my head with the flat of my palm.

'Nothing,' I said.

Keir smiled, clutching my hands. 'Is it cos of what happened?'

'No,' I said firmly.

He looked into my eyes, pleading.

'Just, no.'

4.2

Mum and I were watching *Gogglebox*. We were both quiet and although our faces were pointed at the television, neither of us were engaging with what was on the screen.

'I was thinking,' Mum said during the ad break. 'I like that you are learning how to defend yourself but I want to ask you again – why boxing?'

It was the first time she had brought up the boxing since I'd told her about it.

'What do you mean?' I said, keeping my eyes on an advert for fish fingers.

'Well,' Mum said, leaning across the sofa, so that her hand was on my knee. 'Why don't you learn self-defence, beta? Better yet, what about learning to resolve conflicts through diplomacy? Through talking. Boxing is ugly. Two people who are giving each other permission to hit them. How ugly.'

'Mum,' I said, looking at her now. 'We're not talking about this.'

I had fallen in love with the sport. It was far from ugly in my eyes – I loved the dance of it, the thought and strategy. I loved the power and the movement. I loved how beautiful it was to watch two people spar, even when the thought of doing it myself filled me with dread.

'You're too old for me to forbid you,' she said. 'But I am not happy about you doing this. I do not like you boxing. Understand?'

I hated seeing her unhappy with me like this. It stung.

'Mum . . .' I paused. 'I'm just learning to defend myself.'

'No,' she said, turning to me. 'You're learning boxing. It's different.'

'But I'm doing it properly,' I said. 'I'm not just messing about. I'm taking it seriously. I'm doing it properly.'

And in that moment, I realised I was lying to Mum. Doing it properly meant I had to give myself to boxing. One hundred per cent.

And that meant getting in the ring with Keir.

4.3

It was Thursday morning. No one else was in the gym. I got there early because I knew Shobu, as the first one in, liked to work the bags. Also, I didn't need to be at college till the afternoon. Not that I had much to work towards. Christmas had passed me by. The UCAS application deadline had come and gone. I was not going to uni in October.

I'd never seen Shobu in action before. It was amazing to watch her. She struck with such power. She was like a robot, repeatedly throwing the same punch again and again, till it was perfect, then resetting, and then doing it again and again, checking her alignment every time. It was a lesson in patience. She had such presence.

Watching her fight, I realised how each of her movements meant something. She wasn't just play-jabbing at the air. She had purpose. She struck with passion and with heart. I was so hypnotised I wanted to be in there with her.

Then I remembered the last time I'd been hit.

Give us a bite of your curry thing . . .

It was my fault.

My face fell. I wanted to run out of there. Suddenly, everything felt open and it was like everyone on the posters was staring at me.

But this time, I didn't run. I needed to take the power of those blows away so I could stay in the ring when I was sparring. So I didn't have to be thinking about Sam. Or that night.

Or it being my fault.

I knew what I had to do.

The bell rang and Shobu turned to face me. She nodded like she knew I'd been there the whole time.

'OK,' I said. 'I'll do it.'

'Great,' she said, starting to take off a glove.

'Can you do something for me please?' I asked.

She laughed. 'Sunny, my darling, I do quite a lot for you already.'

'Please hit me,' I said.

'What?' she replied, surprised. 'We're not in *Fight Club*. This is a boxing gym.'

'I know,' I said. 'Please. I want you to punch me in the chest. I will try to block it.'

'No,' she said. 'Go get yourself ready.'

'When they attacked me – when they punched me and kicked me and treated me like an animal – I don't want the punches to mean the same as that.'

'Sunny, I—'

'What we are doing is sport. All I can think about is the horror of that night.'

'Look—'

'I want to spar,' I told her. 'But if every time I get hit I'm thrown back to what happened, I won't get better. I won't own it.'

It was my fault.

I tapped my head, to dislodge the bad thought.

Shobu nodded and moved closer to me. I put my fists up. She punched me, on the shoulder, a jab at full force. I fell backwards.

It hurt. It pushed me off balance and winded me. The impact was like someone slamming a door shut right next to you, the burst of wind over your skin making the hairs rise. The stinging throb came after. But because I'd been expecting it, it wasn't that bad.

'And?'

I laughed. 'It felt good. Thank you.'

'Weirdo,' she said.

Shobu took me to the basketball court that was part of the grounds of the gym. It was sunny but the shade still cast a chill over the court. I was lifting and flipping a huge tractor tyre from one end of the court to the other. When I reached the other end, I had to do five burpees then bring the tyre back. The entire time, Shobu was giving me tips on sparring.

'Always plan ahead. Know what you're doing two or three movements from now.

'Stay at your level. This is the most important lesson when learning how to fight.

'Breathe. Keep breathing.

'Relax.

'Find a comfortable stance.

'Keep your eyes on your opponent.

'Focus on learning, not winning.

'Throw punches.

'Exhale with every punch. You have to retrain yourself to breath differently.'

Burpees were knackering, but with the added combination of having to concentrate on Shobu's pearls of wisdom as well . . . I slept good that night.

4.4

I knew everyone by name but I didn't think any of them knew mine. I was the ghost in the corner trying not to be noticed.

I stood in the doorway to the changing rooms, waiting for my name to be called. The panic was thick all around me. Everyone was going to be watching and shouting and being supportive. I didn't want any of it. I wanted everyone to look away. Or, even better, to go away.

When Shobu called my name, and Keir echoed it, everyone looked around, like, *Where is he?* I edged backwards towards the changing room.

'Come on, Sunny,' Shobu called. 'Come on.'

Everyone cheered for me. I pressed my gloves together as hard as I could and edged forward tentatively.

People parted to make room for me to step up into the ring. Someone patted me on the back. It made me flinch.

'Go on, son,' he whispered, as I stepped up.

As I entered the ring to applause and cheers of appreciative support – especially when Shobu announced it was my first time – I felt an unexpected wave of warmth flood through me. I was seen.

I tried to block everyone out. They were so hard to ignore. Even the whispers, the hushed talking, was deafening. Also, I knew they were all rooting for Keir. He was their big shot. Their up-and-comer. They wanted him match-ready for a few months' time.

Keir walked towards me, his arms stretched out. He fist-bumped me through our gloves.

Shobu grabbed my face. I was wearing a head guard. Keir was not.

'Remember what I said. Concentrate. Breathe. Always plan ahead. Sparring isn't about winning or knocking him out. It's about learning. Got it?'

I nodded.

Shobu went over to Keir and whispered a pep talk to him. She bopped him on top of his head and let go. I wondered how she felt when two of her fighters faced each other. She left the ring.

I suddenly felt alone.

Concentrate!

Keir jumped up and down on the spot. The boxers around the ring whooped and cheered. Shannon even shouted out, 'Go, Sunny!' She knew my name? She was facing a Commonwealth champion next week. When did she take the time out to know who I was?

Without Shobu in it with me, the ring suddenly felt big.

I whispered to myself, trying to calm my rising nerves.

'Stay in the ring. The only people in here are you and Keir. No one else matters. So stay in the ring.'

There wasn't a referee because we were just sparring. This wasn't a match. There was no animosity or competitiveness that needed to be considered.

I jumped up and down on the spot, letting my arms fly free one last time before I held them up to guard myself. Keir and I started circling each other. I was terrified. Everything in me wanted to run out of the ring. I felt stiff, hot, claustrophobic. He looked so loose, sprightly, comfortable. Suddenly, all of the encouraging voices cheering us both on felt too loud and in my face and distracting. I didn't notice Keir step towards me and jab me on the chin.

It snapped me back into focus. This was the first time I'd been punched in the face since the attack, and the surprise and adrenaline jolted me out of my thoughts. I tensed my arms and circled him, aiming to not let that happen again. I knew what to do. I could slip Keir's punches easily. Shobu had worked us both, again and again and again, with speed and with precision. She had been, like, 'Slip or get hit. Don't hold back, Keir.' So, for the last month, she'd had me slipping the full force of his punches and now here I was, suddenly unable to judge the strength and speed of his shots.

He seemed quicker though. Maybe he was nervous too, and this was making him work faster.

He threw another jab.

This time, I remembered to slip. Except not quickly enough because I was still in my head. The blow caught me on the ear as I rolled my shoulders forward.

That one stung.

I needed to wait him out for the round. I didn't want to be here. This was not fun. This was not why I was doing this. It was too much. It was all too much.

He jabbed at me again

I didn't see it coming. It knocked my cheek and I reeled back a step. He followed it up with a cross and bang, which smacked me across my face, sending me to the floor.

I landed elbow first and rolled on to my side to protect myself. I was in survival mode. My breathing was shallow. I was sweating through every pore of my body. I was curling up to let him finish whatever he wanted to do, but so I was protected. I hated myself in that moment. I wanted the ring to be a black hole that sucked me into its nothing.

'You OK?' Keir asked.

I opened and closed my mouth. I could feel a bruise on my cheek.

'Yes,' I said, nodding at him, reminding myself that we were friends. We had both chosen to do this.

'You getting up?' Keir said. 'You don't have to . . .'

'Man cool, Sunny?' I heard Shobu say.

I looked for her. She was standing next to Surinder, her eyebrows raised in concern, leaning on the ropes, clasping her hands. I held my hand out to signal I was OK.

People around the ring applauded. I slowly got to my feet. Shobu and Surinder offered me two thumbs up apiece.

'Nice one, man,' Keir said. 'Keep going – you'll get the hang of it.'

The bell rang. It had been a long three minutes. We had two more rounds to go.

The second round felt longer. Keir was more on the attack. He was throwing shots in combinations I recognised from Shobu. I knew how to slip them. He had practised them on me. He was quicker and this was shaking me. I wasn't throwing punches back, because it meant throwing them with full force, and I wasn't sure I wanted to hurt him. I could have dug him in the stomach, an uppercut to the head, hooks, right and left, up and down the body. But I couldn't do it. I didn't want to hurt him, even though he was giving me every single opportunity to do so. I kept moving, staying on my toes, and always slipping, ducking and weaving. He didn't manage to land a single punch. When the bell eventually rang, everyone shouted encouragement, mostly to Keir for forcing a defensive round out of me, but with the occasional cheer of support for me – that I was doing well, keep going, they all seemed to say.

The third round, Keir seemed tenser. He was a bit looser with his punches, knowing by now that I wasn't going to hit back. My job was to defend. I dodged and slipped and backed away as best as I could but he kept coming. People had stopped cheering for me at this point. They were calling out for Keir to get stuck in. Keir threw jabs and hooks, trying to catch me. I dodged and dodged. I could see us heading into our final minute out of the corner of my eye.

'Go on, son,' I heard one person say.

'Knock him about, Keir. Go on, mate.'

'Hit the jihadi in the face,' someone yelled and they all laughed.

I stopped dead. Jihadi? What?

I paused, scanning the faces for who'd said that word. Then two things happened at the same time.

I heard Shobu shouting, 'Who the hell said that?' as Keir dealt me an uppercut with his right fist, sending me backwards to the floor.

I crashed into the ring. My arms were limp, useless. My legs were deadened from tensing. My chin was burning.

I saw Shobu shouting at someone. My vision blurred. I couldn't focus on anything. I was hot and sweaty and yet there was a chill up and down my spine, pulsing like an electric eel.

The bell rang.

Keir bent down. 'You OK?' he asked, smiling.

'Yeah,' I said. No smile.

He offered his arm so I could pull myself up. I rolled over and got up all on my own.

'I'm fine,' I said.

I started to leave the ring.

'Sunny,' he called after me. 'I did what I had to do. You left yourself open.'

I turned around and then I smiled. I don't know to this day why I smiled at him, exactly. But I did. The crowd was starting

117

to dissipate. I could still hear the echoes of Shobu shouting at someone, Surinder too. The jihadi? Why the hell did whoever it was call me that? I thought this place was safe. I thought here I was free from all that.

'You did what you had to do, Keir,' I said. 'Me? I'm just a jihadi.'

'What?' he said, confused.

I left the ring and headed for the changing rooms.

4.5

Keir texted me later that night.

I'm sorry.

What for?

I didn't know Paul called you that.

So?

So, I'm sorry.

You have nothing to be sorry for.

K.

K.

Wanna come to ours for dinner?

I'm eating dinner rn

Not tonight, dickhead. Tomorrow. My parents wanna meet you

Why?

He called me.

'Hey, man, listen, Mum and Dad are back from Australia and basically gassing me up on my boxing. They really want me to go pro. Think I can go the distance. I've been talking to them about us training together and, like, they just wanna see what you're about. Mum will be offended if you don't . . .'

'Is your brother gonna tell me to eff off again?' I asked.

'He didn't say that exactly . . .'

'What about your dad?' I asked. 'Is he gonna go off on immigrants to my face?'

'No,' Keir said. 'He thinks you're all right. You were born here.'

'Right . . .' I said. 'I'm out.'

'I'm joking, I'm joking,' Keir said. 'Look, it's really important to me. I'm close with my family. They like meeting all my friends. And if I go pro and you're my training partner, you'll see a lot more of them.'

'I dunno,' I said. 'I feel weird.'

'Swear down, man,' Keir said. 'I'll make sure they're on their best behaviour. I'll back you. It's so important to me that you're all OK with each other.'

'It still feels—'

'They're my family. You're my friend,' Keir said. 'You're both helping me on my journey. I can go all the way. I know I can. They just wanna, you know . . . I just think you should meet. Not everyone has to get on with everyone. But you all have me in common. That should be enough.'

'I'll think about it,' I said and hung up the phone.

He texted again after that with an address and a time to meet him but I didn't reply. I felt shook. After Paul calling me a jihadi and knowing what I knew about Keir, I didn't really want to put myself in another situation where I felt exposed.

But it was important to Keir.

And he was my friend.

I replied and asked him to meet me on the way tomorrow.

*   *   *

119

We met at the bus stop. He was wearing jeans and a DAMN. T-shirt. I smiled. I loved that album. He'd got his hair trimmed. He had his earring in. He'd made some sort of effort. I'd just dressed as normal. A black tracksuit and a white T-shirt. He nodded at me.

'Thanks for the invite,' I said, and we started walking.

I was still unsure about going round his for dinner. I hadn't exactly felt very welcomed by his brother that previous time I'd been in his ends. But maybe his brother had been having a bad day. I dunno. Mum had been upset I was going out. It was her night off so she was at home and wanted to make her way through all the sitcoms we'd recorded to watch together.

'Thank you for doing this,' Keir said. 'You know how important family is to me.'

'OK . . . brother,' I said, and laughed. He put his arm around my neck and pulled me close for a hug.

As we hit his street, we were walking in silence, even though we had so much to talk about. I knew he hated silences. I realised he must be nervous too.

'How you feeling?' he said.

'About what?' I asked.

Keir pulled at his ear and looked at me, and then behind us. I followed his eyeline. There was no one there. A cat purred, hiding behind a skip. The distant roar of boy racers hummed across the night sky. The smell of barbecue was thick in the air. I could hear the strains of Kings of Leon somewhere nearby. Despite the crisp weather, Indians still found a way to barbecue.

'You know,' he said. 'What Paul said . . .'

'Shit. Dunno if I wanna go back, to be honest,' I said. 'I don't want people looking at me like that again.'

120

'I didn't realise at the time what a problem that would be for you,' he said, quietly.

'Why just me?' I said, disappointed in him. 'Why isn't it a problem for you too? Why are you sorry? Cos I heard it or cos it's wrong?'

'Cos it's wrong!' he said, urgently. 'Sunny, I swear.'

He extended his hand towards me. I kept my hands in my pockets before thinking better of it and reaching out to shake his.

'Yeah,' I said. 'Yeah, it is wrong.'

'I thought it was just jokes. I didn't know you'd be so shook by it.'

'How would you feel if someone reduced you to your race?' I asked.

'People do it all the time,' he said. 'I read Reddit and stuff. People are always blaming straight white men for everything. We're the enemy now.'

'You really believe that?' I asked, wondering yet again whether this dinner was a good idea.

'No, man,' he said. 'But it makes you think though, innit.'

'You're just talking about anonymous men cry-wanking on the Internet,' I seethed. 'He said it to my face.'

'I'm sorry,' Keir said. 'I didn't think you'd— Look, I'm sorry. It was wrong.'

I stared at him. 'Come on, man, I'm hungry,' I said, leading the way to his house. I didn't want to argue with Keir. His friendship was too important to me. I didn't want to rock any boats. I didn't want him to have a reason to hate me. And if that meant looking past a careless comment or two, so be it.

Friends compromised.

*   *   *

121

He shushed me as we entered his house. There was music playing. It was Westlife, I think. It was loud and upstairs. Without thinking, I took my shoes off.

'What are you doing?' Keir asked.

'Taking my shoes off,' I replied.

'You don't need to do that here.'

Embarrassed, I slipped my foot back into my shoe and smiled and shrugged.

'Sunny,' I heard a loud, happy voice say. I looked up. A woman with a big glass of what looked like wine bore down on me, offering me a hug. I returned it and smiled. When she let go, I could smell her floral perfume everywhere, like she had imprinted on me.

'Hi,' I said. 'Yes, Sunny.'

'I'm Layla,' the woman said, releasing me. 'I'm Keir's mum – welcome to our home.'

I smiled, not knowing what to do next. Keir grimaced, clearly embarrassed by his mum.

'Something smells delicious,' I said, lying. I couldn't smell anything but perfume.

She led us into the dining room. It felt strange wearing my trainers indoors. Keir's dad and brother were sitting at the dining table. Joe was showing his dad something on his phone. They both looked up. Joe shifted uncomfortably in his seat as Keir's dad stood and leant over the table to shake my hand.

'Sunny, right? Short for . . .?'

'Sunil,' I said, with a frog in my throat. No one called me Sunil except my dad, formal to the very end.

'Su*nil*,' he said. 'Su*nil*. Sorry. It takes me a few times to get the pronunciation. Su*nil*, right?'

I nodded.

'Come on, Dad,' Keir said.

'I'm Martin,' he said, shaking my hand.

He clasped it and squeezed, pulling me ever so slightly closer to the table and shaking down hard three times.

'I thought he was a boxer,' he said to Keir. 'Got the grip of a wet lettuce.'

'Dad!'

'You need a training partner, not a side salad.'

Joe stood up and left the room without saying a word. He hadn't even acknowledged me. My stomach flipped. Keir sat at the table and gestured for me to do the same. I sat down on the chair. It dipped in the middle and the back was broken on one side. I steadied myself and crossed my arms.

Martin sat down too.

'So,' he said to me. 'How's my boy shaping up?'

'Keir? He's so good,' I said. 'Really strong. We sparred.'

'I heard he kicked ten shits out of you, lad,' Martin said, laughing.

'It was my first—'

'Yeah, Dad,' Keir said, interrupting. 'Had him on the floor in seconds. Innit, Sunny. Next time, eh?'

I looked at Keir, like, *What the hell, man?* I considered telling his dad about the sucker punch. What good would it do?

Then it hit me – Keir needed to look good at all costs, even in front of family. *OK*, I thought. *Seen. I'll drop it now, but I can use that in future.* It made me want to get back in the ring with him. It made me understand how I could beat him.

Joe reappeared when Layla started serving food. He made an explosion noise as he entered the room and Martin sniggered and pretended to duck. Joe took his place at the table. He started laughing and pointing at the top of Keir's head. Keir kept rubbing at his crown and asking what the matter was. Martin was looking in my direction but I didn't know how to react. It felt malicious to me, not friendly family banter.

'It's a joke,' he bellowed at me. 'You *can* laugh.'

I smiled and shifted in my seat, which caused a squelching noise.

'Pardon you,' Martin said and Joe joined him in laughter. Keir too, but it sounded strained. Layla entered with some knives and forks.

I asked if she wanted any help bringing things in, and she said, 'Sure.' I followed her into the kitchen.

'Thanks, love,' Layla said, pointing to some empty plates. I picked them up and walked back into the dining room. There was an uncomfortable silence as Keir checked his phone and Joe and Martin talked about football. I put the plates on the table and headed back to the kitchen.

'Sunil,' Martin said, seriously. I turned around to face him. 'You're a guest, not the help. Sit down.'

'I don't mind,' I replied.

'Sit. Down,' Martin said.

I did what he said. Keir passed plates to his dad and brother as Layla walked into the room with one full plate of food. She placed it in front of me. It had a burger on it, with some wedges.

'I know you don't eat pork,' she said.

'I . . .' I was about to correct her, but I could tell that Martin was looking at me. 'Thank you.' She smiled and headed back into the kitchen.

'What's the matter?' Joe asked. 'Your lot don't eat beef neither? What do you eat?'

'This is great, thank you,' I said again.

Layla returned with a tray of pork ribs. Martin, Joe and Keir grabbed at them, filling their plates. Layla sat down and sipped at her glass of wine, waiting for them to be done before picking up a few for herself. I lifted the burger and bit into it. It wasn't worth explaining to Layla that I came from a Hindu background rather than a Muslim one, and it was beef, not pork, that Hindus were prohibited from eating. Seeing as I didn't really practise, it felt unnecessary. Besides, the burger was tasty.

'Home-made, you know?' Layla said. 'Left over from a chilli con carne. Nice, yeah?'

'It's not halal though, is it?' Joe said. 'Sorry about that. We don't get halal.'

'Neither do I,' I said.

'What's wrong with halal?' Martin asked. 'Are you not a believer?'

'No,' I replied, quietly, side-eyeing Keir, hoping he'd change the subject. His body language had shifted. He was stiff and looking down at his plate. 'I'm just not Muslim, so, you know . . . Not that it matters or anything . . .' I trailed off, not really knowing what to say because, ultimately, I didn't know why they'd even mentioned it in the first place.

'Oh,' Joe said, smiling. 'Sunil, we've totally misjudged you.'

He laughed and tore at a pork rib.

4.6

Madhu got on the same train as me the next day and waved as she walked towards my seat. I moved my bag to let her sit down.

'How are you doing?' she asked. 'I don't see you so much since . . . you know . . .'

She mimed punching me.

'Sorry, I've been busy,' I said.

'Your mate Keir's not that busy. He's been texting me.'

'Saying what?' I asked.

'Oh, nothing. Just basic questions. Trying to work out what sorta stuff I'm into and telling me about how hard he's training. He's gearing up to ask me out. I just wish he'd do it so I could get on with saying hell the fuck no.'

I was shocked. Keir was a good-looking guy, thoughtful and funny. Why wouldn't she want to go out with him?

I wasn't sure how I felt about Keir asking Madhu out. I was still finding my feet in this new city and it was like they represented two very different parts of it. Maybe two different parts that I didn't want bringing together? And it was weird, especially since the barbecue hadn't really gone that well.

'What's wrong with him?' I asked.

'Who?' she said, standing up as the train began to slow into our stop. 'Keir? Dunno. There's something off about him.'

'That's my friend you're talking about,' I said, my voice rising. I felt suddenly defensive.

'And what am I?' she asked. 'Seriously. I'm not good at a lot. Three things: Beyoncé facts, shading boys and judging people's characters. And let me just say, there's *definitely* something a bit off about him. Be his boxing buddy or whatever, but—'

'But you won't go out with him?'

'Exactly,' she said.

I didn't reply.

We walked into college in silence. I was still processing my dinner with Keir's family. His brother. How aggressive he was to me until he found out I wasn't Muslim. How he made some cracks about Muslims, once he knew I wasn't one. How Keir called him a racist and Joe laughed and said, 'So what?' And how I just sat there, not saying anything at all, letting it all happen around me.

Their dad didn't take his eyes off me. Layla ordered Keir to help her tidy up and I was left in the dining room by myself. Joe and Martin went to watch the second half of a football match. They didn't even ask if I wanted to join them. I just sat in silence, looking at the mantelpiece. It was an assortment of family photographs.

Layla came back in with two teas.

She sat with me. She sucked on a vape that smelled like watermelon and loudly sipped at her tea.

'You be careful around my boy,' she said. 'He likes you. Don't get him into any trouble.'

She picked up her tea and left the room. I wasn't sure what she meant. By this point, I was desperate to leave. Keir came in eventually and told me he thought it was time for me to go home. He was red in the face and didn't quite meet my eye.

Relieved, I sprung up out of my chair and left.

When Madhu met me for lunch she said that she'd been texting Keir again.

'Why?' I said. 'You decided you weren't gonna go out with him. So what's the point?'

'Cos I wanna figure him out. He's spending more time with you than I am, so . . .'

'Oh,' I said. 'OK.'

'I'm not gonna lie,' Madhu said. 'I feel replaced.'

'It ain't like that,' I said. 'We're just . . .'

'He said you went round for dinner last night.'

I smiled evasively and pulled a samosa out of my bag.

'Yeah,' I said. 'I did.'

'You don't sound sure, man. What happened? Are they weird? Is he into God? Are they hippy-dippy types who namaste'd you? What? Come on, spill.'

I told Madhu bits of everything. I steered clear of Keir and concentrated on how horrible his brother was and how his dad got nicer to me once he'd found out I wasn't Muslim.

'Oh,' Madhu said.

'Oh, *what*?' I asked.

'It means . . .' Madhu paused. 'It means they sound like bad news, man. Keir needs to disown them or something.'

'They're not . . .' I realised I was about to defend them and say they weren't that bad. But I stopped.

Madhu punched me on the arm, hard.

'Muscles, bruv!' she said as she flexed her knuckles, clearly surprised at how hard my bicep was now.

'Keir is fine,' I said. 'He's fine.'

'Yeah, he may be fine, but you get too close and you have to deal with that family. The only reason I haven't told him to piss off is because he's been relatively polite, you know?'

'OK,' I said.

128

'I mean, he's peng for a white boy,' she said, laughing. 'But I bet his dad would say me saying that was racist, right?'

We looked around us. People were standing around listening to music on someone's phone and talking loudly about a party. Who got with who. Who was meant to get with who. Who didn't show. Who knew who got with who. Madhu smiled at one of them and I sat awkwardly as the friend came over to say hello.

Feeling my stomach rumble, I lifted my samosa, biting into it and feeling the spices tease my mouth.

A teacher walked past me. 'Obnoxious food smells should be kept outside,' she said as she passed.

'Pardon?' I said.

'You know what I mean. Take it outside . . .'

I was angry and gestured at her with the samosa. 'It's a bloody samosa,' I said.

'Sunil, I do not appreciate your tone,' she told me.

'And I don't appreciate what you're suggesting, miss.' I stared her out. She eventually strode off, back the way she came.

I felt a shiver of pleasure. I had never stood up to anyone like that.

After lunch, I sat in my usual seat in class and waited for Madhu to join me. I texted Keir.

SHOBU SAID YOU WANT A REMATCH

Yea

This time I'm gonna win.

k

what's wrong i was joking

am fine

wevs

I stared at our exchange until Madhu arrived. She sat down and got her things out of her bag, then turned to me, a serious look on her face.

'Your mate literally just texted,' she whispered. 'He asked me out. I told him to fuck off.'

'What?' I said. 'Why?'

'I didn't give him a reason. I don't really need to get into my reasons with him, do I? Seriously though, I thought about it and what you said about his dad makes my skin itch.'

'Keir's not like them,' I said, loud enough for our neighbours to hear. Madhu didn't reply. Our teacher walked into the room.

I rolled last night around and around in my head for the rest of the lesson. He definitely wasn't.

*   *   *

I decide to frustrate Keir. I keep moving, letting him come to me the whole time. I never let him land a punch. I am always on the move. He gets more and more tired, more and more pissed off, as I dance around him, never ever letting his gloves even graze my skin. He even screams out in frustration as I slip and swivel so that I'm behind him.

I do it for five whole minutes.

Round 5

I can see Keir's trainer shouting something at the referee. He is pointing at me.

'What's this now?' Shobu asks. 'You OK?'

'Yeah, fine,' I reply.

'Good round there – you really pissed him off. You know he's gonna come at you even harder in the next round, right?'

'I can take it.'

'I know you can. But remember, when he comes at you hard, he's angry. He won't be thinking straight. Be smart. Keeping moving. Make him work for every punch. Got it?'

I nod.

The referee bounds over to us.

'What's wrong?' Shobu asks him.

The referee bends down and shines a pen torch into my eyes. It blinds me slightly.

'Look up,' he says.

'Sunny's fine,' Shobu replies.

'Follow my finger,' the referee says, tracing his index finger in a line in front of me.

'Ref,' Shobu says. 'He is fine.'

'There seems to be concern that Sunny is concussed. You OK there? Took a few blows. You can bow out now if you're feeling faint.'

'I'm fine,' I tell him.

'OK,' the referee says. 'OK, that's fine. Let's crack on then.'

The referee turns around and walks to the middle, giving the other side the thumbs up. Keir smiles. So does his trainer.

'They're messing with me.'

'Of course they are. They're being smart. They want to get inside your head,' Shobu tells me. 'So now you're gonna worry you're concussed and not thinking straight. You're fine. Remember: keep frustrating Keir. You got that? You'll find an opening.'

The bell rings. I stand up and walk to the middle.

'Nice try, dickhead,' I tell him. 'I'm not concussed.'

'Yet,' Keir says and bangs his gloves against mine.

5.1

The second time we sparred, half the amount of people stuck around to watch it. We were the last to go up against each other, there was a big fight coming the night after and I think everyone remembered the previous time being a bit of a let-down. Looking back, I think Keir was disappointed by the lack of support. I was just grateful to not be looked at by so many people.

He arrived wearing sunglasses and grabbed me by the shoulders as he entered the changing room. I said hello to him a few times before he looked up at me and nodded.

I asked how he was and he sighed and cleared his throat. He did everything to avoid looking in my direction.

'Keir,' I said, sternly. 'Are you OK?'

'Let's get readeeeeee to rumbleeeeee,' he announced.

'Man cool?' I asked.

'All good, baby,' he said, taking off his sunglasses. His eyes were bloodshot. He had a bruise on the side of his face that hadn't been there the day before.

'What happened?' I asked, pointing to the bruise.

'Nothing,' he said. 'Nothing you need to concern yourself with, man.'

'Keir,' I said. 'I saw you last night and that wasn't there. Did someone hit you?'

He didn't say anything and instead busied himself taking his shorts and a vest out. Then his wraps.

'Who hit you, Keir?' I asked, softly.

'No one,' he shouted. 'Leave it.'

'Your dad?' He shook his head. 'Joe,' I said, not as a question, as a fact.

He looked up at me. 'It's nothing to do with you,' he said, firmly. 'Sometimes I talk back one time too many. Anyway, let's get ready. Come let me punch you up.'

He put his sunglasses back on for the entire time it took him to get changed.

We dapped our gloves together and the clock signalled the first of our rounds of sparring. Before the bell had finishing ringing, and before Keir had put up his gloves, I jabbed at him, catching the side of his nose.

Blood streamed out. He lifted his fists to wipe at it. He looked at his bloody glove and then at me. He was angry.

'Sorry,' I started to say but he threw some shots at me, clipping my ear and forcing me on to my back foot, trying to dodge him.

He was fierce, punching and growling at me as the blood trickled down his face. He pushed me and then kicked at my legs. I fell to the ground.

'Stop! Keir, what are you doing?' Shobu shouted, entering the ring.

'He bloody sucker-punched me,' Keir shouted, pulling off a glove and properly wiping at his nose. People around us started to disperse.

'Keir, he did nothing wrong. You hesitated; you paid the

price. What's the matter? You don't like being punched, choose something else to do. Maybe competitive yoga or something,' Shobu said.

'Whatever, Shobu,' Keir said. He glared at me. 'You gonna apologise or what?'

'Sorry, man,' I said.

Shobu looked at me. 'The hell? Why are you apologising? Keir's being the baby. You did exactly what I trained you to do. Don't apologise.' She paused. 'If anything, Keir should apologise to you for breaking the combat rules of a sparring session and kicking you.'

'Nah,' Keir said. 'Highly unlikely.'

He took his gloves off and left the ring, strutting back into the changing room. Shobu helped me up.

'You OK?' she asked. I nodded. 'Good. Now if I ever see you apologising like that again, we are done, do you get me?'

I nodded and looked at the door of the changing room. If I hurried, I could still catch Keir.

'Keir,' I shouted.

He had reached the edge of the car park and was on the main road. I knew he'd heard me but he kept on walking. I ran after him. It was cold and the wind blew around my knees and into the core of my sweaty armpits, making me feel cold. I caught him at the gate.

'Keir,' I said again.

He spun round.

'What the hell do you want?' he said.

'I said I'm sorry. We cool?'

Keir laughed and put his hands in his pocket.

'We cool?' he asked. 'We are not cool, bro. We are definitely not cool.' He paused.

He turned to walk away. I grabbed at his arm. He whipped round again, his fist raised.

'I will deck you,' he said. 'Out here, I'm not bound by no combat rules.'

'Keir, what is wrong? I'm so sorry I clipped your nose . . .'

'You think I care about that?' he shouted, talking over me. 'I don't care about that. You know what your friend Madhu texted me? You know what she said? She said she doesn't date people with racist families. Like she knows everything about me because of what you told her. What the fuck did you tell her?'

'Come on, man,' I said. 'You were there . . .'

'Everyone thinks they know me. Because of my family. Or because of what I do. None of you know me.'

'Keir,' I said, welling up. 'We're friends. But you know what happened at yours. And how Joe was with me that first time.'

'You know why Joe hit me? I told him I blamed him for what Madhu said and he punched me. Told me to stop being so wet. That I was crying over a paki. And that he could fuck her up for me if he wanted.'

'Your brother said . . .' I couldn't breathe. I sat down, right there. Hurt Madhu? And that word. Rattling around in my brain. It was sinewy. It had a hold over me.

'I get it,' Keir said, standing over me. 'I get it. We have to side with our own, man. See you around.'

He walked away. I sat there in the car park, trying to breathe in the cool air, holding on to the gate, feeling like my legs had been swept from under me. I watched Keir's back as he moved further and further away from me.

I sat there for a few minutes crying, until a car beeped me to move and I ran back inside to change.

5.2

'We're going to see your father,' Mum said.

I was lying in bed, staring at the pictures in a comic but not reading the words. I was trying to avoid looking at my phone to see if Keir had texted me back. He hadn't. I was at the lower level of freaking out. He was always quick to reply. Except when training. But we only trained together, so he was clearly screening me.

It was the weekend now and I wanted to know if we were doing our weekly long run along the river.

'I'm busy,' I said, lowering the comic.

'No, baba,' Mum said. 'No, you need to see your dad. He has been asking after you. Please come with me.'

'Mum,' I said. 'I don't want to see him.'

'Why?' she asked. 'He's your father.'

What could I say to my mum? She always defended him. Once when he had shouted at me for an A minus in an exam because it hadn't been an A, she'd backed him up and sent me to bed with no dinner, to study. Hours earlier when I'd told her about the A minus, she'd been so overjoyed that she'd cooked me theplas, my favourite.

'Mum,' I said. 'I don't want to see him like that.'

This felt like the easiest way to dodge it. It meant I could avoid a conversation where I might find myself saying the words, *I hate that man because he has never been there for me when I needed him and now he's dying. What's the point of trying to force us to have any sort of relationship?*

'It's the weekend. You're coming,' Mum said. 'He's been asking after you.'

I stood up slowly, sighing. I didn't want to let her down. Mum threw a clean pair of socks at me. They were still warm from the dryer. Checking my phone, I saw that Keir still hadn't messaged me.

'What time are we going to be back?' I asked.

The club's big fight night was tonight and I hadn't planned on going. I still couldn't stomach the idea of being in a noisy crowd, nor did I want to socialise with people like Paul who thought calling me a jihadi was bants. The whole thing made me feel nervous as hell. But now I was torn because not hearing from Keir meant I needed to accidentally run into him. And I knew he was going to be ushering. I could check in with him, make sure we were OK, make things right between us.

The more he had ignored my texts, the more I'd started to feel like what I had done was the problem, not him. Maybe he was right to be pissed off that Madhu had judged him cos of his family. But at the same time, she was right. I was so scared to not have him as a friend that I was willing to overlook this. And that was eating my insides. I had torn myself up thinking about it. I even texted Madhu to ask what she thought. She just replied with a LOL and an emoji of a gun pointing at an exploding head.

Despite everything, I knew I still liked him too much to walk away.

'Come on, Sunny, baba,' Mum said.

'OK, OK. But what time . . .?'

'We'll spend an hour there. No more. He gets tired.'

I moved so slowly. I didn't want to go. I didn't need to see a dying man. In my head, he was already gone. I didn't need to spend time with someone who was already dead to me.

We walked to the bus stop. I checked the times on my phone.

'Mum, we just missed one,' I told her.

'We'll wait for the next one.'

'Mum, that's half an hour away. I need to be at the venue later for fight night.'

Mum sat down on the bench and looked up and down the road. A taxi approached, blaring bhangra. It slowed as it pulled up to the bus stop like it was waiting for us. Mum waved it on.

'Bruv,' I heard. 'Sunny!' I looked up. Surinder was leaning out of his window. 'I heard you did good in sparring. A real fighter now.' I looked at Mum. She was staring at Surinder and gesturing to him, like, *What are you even doing?*

'Safe, Surinder,' I said.

'You going to the fight? Was gonna see if you wanted a lift later. Realised I didn't have your digits so I thought I'd pop in.'

'Haven't decided yet.'

'Safe. Where are you guys going? Want a lift? I just finished a shift. Free as a bird.'

'Nah, we're cool. Thanks, man,' I said.

'No thank you, young man. We cannot afford a taxi,' Mum said.

I felt my skin burn with embarrassment.

'Free, innit. For my mates. Hop in. Where are you going?'

Mum smiled at the word 'free' and stood up. She crossed to Surinder's car.

'Mum, wait . . .' I called. 'Surinder, we're fine with the bus, thank you . . .'

I was pressed for time and the bus would add two hours to our journey but I didn't want to mix worlds.

'Come on, baba, get in,' Mum said.

I grunted in annoyance and got in the back. I slammed the door shut and Surinder raised his fist for me to dap it. I did.

'Where to, baba?' he asked, sniggering.

'The hospice. Chatterton Farm,' Mum said.

Surinder looked back at me, the smirk firmly off his face, and I looked at him, nonplussed, like, *I do not want to talk about this*.

'Seen. OK, auntie,' he said, clearing his throat.

We hit the A road leading out of the city to the farm on the outskirts where there was a cancer-specialist hospice. It was mainly for kids but they had a wing for people from South Asian communities who didn't speak English as a first language. A heap of staff spoke Punjabi, Gujarati, Hindi, Urdu, Bengali, Tamil, Telegu, even Swahili.

'Your dad out there, man?' Surinder asked.

'Yeah, man,' I said, quietly. I carried on looking out of the window, watching Bristol dissolve behind us. I could feel Surinder looking at me in the mirror.

'How do you, a grown man, know Sunny?' Mum asked Surinder.

'Mum . . .' I groaned, embarrassed.

'It's a fair question, no, Surinder? You are in your late twenties . . .'

'Early thirties actually . . .'

'And my boy is only just eighteen. How are you friends?'

'Ah, auntie. Sunny's the best. I told him about the boxing club I go to. Next thing I know, he's being trained by my

142

flatmate, Shobu, and I'm just standing there watching him improve week on week, with my chest inflated, you know? Like, I did this, you know? Really proud of him. What a lovely boy you have. He's fam, innit. All the Asians in this city know each other. We all look out for one another.'

'Yes, yes, OK, fine, fine – this is all very nice,' Mum said. 'But how did you meet to tell him?'

'Oh, you know,' Surinder said, indicating, casual. 'I gave him a lift to school just after he was attacked by those racists.'

I froze.

How did he know that detail? No one knew. Not Mum. Not Madhu. Not even Keir.

Shobu.

It had to be.

Shobu had told Surinder what I'd said to her. And now Surinder was telling my mum. I still hadn't given Mum any details. As far as I was concerned, it was a distant memory and didn't need to be dragged up again. Mum looked back at me and raised her eyebrows, like, *Is this your big secret? How can you tell him and not me?* I shrugged, pretending like I had no idea at all.

But for Shobu to tell Surinder the one thing I'd asked her to keep in confidence, that the people who attacked me did it because I was brown, that was such a betrayal. How dare she? Who the hell did she think she was? How could she demand my trust in her when she couldn't even be trusted to keep the things I told her to herself? I was still dealing with it. Everywhere I went, I was hyper-aware of my surroundings, desperate to not be seen in case those men were around. I hadn't even reported them to the police, even though that was what you were supposed to do. I didn't want to be in a situation where I had to see them again, in court or whatever. Not that I had any faith that the police would catch them or even be interested in catching them. Also, it'd been nearly three months. They'd wanna know: *Why did you wait so long before coming forward? Is it because you're lying? Can you even be sure of the details any more? Did it happen the way you think you remember it did? Did it actually happen another way?* There were so many reasons for not taking this to the police.

'My boy used to be lovely,' Mum said, looking at me. 'But I wouldn't know now. He doesn't tell me anything any more.'

'Of course he doesn't, auntie. He's your son, innit. He wants to protect you. So if bad things happen, he wants to deal with them himself so you don't worry. I get that – that's like what I am with my mum.'

'Do you lie to her?' Mum asked.

'Mum,' I said, interrupting. 'Can we deal with this later?'

'No,' Surinder said, smiling at me in the mirror. 'I tell her the truth. But I don't tell her everything. She's the last one I want worrying.'

'Surinder,' my mum said. 'Omitting the truth is tantamount to lying. You are lying to her.'

'OK, auntie,' Surinder said, laughing. 'OK.'

The rest of the drive was in silence.

5.3

Surinder pulled up outside the entrance to the Jhalak Wing for people with different language needs. *Jhalak* meant 'beam' in Hindi, Mum had told me when she'd first left Dad there. The hope was that despite the hospice being what it was, there was still a ray of light. Whether that was family, or medical care, or just time to reflect, I don't know. I couldn't see it myself.

He turned off the engine as I got out.

'See you in a bit,' he said.

He pulled out a book and moved his seat back.

'No, Surinder, beta,' Mum said. 'You go. It's getting late. We will take the bus home. There is one every half hour.'

Surinder pulled out a Nicola Adams book from his door and held it up.

'Don't be silly,' he said. 'I was just gonna finish this book off at home anyway.'

'We will take the bus.'

Surinder looked at me and mouthed, *Sorry.* I wasn't mad at him. Surinder was just one of those nice big bears who liked doing things for people. There was no malice to him. Shobu was the one I was screwing at. How could she have done that to me?

'I'm going to wait, auntie. I've spent many an hour in this car park. I've given so many people lifts back to the city in my time, people who'd been let down by the awful buses. It's cool. I have my book. I have time. Say hi to Nurse Paula – ask her if she's still making them banging cups of tea, and if she is, Surinder would love one.'

Mum made a noise and stomped towards the door. I could tell from how quickly she walked, a few steps ahead even with her short stride, that she was annoyed with me.

Mum signed us in at the reception. The nurse looked at me and smiled sympathetically. Mum came every few days and so the nurse knew her to say hello to. But she was definitely looking at me like she knew it was my first time and it'd probably been a mission to get me here.

Truth was, Mum had never once asked me to come and visit. This morning had been the first time. She knew the idea of it was difficult for me. She had clearly been waiting for the right time. But why now? Why today? Maybe it was finally happening. The old man was going to kick it, go, be gone, like I felt he already had been all this time.

And now I needed to get this over with as quickly as possible so I could head to the fight night and see Keir.

'Be the best at whatever you do,' Dad once told me. He repeated it many times over the years. When I was younger, I used to have lots of different obsessions. One week, I'd be drawing everything, desperately trying to teach myself to write comics. Then when summer term approached, and a teacher told me that Indians were the best spin bowlers, I became obsessed with doing that. When I wasn't practising in the courtyard in front of our building, I would sit in front of the television, ball in hand, spinning it repeatedly till calluses formed in my palm. Then I decided I wanted to learn guitar and join a band. At this point, Dad declined to buy me a guitar.

'I will only do it if you become the best. Be the best at whatever you do,' he told me. And that was that.

I overheard him in the kitchen later complaining to Mum that I flitted about, that everything I chose to do was expensive, and that he couldn't afford for me to have weekly obsessions. Besides, he supposed, I was old enough to get a job myself. I was only twelve.

When my cousin gave me his old acoustic guitar as a

hand-me-down, having upgraded to an electric one, I just let it gather dust in the corner of my room.

The nurse swung her head round to say hello to a colleague and her braids shifted up off her name badge.

Out of curiosity, I looked down at it.

Paula.

'Hello, Paula,' Mum said to the nurse as she led us away to the corridor. 'Surinder's outside. Asked if you're still making those banging cups of tea.'

Paula laughed loudly and shook her head.

'Bless that boy. I'll go say hello.'

I followed Mum down the corridor. Every step was laden and loud in the quiet corridor. I wanted to scream, just to cut the tension in my head. She was walking quickly. I followed her. She stopped and turned to me. She was looking at me weirdly, like she was placing eyes on me for the first time in a long while, like I had been on a world trip or something.

'Beta, why didn't you tell me?'

I looked at the floor. Mum wore sandals everywhere, in every weather. Today she wore them with special socks she'd had shipped over from her sister in Baroda, where the big toe was separate from the rest of them. I hated those socks. I hated those sandals. She claimed to always have hot feet. Socks and flip-flops – it was so cringey.

'Mum, I don't want to talk about this now.'

She sighed. Looked sad. 'OK. But only because we have to see your father.'

I stopped dead. Suddenly afraid.

'I can't. Mummy, please don't make me . . .'

'He's your father, baba?'

She touched her hand to my face.

'Mummy, it's . . .' I stopped. I didn't have anything to say. In these intense moments, my mind tended to go blank and I desperately counted the seconds till the other person felt too awkward to be silent and spoke.

'Whatever you think of him, he's your family. Family is all that is left when everything is done.' She thought about it and then smacked me on the shoulder for emphasis. That was more like Mum. 'And don't tell him what happened to you. You and I will talk about it at home. I don't want him to worry.'

'OK.'

'Sunny,' she asked, breathing in slowly. 'Why don't you want to see him?'

I hate him so much, I thought. And I immediately felt shame.

It was my fault.

5.4

I paused at the entrance to Dad's room. The door was open and I heard a quiet beeping from inside. There was the low hum of the radio. He was listening to cricket. Except, I didn't think there was a match on at the moment.

Maybe he was listening to old recordings.

Mum went in and looked back at me. I held my hand up as if to say I needed a moment.

'He's your daddy,' she said, quietly. 'Not the president. You don't need to compose yourself.'

He was never really a proper dad though. He was never present. But he was all too happy to order me to live my life a certain way, see certain people and cut certain people out.

The six months he made us all vegan. The Saturdays he insisted I volunteer at the *mandhir*. The choice of senior school. My GCSE options. All of it. And each time, I had absorbed my fury with him and done what I'd been told.

I could feel the bubbles in my chest, a burning fizz of tears. It was finally coming. The anger, and the frustration. Everything in my brain was urging me to stop myself crying. I looked around. There were nurses and there were porters. The corridor was far from empty. And they were used to this sort of behaviour. But I didn't want my father to see me cry.

I turned and ran to the exit. Outside, I spotted Surinder's car. He was still laughing with Paula. I went back inside and found a toilet to hang out in. I would give it five minutes and then go and wait in the car.

When Mum joined us, I could tell she had been crying. Surinder ran inside to take back the mug he'd been drinking from. I wanted to tell Mum I was sorry. I was just struggling to find the words.

'Mum . . .' I said, tentatively.

'Don't,' she said.

The car door opened and Surinder got back in. As he started the engine up, a song by Queen came on, 'London Thumakda'.

'I love this song, Surinder, beta,' Mum said and he turned up the volume as we sped away.

I closed my eyes. I hadn't felt so tired since the attack.

I am tiring. I know the fight is halfway through. But I am tiring. My responses are slower. And Keir is starting to feel my sluggishness. I am slow to slip a cross and I am slow to counter the cross with a hook to the side and I am slow to move out of the way of another combo that is Keir's favourite and I am slow to respond in kind.

I look at Keir's face, and I try to understand how we got here. Everything has changed.

One-two – he lands shots across my face.

I don't defend myself.

The crowd cheers. I can hear banging on seats. I can hear whoops. I can hear Keir's name. No one is calling for me. No one at all.

Even Shobu is quiet.

I feel like I am alone. I feel like everything that led me here has been a path to embracing solitude. How can you feel so alone in a room full of people? When you realise that none of them are looking at you, I guess.

But isn't this what I always wanted?

To not be seen?

What changed?

Bang: a shot to the side of my head sends me crashing to the floor. Everything goes black.

Round 6

'I want this to stop,' I say to Shobu, after I come to in time – before I am counted out.

'Are you kidding me? All that training? All that aggro? Everything that led you to here and you want to give up?'

'He's so much stronger than me,' I tell her, looking at her.

'Then he's already won.'

Even though my face is dripping with sweat, I can feel a cut leaking blood down the side of my cheek. It's an old wound. From the racist attack. Keir has managed to open it again. I will always be reminded of that moment because of these little trinkets dotted around my body. How my right heel is in abject pain every morning until I reach the bathroom and have somehow walked it off. How I can only straighten my little finger on my left hand when I concentrate, otherwise it bends involuntarily at the middle knuckle. How I have a cut near my temple that bleeds when struck. We found that out sparring. We found that out training. We found that out now. How I have a chip on my front tooth. How I've developed a squint in my left eye.

All these things remind me of what happened. All these things tell me that for a vital few minutes people took ownership of my body and inflicted hate-fuelled violence on it. I wonder to this day whether they think of me. I think about them every single day. Even the days when I force myself to push it down. They are all there. Lurking in the background. There. Present. They own me. And I cannot shift any of them from my head. Even the one who walked away. Actually, especially the one who walked away. Because he knew what was going to happen. He didn't want to be involved but also, crucially, he did absolutely nothing to stop it.

Keir knows all of this now.

And he is using it against me. He went right for that cut near my temple. That gets me mad. I'm in two minds. Part of me wants to run. Part of me wants to give him a beatdown for using my trauma against me. He knew what he was aiming for. He'd hit it before and he'd caused me damage before. Except, we were in a different place then. We had a bond. We shared things. This hurts.

Shobu squeezes my shoulder and squirts water on my wound.

'Well, what do you want to do?'

'How do I get him out of my head?' I say.

'You get into his.'

'How do I do that?'

'What is Keir most afraid of?'

I know the answer. I know him. I know exactly what his worst fears are.

I look around the crowd. I can't see who I'm looking for. His trainers are shouting at the referee that we're stalling. That we need to hurry up. That this is unacceptable. Keir is looking at the ground. Almost like he has been switched off.

I realise what I have to do. I know how to get in his head.

The bell rings and it's like that's Keir's wake-up call. He springs up from his seat, and waits as his coach pushes his mouthguard back in. He bangs a glove against the side of his head and jumps up and down a couple of times. He bangs his gloves together.

I get up slowly and I walk towards the referee.

'Did your brother come and watch, Keir?' I ask, smiling. 'I can't see him in the crowd.'

Keir growls and punches out at me. He clips the referee's hands and the referee pushes him backwards. Keir runs at me again, screaming at me.

'Easy, easy. Do that again and I'll disqualify you, you hear? My ring, my rules,' the referee shouts at Keir. He turns to me. 'And you. You watch your mouth, OK? Joe Radley is good people, you hear?'

The referee makes us bang gloves together. Keir smashes his against mine. I smirk. I know what I did. I know why I did it.

6.1

I arrived at Ashley Road Boxing Hall desperate to find Keir but also afraid of what I might encounter when I did. I was nodded through by Jimmy, one of the trainers at the gym. He probably thought I was here to usher.

'Mike and Steve need some help taking food orders in the Francis Suite,' he said.

I smiled and nodded.

'Have you seen Keir?' I asked.

'No,' Jimmy said. 'Not tonight I haven't. He's always running late though.'

'Innit,' I said, and went inside.

It was heaving. Loads of men in suits, some even in tuxedos, like it was a wedding. They all walked past, ignoring me and chatting amongst themselves. I was invisible in that crowd. I headed to the Francis Suite. I was pushing against the swell of people heading to the bar, heading into the arena, heading to the toilets. There were cries and roars from the crowd around the ring. I wanted to watch some of the match but I needed to find Keir. I needed to see him. I'd be restless, stressed, until I made sure we were OK. I had pissed him off. I shouldn't have told Madhu about his family. I shouldn't have shown him up in front of everyone at the gym. It was my fault he was mad. And now I needed to make it all better.

I couldn't see anyone from my crop of fighters anywhere. Not Femi, or Heather, or Max, or any of those guys.

I saw Surinder standing in front of the toilets. I bowed my head so he couldn't catch my eye, and I carried on walking.

I finally reached the Francis Suite.

Ruchi was standing on the door.

'Hey,' I said.

'Hey,' she replied. 'You helping out?'

'No, I was looking for Keir,' I said.

'Oh, he's not here,' she told me. 'You don't know?'

'What?'

'You should talk to him yourself.'

A couple, both of them in suits, arrived and Ruchi introduced herself to them, as well as offering to take their coats. I left her to it and headed back down the corridor.

Why should I talk to Keir? Was he OK? Was he in trouble? Was it to do with me? I ran towards the exit.

Back in the lobby, I heard my name being called. I ignored it, despite it getting louder over the throng. I finally felt a firm hand slap down on my shoulder. I swung around. It was Shobu.

'Hey, mate,' she said.

'Hey, Shobz,' I replied, looking over my shoulder at the exit.

'I didn't know you were coming tonight,' she said.

'I'm just heading out,' I said.

'One second,' Shobu said. 'I wanted to introduce you to one of my fighters.'

She turned around and tapped someone on the back. I froze. It was Hari Ramsaroop. I felt my mouth dry. He was smiling. Which was weird cos all the photos of him looked so serious. He had a thick stubble and his messy hair fell about his face, instead of tied into a ponytail like in his press shots. I felt nervous, immediately. He was so beautiful. He was who I wanted to be. He smiled at me, quizzically.

Shobu raised her hands as if to indicate we were both her boys.

'Hari, this is Sunny. Sunny, this is Hari.'

'Hey,' Hari said. 'I've heard a lot about you.'

'Me too,' I said. 'I've seen your YouTube videos. You gonna fight in the next Commonwealth Games?'

'Yeah, dude, that's the plan,' Hari said, smiling. 'I have a fight next month. You wanna come? Come with Shobu. Surinder probably needs company.'

I nodded. I couldn't quite believe I was talking to Hari. There were all these other role models for sure. Prince Naseem. Uzzy Ahmed. But Hari Ramsaroop was from Bristol. Knowing you could look like me and still stand tall in this city, it made it feel more like a home.

I stood there, frozen, not knowing what else to say. He'd invited me to a fight. That was cool.

'Sunny just started sparring,' Shobu said to Hari. 'We'll have him match-fit in no time.'

'Ah, seen,' Hari said. 'I hated sparring. It was the first time it all felt real. Like, now I have to hit someone and wait for them to try to hit me back real. You know?' I nodded, feverishly. 'The best thing to do is to remember that whatever happens, in the ring you're not friends. Spar as much as you can. With people heavier than you. Lighter than you. Never the same person. You need to study everyone's behaviour.'

'Thank you, Hari.'

'Stay tough. Maybe we'll fight one day.'

He held his fist up for a spud.

'Thank you.'

I dapped him. 'See you,' I said, turning and heading towards the door.

Shobu ran after me.

'Where are you going? You not staying?' she said.

I shook my head, staring at her feet. She was wearing open-toed sandals. It was strange seeing her feet. They didn't look like they belonged to her.

'I have to go,' I said. 'I need to find someone.'

Shobu placed her hands on her hips and sighed.

'He's not here,' she said.

'What?'

'You're looking for Keir, right?' she said, smiling, wiping hair from her forehead and putting her fists on her hips.

'Yeah,' I said, looking over her shoulder at Hari laughing at something Surinder had said.

'You need to forget about Keir,' Shobu said. 'Seriously. It's not worth it. He's got a lot of stuff going on. Stuff neither you nor I can help him with.'

'How can you be so heartless?' I said.

'Excuse me?' Shobu replied, tensing her shoulders.

'He's my friend. You're his trainer. Just because he's in trouble, or having a bad time, we don't abandon him, OK? So I'm going to go round his house and I am going to check in on him, because I am his friend and that's what we do.'

'Sunny, my friend, you have the sweetest heart,' Shobu said, rubbing her hand against my cheek. 'And I totally respect that. But you need to understand that what's going on is bigger than you, me or Keir.'

'What's happened?'

'His uncle . . .' She paused. 'Look, just stay. Hang out with Hari, Surinder and me tonight. We'll have fun, watch the fights, go to Tiffins after for some khichdi. Then Surinder can drop you home. And if in the morning you still want to chat to Keir, then go ahead, but go easy. OK?'

Quietly, I was freaking out. What was she talking about? What had happened?

'I'm sorry, Shobu. I'll see you at training on Monday. But I need to do this.'

Shobu called my name, angrily, as I ran out of the building.

6.2

It took me half an hour to run to Keir's house. It was cold, and I was wearing my dad's formal shoes. They were too tight for me, so I kept tripping and grimacing as they pinched my toes. I'd gone to the effort of wearing a suit to the event, like we'd been told, because everyone had to dress smart. No tracksuits. Dad's suit was loose on me. His shoes too tight. Our bodies were in opposition to each other.

With every step I took, I was sifting through all the questions rattling around in my head.

What's happened?
What about his uncle?
Is Keir OK?
Is it what I said to Madhu?
Has his brother hurt him again?
Is it my fault?

I passed people coming and going from nights out. In T-shirts and jeans and shoes. Groups of lads, four or five large, all shouting their enjoyment to each other. Each group seemed to make a passing comment about me running. I ignored them all. I felt breathless even though I'd been training so hard. It was the mixture of the cool night air and nerves making my lungs feel bubbly.

Why was I doing this?

As I ran up Keir's street, everything felt suddenly quiet and eerie. Like the street lamps cast a thinner radius of light over the street. Cars were still. There were no pedestrians. It was like Christmas Day two weeks after a zombie apocalypse.

I slowed to a walk, regulating my breathing, breathing in for four, breathing out for eight. After four rounds of that, I was no longer panting. I approached Keir's house. The acrid smell of fags was thick in the air.

In Keir's front garden, sitting on the wall while his dog sat by his feet, was Joe, head bowed, cigarette clamped in his lips. Another friend sat next to him, head in his hands. I walked quietly, hoping I could make it to the front door before these sentries saw me.

No chance. My movement was enough to make Joe look up.

I kept on walking, feeling him staring at the back of my head.

'Excuse me,' he said. 'The fuck are you doing here?'

I turned around to face him. His friend glanced up. He looked familiar. I couldn't place him though. He had a shaved head, wore a football shirt – Chelsea, I thought. It was blue. He had an earring, a nose ring and an eyebrow ring. He was holding a cricket bat.

'I'm here to check in on Keir. How's he doing?'

Joe stood up and walked towards me, pointing.

'You are not bloody welcome around here. Go home. Now.'

'Is Keir OK? Can I just see him?' I asked, trying to keep my voice as quiet and as calm as possible so Joe couldn't hear the tremble in my throat.

'Did you not hear what I said, paki boy?' he asked, stepping closer to me.

'What did you call me?' I replied, as if on autopilot.

I stood rooted to the spot. I could feel my shoulders rounding, my fists clenching and raising to my stomach, ready.

Joe took a long drag of his cigarette and blew the smoke into my face. I coughed.

'I called you *paki boy*,' he said, slowly.

I felt it. That anger spill out of me. That visceral synergy between my heart and my body took over. And flooded, red, all through me. My entire body was tense. I wanted to scream. I wanted to shout. I wanted to beat Joe to a bloody pulp. He had called me that word, stripped me of any agency. Made me that thing. That word. That nothing. Everything in my body flowed into my fists and I launched an uppercut with my left hand towards his chin. I was ready to catch him off guard with a cross.

My uppercut didn't connect. He ducked and slipped out of it. And with his open palm, he slapped me in the side of the head and pushed me till I tripped over a hedge and fell on to the small patch of grass in his front garden. Within seconds, as my eyes adjusted to the dark, and with his dog barking, he and his friend were on top of me. He was laughing manically, spit dripping from his mouth on to my cheek. Joe squatted over me and leant down, punching me in the face. My head whacked against the grass. I could feel blood fizzing in my nose. He landed another punch in the same spot. I remembered myself and punched at his thigh. He grimaced and stood up. His friend hit me in the side with his cricket bat. This stung, pushing all the wind out of me. I wanted to cry. Instead, my body was insisting on spread-eagling, taking up more space.

Joe recovered and came in for another punch. I was squealing for air, trying to get on to my side to make it easier to breathe.

Joe grabbed the cricket bat from his friend and lifted it high, about to bring it down on me like an axe, when I heard another voice.

'Joe, leave him.'

Joe stopped and looked at Keir, who had stepped out of the house and run over.

'Fuck off, Keir, he needs to go home. Right now. And I ain't talking about Easton.'

'So, what? You're gonna beat him up in our front garden with everyone watching? That won't bring Uncle Steve back.'

Uncle Steve?

I was shuddering, squealing for breath. Back to the four-eight-four method. In for four, out for eight, four times. I managed to get some air back into me.

Joe threw the bat on the floor and he and his friend stomped into the house, dragging the dog inside and slamming the door behind them.

Keir helped me up.

I stood there, in front of him. I wiped the blood from my nose. He looked around furtively.

What had happened to Uncle Steve? I knew family was everything to Keir. I just didn't know what to say to him.

162

'You OK?' I eventually asked. 'I'm . . . I'm sorry for your loss.'

For a second, in the flicker of sadness in his eyes, I saw my friend. Just for a second. Then he remembered himself, pursed his brow and squared his chin.

'You need to leave,' he told me. 'Right now – just go home.'

'Keir, text me later, yeah? Just tell me you're OK.'

'I'm fine,' Keir said, walking back into the house. 'Go home, Sunny.'

6.3

'Keir's uncle got killed in prison,' Madhu said, slamming the local paper down in front of me. Amanda looked across the classroom and I shushed Madhu.

'I know,' I said, picking up the paper and staring at the front page.

It showed a police mugshot of a man – he looked a bit like Martin, Keir's dad. He was balding, red-eyed and smirking. The headline said: 'LOCAL RACIST KILLED IN PRISON OVER BOOK'. I glanced up at Madhu.

'I looked it up last night.'

When I'd got home, I'd gone on the *Bristol Post* website. It was on the home page. The first item. There wasn't a huge amount of information, but enough to tell me what I needed to know.

'Turn over . . .' Madhu said.

I opened the paper and there was an array of photographs. I'd seen some of them last night, aimlessly googling Steve Radley while I'd waited for Keir to message me. It hadn't taken long before I'd felt sick and shut my laptop.

I scanned the paper. Steve Radley in a suit going to court; one of him showing off a three lions tattoo that had been screen grabbed from his Facebook; him laughing with some friends on an EDL survivalists' training weekend that had been found on another Facebook group and used as the main image on page two of the paper. And there he was, hugging Keir and Martin at what looked like Wembley Stadium. Poor Keir.

I felt queasy all over again.

I heard Amanda clear her throat and stand up, ready to start the class.

'That's his family, man,' Madhu said, and hissed.

'It's not *him* though,' I hissed back. 'It's his uncle.'

I sat through the hour and half lesson like I was in a fog. Everything around sounded muffled and distorted, far away. I didn't take anything in. I kept my phone on the table in case Keir contacted me. I felt myself wanting to reach for it every few minutes.

Steve Radley stared at me from the front page. Smirking. For ninety slow anxiety-filled minutes.

I found my quiet spot in the library and sat down, logging on to the computer, waiting an age for it to load before opening a browser and typing in 'Steve Radley'.

I hit return.

There he was again. A BBC interview on YouTube. The quality was grainy, but the house he stood in front of was unmistakeable. He spoke loudly and in short sharp bursts. He smiled at the end of each of his points. He pressed his index fingers together and rubbed them lightly on his lips when he was being spoken to.

Steve was talking about Brexit: *The thing is, I look around here and all I see is halal shops. This isn't the city I grew up in. The way of life for simple British people like me has changed. My brother used to run the chippie shop over there . . .'* He pointed. *'Had to close it cos, well, who eats fish round here? We are losing our way of life.'*

He seemed so reasonable. He just wanted a fish and chip shop. His brother was out of work. Everything about what he said came across reasonable. And that was the scary thing.

Seeing Steve standing in front of Keir's house really shook me.

More news footage. Sentenced to thirteen months in prison for a hate crime. There were shots of him going to court and shots of him that had been grabbed off Facebook. The hate crime? He and his mates had got drunk one night and spray-painted swastikas on the shop windows of Muslim-owned businesses in Easton. A travel company, a butcher's, an assorted goods store, a coffee house. They'd written 'GO HOME IMMIGRANT SCUM'. Keir's uncle was caught doing the last one, a chicken shop, the spray can in his hand and his mates filming. They ran when the police arrived. A guy cashing up his till in a shop across the road had called them. As they reached the scene, the one filming dropped his phone as he ran off. They all, the report says, failed to warn Steve.

He went to jail.

Another report: Steve Radley was killed in prison.

I skimmed the article. The details on what had happened to Steve were light. All we knew was that he had been suffocated with a pillow in his room after a disagreement with his cellmate about a book escalated. The article mooted that perhaps he should not have been in prison in the first place. It contained a quote from Martin:

165

'This is proof that the law cares more about protecting the rights of immigrants than of its naturalised citizens. My brother should not have been in jail. He should not have been put in this dangerous environment to begin with. The state has blood on its hands. It will pay.'

I felt a searing chill down my spine.

I sensed someone shuffling behind me. I looked up. It was Madhu. She put a hand on my shoulder.

'People are angry, man,' Madhu said. 'How's Keir taking it?'

'I don't know,' I said. 'I haven't heard from him since I went round.'

I looked at Madhu. She smiled sadly and nodded.

She showed me her phone. She was scrolling through Twitter.

'I've been doing some research. There's a hashtag,' she said. '#justice4SteveRadley. Look at the shit they're saying.'

Kill the immigrants #justice4SteveRadley

Banged up for telling the truth. #justice4SteveRadley

A reckoning is coming. The state has blood on its hands.

Time to mobilise. #justice4SteveRadley

We need to march for Steve. This Saturday. Who's with me?

#justice4SteveRadley

This last post had been retweeted hundreds of times.

I logged on to Facebook. I put '#justice4SteveRadley' into

the search bar and found an event. A march in honour of Steve Radley. It was organised by Joey Steven Radley. Jesus. Reading through the comments from people attending the march, it was definitely being turned into a bigger thing – for lots of far-right parties. There were loads of slurs in the comments too, calling out pakis and terrorist scum and other horrible words. I looked at Madhu. She shrugged.

'He's your mate, innit.'

'Madhu, he's not doing this.'

'He might not be,' she said. 'But it's still his family. You think he'll be there?'

'I don't know,' I told her. I wished I did.

Keir was grieving for his uncle and there was still this weird, unresolved thing between us. I didn't know what to do next.

Sure, his uncle was clearly a monster, but Keir would have to watch as other racists twisted his family's grief to suit their own agendas. I knew he'd be scared, even if he couldn't show it. I knew how that felt.

'You know,' I said to Madhu. 'Until what happened to me, I'd never thought about any of this stuff before.'

'What do you mean?' she asked.

'Where I grew up, we all were just people. I was surrounded by Asians. I didn't think of myself as a brown person or a paki or even an Asian. I was just a person. It was when I moved here and found myself the only brown person in the room the majority of the time, that's when it started to dawn on me that some people believed I was different in a bad way. I hadn't thought about it before.'

'Sunny,' Madhu said. 'You knew racism existed right?'

'Yeah, of course I did. People used to make terrorism jokes at school all the time. I thought it was just kids being dicks. Like, they'd say anything to get a rise. If they'd known I was gay, they would have called me something awful about that too. I just didn't think there was anything more to it. I remember walking home with my dad once, and people in a car drove past squirting red ink at us from water pistols. They actually shouted, "Kill the immigrant scum," but I genuinely didn't think they were racists, just idiots being idiots. Bants or whatever. Just trying to piss us off. Maybe I was too young to realise. Maybe it's cos my dad didn't call it out for what it was – I dunno.'

Dad had kept on walking, not missing a step. I'd wanted to ask him about what had just happened, but I never did. He was so composed. Almost like he didn't even notice it happened at all. When we got home, he made me change, and he stood at the sink in his white vest and trousers, soaking our clothes to get rid of the red ink. He wasn't able to get it out of his shirt. He silently put the shirt in the bin and left the kitchen. I sat there wondering if I had imagined the whole thing.

Madhu put her hand on my arm.

'Sorry about the attack. I didn't realise it was racially motivated . . .'

'I don't want to talk about it,' I said, curtly, and she was quiet.

I could feel the perimeter walls beginning to break. Their faces were starting to skulk around my brain again, calling my name. They had been waiting for me. They had been waiting for me to slip up and let them back into my head. They knew that I was weak. That my coping mechanisms were tenuous. I couldn't really see the detail of their faces any more. It was like they were all wearing flesh-coloured stockings on their heads, obscuring my view of them.

Go away, I wanted to scream into the void of my head. I replaced their faces with Keir's. I needed to find a way to talk to him. I needed to know if he was OK.

Madhu put an index finger to her lips. She usually did this when she was desperate to say something but was shushing herself.

'But, like, you know the world is fucked up and racist,' she said, slowly.

'Yeah, of course,' I said. 'I'm talking about when I was younger. I didn't understand this stuff. But . . .'

'But being beaten up for being a paki changes stuff, huh?'

'Yeah,' I whispered.

'OK, OK, look – this march sounds serious. I know you, man . . . You stay away from it, OK? Don't go looking for him. He'll find you when he's ready.'

'I can't abandon him,' I found myself saying, yet again. 'He's my friend. I know he's a good person.'

'I get you,' Madhu said. 'But part of being a friend is giving your friend the space to choose their own path, even if it is the wrong one . . .'

'I know.'

'And part of being a smart person is staying well away from people who want you dead . . .'

I couldn't take any more of Madhu's prodding, so I stood up and walked out of the library, bumping into Amanda as I went.

'Sunny, where are you going?' she called after me.

I broke into a run.

6.4

I ran to the station, catching a train at the last second, taking me home. I needed to be by myself and get some space to think. I had four missed calls and seven text messages from Shobu. All wanting to know why I had missed training. I ignored them.

I sat at Mum's computer in her bedroom, reading through Facebook groups discussing the march. I clicked on Keir's profile to see if he had engaged with any of them.

He had unfriended me. What the hell?

I couldn't see any of his profile now.

Why had he unfriended me?

I found Joe's profile. He was happy to put most of his business online so I was able to see what he had been up to at least.

He had created the event page for the march. He belonged to seventeen groups that veered between far-right organisations, anti-liberal memes, anti-immigration chats and justice for Steve Radley. And those were just the public ones. He linked to a couple of 4chan threads about prominent Muslims who were spreading Sharia law in the UK and needed dealing with.

I moved on from Facebook and started trawling through more 4chan threads about hating everyone. Every single one seemed to end with someone declaring that they were going to exterminate all the Jews. I saw every single slur possible.

I was on the computer for hours. I didn't hear Mum come home. She must have assumed I wasn't here because I didn't realise she was in until she put on Asian Network and started singing along. Panicking, I starting closing browsers and clearing my search history. Mum didn't need to know I'd spent the entire afternoon on a deep Google search into alt-right Bristol. I'd barely scratched the surface, but I'd at least got the number for a WhatsApp group that I could be added to. It was at the end of the Bristol thread.

But first I needed to eat something. I'd forgotten to have lunch.

I closed down the computer and went into the kitchen.

Mum screamed and held a hand to her chest.

'Sunny,' she said, panting. 'You scared me.'

Spook.

'Sorry, Mum, I was doing some research. My laptop was so slow.'

'I'm glad you're home,' she said. 'We need to have a talk. A serious one.'

'Mum,' I said. 'I need to finish this—'

'No,' she replied. 'No, you don't.'

She pulled out a chair for me. I sat down with a slump.

'I am sick of not knowing what is going on with you. You're not being told off, my boy, but you *are* finished with not telling me what is going on. That has to end. I am your mother. I deserve to know what is happening in your life. You used to tell me everything.'

Mum's eyes flicked to the door. I suddenly realised she was stalling.

There was a knock.

I stood up.

'Mum, who is that?' I said.

She silently walked out of the room. I was left with the sound of the kettle gurgling to life. I noticed she had put out three mugs. And the nice coffee. And sugar. We never had sugar. She had invited someone over.

I heard her open the door and greet someone. I heard her ask them to remove their shoes. I heard a low murmur of conversation.

I faced the doorway and clutched the back of the chair, tightly. Mum came back into the kitchen. Behind her, clutching his uniform hat, was a policeman.

I felt like my chest was light and fuzzy and my legs wobbled. I sat down. *A policeman? Here? In our house? The hell you doing, Mum?*

'Sunny,' she said. 'This is Detective Roberts. Steven, beta. This is my son, Sunny.'

'Mum, who is this?'

'He gave me a lift home a few weeks ago when I had a lot of shopping and it was raining. Very lovely man. I asked him to come and talk to you.'

'Mum,' I said. But I knew I had nothing to say. I had avoided a few messages from the police officer who had spoken to me when I was first attacked a while back. I had avoided going in to file a report. I had avoided giving them any more information. And eventually the officer had stopped trying to get in contact. Which was fine with me.

'Mum, what have you done?'

'Steven,' Mum said, addressing the police officer. 'As I told you on the phone, my son was brutally assaulted and attacked by some racists. He won't talk to me about it. I don't understand why. But I wondered if you could get the information out of him so you can lock those bastards up.'

Detective Roberts listened to Mum, paused to accept a tea from her and then sipped it a few times.

'Auntie,' he said. 'Please could you let Sunil and me talk alone please?'

'Detective, I know he is eighteen, but I would feel more comfortable if he had an adult present.'

I hated them both talking about me like I wasn't even in the room. How dare they? I hadn't even consented to have any sort of conversation with Detective Roberts about anything.

'If this was an on-the-record talk, I would ask him if he wanted someone present, maybe a legal representative or parent, but hey, me and Sunny, we're just having a chat. Informal. Off the record. It goes nowhere if you don't want it to. What do you think?'

He made a finger gun at me. I stared at his hand.

'Sunny,' Mum said. 'Answer the man.'

'You don't even have to tell me anything,' Detective Roberts continued. 'You control the conversation. I think it'll be helpful, auntie, if you weren't here though. Don't want you to accidentally lead it.'

Mum sighed, picked up her tea and left the room. Thirty seconds later, a Bollywood song blasted from the television. Purposefully loud, I thought. Making a point.

'May I?' the policeman said, sitting down.

I nodded. I was wary. I had never really been this close to a police officer. Certainly not on my own.

'You don't remember me, do you?' I shook my head. Even when he'd been texting me, this wasn't the face I ignored. 'I saw you that night. In the hospital. I wanted to talk to you. The paramedic, Shanai, told me off for being too aggressive while you were vulnerable. Totally fair. Shanai said she would leave you my card. Did she?' I couldn't remember. 'I hoped to hear from you and then work got really busy and I let it go. I'm sorry. But what you went through – there's zero tolerance for that. I can help you, Sunny.'

I could feel them, my attackers, back in my head, beating their fists against the glass wall I had built between me and them. Their facial features were starting to be drawn in now.

'Shanai's my girlfriend,' Detective Roberts added, almost like he was reminding himself rather than telling me as if I should care.

'I liked Shanai,' I said.

I was sure I did. I couldn't remember. She must have been kind. Everything was hazy. Everything else that wasn't had been locked away.

'I like her too,' Roberts said. He paused then looked away. 'Look, you don't have to tell me what happened. I saw.'

I froze. A shiver made my neck tense up. I suddenly felt like my legs were weightless and I grabbed the table in front of me. Roberts reached out to steady me. I gulped but my mouth was dry.

'What do you mean?' I stuttered.

Roberts clasped his hands in front of him on the table.

'I saw the CCTV,' he said, before pausing. 'After I spoke to your mum, I remembered that we hadn't reviewed the CCTV. Because you hadn't filed a report. So I went back and watched it.'

I put my hands over my eyes. I was there again. I was in it. The wall was down. They were loose in my head. I was back there, on that bench, replaying everything in crystal-clear detail.

Sam smacking at my mouth. Me biting down on my tongue and my cheek stinging with the smack. Me dropping the

174

samosa and crying out in pain. Me leaning forward, cupping my mouth. I was in so much pain. I'd never been hit before.

Stand up. Walk down the platform. Just stand up, *I thought*. Make your legs work. Why won't your legs work? Stand up. Walk away.

Me whimpering in pain.

One of them saying, 'I said I wanted a bite, you shit-skin paki bastard.'

Something landing hard on my back. It feeling like an entire body. It being so heavy. My nose being whacked into my knee and me having the wind knocked out of me as I slumped forward off my seat. Me falling into Sam, who kicked me off him.

'Leave him, Sam,' one of them saying. Probably the one sitting on the bench. 'CCTV, innit.'

It was my fault.

I blinked twice and looked at Roberts. My chest was tight, my paws clenched, my knees locked. My right foot cramped.

'I need to go,' I said. I couldn't breathe. The room was airless. The sound of the fridge was deafening.

'Sure,' Roberts said, standing up. 'Let's go for a walk, get some fresh air.'

'No. Don't follow me,' I told him, holding my hand to his chest.

I stood up and walked to the front door. I grabbed my trainers. I could slip my feet into them outside. I just needed to be out of here. Roberts had come out of the kitchen behind me, taking up space in the hallway.

'Sunny, wait,' he said. 'I'm sorry.'

Mum stepped into the corridor, lowering the volume on the television with the remote control.

'I'm sorry too,' I said. I looked at her. 'Mum, I can't believe you did this to me.'

I left the flat, slamming the door shut behind me.

Detective Roberts caught up with me before I reached the corner shop. I'd been planning to buy a packet of crisps. Shobu had banned junk food when we'd started training. All I was allowed was protein, fruit and vegetables in between meals. But I needed some Hula Hoops. Original flavour. The only flavour. I was salivating at the thought of all that delicious salt on my tongue. Maybe I'd wash it down with a corner shop keema samosa.

'I didn't mean to drop that in like that,' Roberts said as he grabbed my elbow.

I wrenched away from him.

'Don't touch me,' I hissed. 'Are you even allowed to do that?'

'Sunny,' he said, stepping in front of me and blocking my path. 'You could help us identify these guys. We could put them away. Where they belong. What they all did to you was horrific ... Look, the CCTV doesn't show their faces too well, so any information would be useful. How did the fight start? Did you hear anyone's name? Anything you can tell us. It might help us find these scumbags and put them away.'

'I should have just let him have my bloody samosa.'

Roberts tilted his head.

'Oh, Sunny, no,' he said. 'No. It was not your fault. You know that, right?'

'Of course it was,' I said, looking in the window of the corner shop. The owner was staring at me.

Roberts smiled. 'Sunny,' he said, softly. 'You did nothing wrong, mate.'

'Sam,' I said. Roberts raised an eyebrow, confused. 'One of them was called Sam.'

I tried to walk on but Roberts gently placed his hand on my chest.

'Wait,' he said. 'Just wait, please. Sam what? Anything else?'

'Sam wanted a bite of my samosa. I ignored him so his mate called me a paki and they both beat the shit out of me. End of story.'

'No,' Roberts said. 'It's not.'

I was furious now. He had pushed me to melt away the ice wall I'd been using to keep myself safe, away from the bad thoughts. He was unleashing terror in my head. These men were now free in my mind. Running around. Causing terror.

'Go away!' I erupted, pointing a finger at him. 'How dare you? How dare you do this to me?' My voice got louder and louder till I was shouting.

'Sunny, please. I can help you,' he said. 'We can put these people away for what they did to you.'

I tapped my head.

'It won't get them out of here though, will it?'

Each round feels like a lifetime. Every second is like a dragged-out, slow-motion video. Every punch feels like a laboured throw I see happening in front of me for thirty seconds before it lands. A lifetime. Every. Single. Round.

I have to push everyone out of my head.

I lean back and throw my shoulder at Keir.

BANG: I land a straight right in Keir's side and, as he doubles over, I recover my right hand and send him to the floor with a hook. I stand over him. He raises himself to all fours, hesitating before getting up.

The bell rings.

I walk backwards to my corner, letting Keir know I am watching him at all times. I spit into the bucket, watching him. I let Shobu squirt water into my mouth, watching him. I bang my gloves together, still watching him. I wait, my hands on my knees. Watching him. Watching him. Watching him.

'Whatever was going through your mind just then? More of that, yeah?' Shobu says.

Round 7

When the bell rings, we're both going at it. This time, we both mean it.

Punches are flying everywhere.

Jab-jab cross. Duck, uppercut.

We trade blows like we have nothing left to lose any more. Every single punch tells a history. My shoulders hurt; my knees are so tensed they might snap. My knuckles are drawn. Every single slip tells the story of us. Every punch says why our friendship was doomed from the start. Every single bead of sweat lost makes us lighter. Every single bruise, cut, grunt, yelp – everything is us, coming together to say what we feel.

7.1

I'd missed four days of training by the time the day of the march arrived. I'd ignored my trainer's every text asking me what was going on. Even a few missed calls. I was starting to prang at how much I had left behind my new routines and systems. I could feel the bad thoughts creeping back in.

I'd been spending every evening trying to understand these people. The two things had conflated in my head. What Roberts said about it not being my fault and how everyone was blaming Steve Radley's death on immigrants. It was all one huge mess that I needed to understand.

Why did they hate us? Why did they think it was OK to treat us as less than human? I watched training videos and vlogs, all spelling out the end of the country due to immigration and Muslims and pakis and people who refused to integrate. I thought about my silent dad. He'd never spoken to anyone. He'd run his shop, in silence. He'd paid his taxes. He'd done everything that had been asked of him. Never spoken up. And yet according to the things I was finding online, he was still not welcome here. *He was born here*, I thought. *I was born here.* Mum was the one who came over, and she worked three jobs to make ends meet. She did everything she was supposed to and still she wasn't enough.

I was still upset Keir had unfriended me on Facebook. His Instagram hadn't been updated in a week. Without any physical access to him, with him ignoring my messages and offers to meet up, I obsessively hunted my friend online. But he was nowhere. I hunted for him in Facebook groups, Reddit, 4chan, Twitter, MailOnline, even the *Guardian* comments.

I couldn't find him anywhere.

I even had Madhu, who had more patience with deep searches, helping me. She'd messaged to say that a learning support worker had cornered her, asking about me, and so had Amanda, and so college basically wanted to know what was up. I didn't know how to answer, so I'd distracted her by describing some of the stuff I'd found online.

why u looking?

Curiosity.

But you know they're all racist. whats to be curious abt?

Whether Keir is with them.

Why? Are you two not friends any more?

I don't know. I'm worried about him. I've seen scary stuff. I hope he's not buying into this shit.

Madhu didn't reply for about ten minutes, then:

I can't find him neither.

He had become a ghost. I knew he hadn't spoken to Shobu since our sparring match and then he had been awful to her. The #justice4SteveRadley march event now had six thousand people marked down as attending with a further thirteen thousand interested in going. It was going to be big.

It even made the local news. Madhu texted me, furious.

Why is BBC Points West covering this? It makes it real. More people will attend.

181

19,000 people interested in attending a racist march, that's terrifying . . . I'd wanna know about it, I replied.

Yeah, man. But it's like free advertising and stuff.

I didn't want to be afraid. I normally avoided going into the centre of Bristol. It was like twenty minutes away by foot, but still, it felt like somewhere I didn't really belong. My entire life was between the gym and my home in Easton and college in Filton. And that was fine. That was totally fine to me. My worlds were carefully constructed, according to my own boundaries and what I was comfortable with.

And then Shobu turned up on my doorstep.

7.2

Mum answered the door, cos I was in the shower. I didn't even hear it. I walked into the kitchen in my towel, fresh boxers in hand, singing to myself, and was greeted by Shobu, sitting at the table with Mum.

'Hey,' I squeaked. I was so surprised to see my trainer there, my two worlds colliding. I was suddenly exposed, clutching my pants, wrapped in a towel.

'Hey, Sunny,' Shobu said, her arms folded. 'What's going on? You don't call, you don't write . . .'

I held a hand up and ran back to my room to change.

'You missed training four times?' Mum called.

'What? Mum . . . Come on!' I erupted back into the kitchen. 'You hate me boxing.'

'I do,' she said, standing up. 'But I didn't know that your trainer was this amazing woman. You want to know a funny story?'

Mum got some gathia out of the cupboard and poured it into a bowl.

'Mum, please, not n—'

'Do you remember some years ago, when your aunties and I went to watch the Olympic Games? We got the tickets in the lottery. You remember what we got? Women's boxing? Remember?'

I nodded my head. 'Vaguely.'

'Well, none of us wanted to go. We didn't like the sport. It was brutish. But we went because it was in our city, and it was the Olympics. And we watched an Asian woman stand up there and beat a Russian woman. It was this woman here, Shobu. Shobhana. She was so beautiful to watch, so elegant and powerful. Not brutish at all. I still do not think it is good for your health to be boxing, but if this wonderful role model is your trainer, then you are in good hands. You have my blessing.'

A grin spread right across my face. I was kinda relieved.

'I lost in the next match,' Shobu said. 'It was Nicola's year that year. And too right.'

'But still, you were good enough to go to the Olympics,' Mum said. She pointed at me. 'What about our boy?'

Shobu looked at me and smiled. 'Our boy is fighting too many people in his head right now. He needs to fight them in the ring. And understand that he can beat them. Then we can see. But, he's not bad, auntie. Not bad at all. I don't train that many people. I'm very selective.'

'Why me though?' I asked, mumbling.

'You remind me of Hari,' Shobu said. 'When he first came along, I could see what was missing in his life – it was the confidence to be in a room and take up the space he deserved to. Same with you.'

'I'm still not very good with either of those things,' I said. 'I just want to be left alone.'

'I know,' Shobu said, smiling at Mum. 'Who doesn't . . .?'

Mum went off to get ready for work. I leant up against the fridge and put my hands in my pockets. Shobu stood up.

'You think I'm mucking around?' she asked, coming right over to me.

'No,' I said, standing up straight so that our faces were level. She was in my space. I didn't like it. I wanted her to step back. 'Neither am I.'

'Look, whatever is going on in your private life, I understand you can't always leave it at the door when you come and train with me. I get that. But you know what you are lacking at the moment?'

'No,' I said.

Shobu pushed me lightly and I fell back against the fridge. 'Respect, Sunny. You are lacking in respect for me. I don't expect life to stop when you're training. But I expect you to be transparent with me. You make it to training, or you let me know.'

'I'm sorry,' I said. 'I had stuff on my mind.'

'I get that, buddy,' she said, softening, stepping backwards. 'I really do. And I don't necessarily want to force you to talk to me about it. But you just have to tell me and I'll understand. If it's college or if it's mental health, or whatever, it'd be good to know.'

'I-I'm . . .' I stuttered, not entirely sure what I wanted to say. I took a deep breath. 'When things get really rough, I sort of put myself in this glass box, like on *The Cube*, and no one can get in cos there's no door – no one can get to me. They can't hear me and I can't hear them. And they all sound muffled and far away and I'm just in the glass box watching people.'

'Sunny,' Shobu said, putting a hand on my shoulder. 'I'm so sorry you feel like you have to do that.' She paused. 'Look, I have to ask . . . what's going on between you and Keir?'

'Don't talk about him,' I snapped. 'And while we're at it, why did you tell Surinder about the attack? That was supposed to be between us!'

Shobu sighed. 'I'm sorry. He was concerned. I thought I was—'

'You talk about respect, but you disrespected me by gossiping behind my back,' I told her.

Shobu held her hands in the air.

'Fair enough. We all have the capacity to muck up,' she said. 'I'm not perfect. Just know I told him out of concern, not cos I was gossiping.'

'I don't want people pitying me,' I said.

'No one is pitying you. People care about you. Is that so hard to accept?'

We fell into a silence. Shobu sat down again.

'Look,' she said. 'I know Keir's your friend and whatever's going on with you is your own business, but I need to talk to you about him. I'm worried.'

I sat down at the table with her.

'Keir came into the gym this morning to collect some stuff he'd left. He's . . .' She stopped talking.

'He's what? Is he OK?' I asked.

'He's had his uncle's name tattooed on his arm. I didn't say anything about the tattoo, but he was just really off with me. Wouldn't talk to me. Didn't want to train. Look, he's your friend, you know him better than I do – I get that.

But you need to understand that when I took him on he was in a bad way. You know why he was kicked out of college?' I shook my head. 'Again, I'm telling you this out of concern, not to gossip.' I nodded. 'He had big anger issues, Sunny. He was put in a PRU, sent to anger management. And that was how I found him. He's not a bad kid. He's just spent too long around the wrong people. Like his dad. His dad hates me. Sends me annoying pushy-dad texts every day. Always aggressive. Always knows better. But I let him, cos I care about Keir a lot. And if I can focus his mind, I can get him away from the people in his life who aren't good for him . . . Keir has the talent to go all the way. And he changed when he met you. He became the Keir I always knew he could be.'

Tears pricked at my eyes. 'I need to find him,' I said. 'He's going to be at that rally, isn't he? It starts in an hour. You're right, we need to get him away from those people. I've seen what they're saying online.'

'You're not going down there,' Shobu said. 'No bloody way. You don't understand – they will kill you, love. I've seen marches like that. These men are drinking, they're taking uppers, they're riled up. They already hate us. Please don't go.'

'I have to,' I said. 'I have to get Keir out of there. We can save him.'

'Darling,' Shobu said. 'He has to *want* to be saved.'

'But he can't see straight right now – how can we help him unless we're there?'

'Just forgetting the danger for one sec, you've got stuff going on too. Sure you're the one who can do this?'

'Yes,' I said. 'He's one of my closest friends.'

186

'Sunny, I'm sorry to be such a downer, but I've seen it before. Something bad happens to a person and that makes them sad and angry. Then someone gives them a hate figure to point their sadness and anger towards, rather than accept the events that led to the bad thing and the consequences afterwards.'

'Like blaming immigrants?'

'Exactly. You know, I went to Steve Radley's trial. My cousin's shop was one of the ones that got tagged with swastikas.'

'Shit. Sorry, Shobu . . . Was Keir there at the trial?' I asked, shocked at this news.

'No, but I saw his brother – god, he's a piece of work. And his dad. But you can see the way it's gonna go. They point the finger at immigrants and "people coming over here stealing our jobs". And all the vulnerable people like Keir, who aren't bad people, but they're sad and they're angry and they're skint – now they have someone to blame.'

'But that's even more reason to go!' I jumped up from the table.

Shobu grabbed my hand and I retaliated by swinging for her head. She dodged me and hung on to my hand.

'Let's work together on this,' she said. 'Or we could lose him for good.'

She had this confused look on her face, like, *I can't believe you swung for me.* I had disappointed her. I looked at the floor and she squeezed my hand.

I growled in pain and she let go.

'Sunny,' she said. 'I know you're going through a tough time. I'm going to look past that swing you just took at me. But listen, please. Whatever you're feeling, you have to try to

187

find a sensible path. You need to stay here. I can stay here with you. It's a good day to stay indoors and watch telly or something. But, please, stay here.'

'OK, fine,' I said. I paused. 'I need the loo.'

Shobu nodded and sat back down at the table. She grabbed her cup of tea. In that second of distraction, I was running for the door.

Grab hoodie, cap, shoes, keys and wallet; open door; slam door shut. I was running.

Keir, I thought. *I'm coming.*

7.3

The bus journey into the centre of town was horrible. Four men, all carrying Union Jack flags and drinking beer, were standing in the middle of the bus, singing a football song at the tops of their voices. They were constantly looking around, like they were challenging the rest of us passengers to say something. I'd squirmed past them as I'd got on and headed to the top deck, hiding at the back – the furthest point away from the men that I could be. Up there I'd found a deck full of silent people of colour. Everyone had nodded at me, like we were in solidarity. The bus driver hadn't said anything. It seemed obvious to me that they were going to the march.

According to the Facebook group last night, the plan was to meet outside Steve Radley's favourite pub, the Maker's Arms, right in the centre of town, and march in a loop to finish at College Green where they would do a vigil in front of City Hall. They had all been instructed to bring flags and dress in white out of respect.

I knew where the pub was. I hadn't ever been inside it, but the few times I'd walked past, I'd crossed the street because it was always so busy and loud in the smoking area outside.

I called Keir one more time from my phone. It went straight to voicemail. I checked the Facebook event again. It had been made private and I couldn't access it.

That was strange. Why was it suddenly private?

I checked Twitter and the local newspaper's site. On the home page was a warning about the march and tensions in the area. It asked people to avoid the city centre as they anticipated a big turnout and a huge police presence.

I was sweating. It was an unseasonably hot day. Black wasn't the best choice of colour for my hoodie and cap, but I hadn't exactly had time to think about it when I'd run out of the house.

What do you wear to a far-right rally?

Especially when you want to blend in.

Shoulda worn white.

The shouty singing men got louder and louder. Now they were yelling, 'Immigrant scum, go home!' in a sing-songy way. Which made it sound even more sinister and threatening. I felt an itch under my cap. I scratched it and looked around me. Everyone was shifting about in their seats, nervous. We were approaching the centre of Bristol. People would be getting off soon. And they would have to go past these men.

The bus arrived in the centre. The person closest to the stairs hovered at the top, tentatively moving downwards when it was obvious the men were getting off.

I heard one of them shout at the bus driver, telling him to eff off. A line of us followed behind them. The driver, an old Indian man, nodded at us all as we passed him.

'Cheers, driver,' each of us said, and as we parted ways, we all nodded to each other again, like, *Goodbye, stay safe, yeah?*

I watched the men walk up the road. Their flags unfurled and now draped over their shoulders, they were still singing, throwing beer cans on the floor and taking more out from a box one of them carried.

I followed them. With my hoodie zipped right up over my mouth and my hands tucked into my sleeves to obscure that I was brown, I felt like I was probably going to pass out from heat exhaustion. I couldn't afford for anyone to see that I wasn't white. I kept my distance. The centre of the city felt weirdly quiet today. Hardly any people walking about; no skateboarders or shoppers. The men walked through the fountains. I couldn't hear them now they'd stopped singing but I could see them gesturing at people who were walking or cycling past.

They kept to the middle of the pedestrianised bit in the centre. Technically this was the cycle path and they were very much in the way, four abreast, taking up the whole lane. At some traffic lights, they joined a bigger group of men. No women, I noticed. They were all white. They all wore polo shirts or football shirts, and hardly anyone had placards.

One of the first things I'd done when I became friends with Madhu was go with her and some of her friends to a Black Lives Matter march from the Malcolm X Community Centre through to City Hall. Mostly everyone there had held home-made placards, not flags. They'd all been showing supportive messages of solidarity and political statements.

Maybe this lot were just not very well prepared.

As we turned the corner on to the road where the Maker's Arms was, the atmosphere changed. It was suddenly teeming with people. They were drinking and talking and waiting. There were randoms dotted around recording videos. There were proper broadcast cameras filming the march. And a woman in a power suit carrying a big wooden cross was doing a photoshoot in the centre of the throng. The noise was making me feel dizzy.

I couldn't count how many people were there.

My phone rang. It was Shobu. I cancelled it.

A few seconds later, a message arrived.

Ur an idiot for going. Stay safe. I'm coming to find you. Please phone me. Now you're putting us both in danger by being there.

go home, Shobu.

Now you're talking like one of them 😳 I'm coming.

I looked up at the sound of a siren in the distance. The street was lined with police officers, all wearing yellow jackets and hats, 'POLICE' written on their backs. They stood facing forward, hands clasped in front of them, like they were showing respect at a memorial. Men spilled out of the pub into the street. Many clutched plastic cups of beer. Some stood in a circle together receiving instructions. There were three or four camera operators and presenters doing interviews and using the scenes on the blocked-off street as their backdrops. The men from the bus quietened down as they neared the pub. They must have seen people they knew because they all shook hands. I kept my distance, not wanting to be spotted by them. I walked behind the police officers.

I lowered my hoodie a little so you could at least see my nose. I didn't want the coppers to think I was a member of the Antifa and detain me in case I started raging on the fascists . . . I was only looking for Keir. Nothing else.

The atmosphere on the road was like the day of a big storm, everything quiet and tense. My fists clenched tightly in my hoodie pocket. I felt sweat collating around my temples. I put my earphones in but didn't put any music on. That way I could look like I was passing through. It seemed that the men were lining up to march because a swarm of them started to swell up the street. Songs were starting to emerge from their pockets: 'Is This the Way to Amarillo?' and 'Three Lions'.

I was desperately scanning the crowd for Keir. They were all wearing white T-shirts. Keir always wore a white T-shirt. Without fail. It was gonna be impossible to single him out.

Suddenly, all the police officers were rushing away from the line they had created. I looked where they were headed. Two men at the head of the march were pointing and shouting at a police officer, who was talking into a walkie-talkie. I couldn't quite work out what they were saying, but the men's body language was angry.

I realised that one of the men was Martin, Keir's dad. The recognition made me feel suddenly exposed and I backed into the doorway of a hotel. I felt the automatic door open behind me. I could just step inside and wait for them to walk away. But if Martin was near, Keir definitely would be too.

I heard a couple of men talking as they walked past the hotel doorway.

'I can't believe those pigs won't let us march for Steve.'

'Fucking Muslamics probably complained.'

'I'm gonna remind 'em who we are.'

One of the men picked up a plant pot at the entrance of the hotel. He emptied the contents of the pot on to the floor and headed for the crowd, which was getting louder. I could feel the aggression in the air, simply from the loud noises. I couldn't make out any words. Just a chilling deep roar. I stepped back out on to the street. Martin and his friend were still shouting at the police officer. All the other police had lined up behind her. She was motioning for Martin and his friend to go back, but neither of them was listening.

She turned around for support.

In that moment, I saw something fly through the air and land next to her, smashing on the ground. It was the plant pot. I looked towards the crowd and tried to see where it'd come from. But everything had changed. The men rushed forward, yelling.

A chant rose: 'WE MARCH FOR STEVE. WE MARCH FOR STEVE,' repeated again and again as they charged forward. The police, not expecting a riot, were dressed in standard uniform. I watched, not knowing what to do as a huge mob rushed at them, shouting. A glass bottle was lobbed. As the crowd reached the line of police, a few of them picked up the metal barriers separating the road from the pavement and were using them as battering rams. The police officers scattered in fear. More people were streaming round the corner. This march was massive. Where were all these people coming from? Were they all here for a racist? What was going on? I was bewildered by the sheer numbers. I didn't know what to do. Seeing the amount of people I realised my mistake. I had to be out of here.

But I still couldn't bring myself to believe that Keir was a part of this.

I finally saw some placards:

BANNING IMMIGRANTS DOES NOT MAKE ME A NAZI
ISLAM IS EVIL
GO HOME, IMMIGRANT SCUM

It was hot. I pulled my zipper down so my mouth was clear, freed my hands. Suddenly, I felt the rush as men jumped the remaining barriers and streamed over the pavements. They were heading towards me. I tried to step back into the hotel but wasn't quick enough and I was pushed to the floor. I fell on my elbows, hard, and protected myself as the men ran past. They weren't paying any attention to me.

PAKIS, GO HOME

It was my fault.

I was suddenly that word again. *You don't have to be.* I tried to stand up but the crowd around me was too thick. I couldn't breathe.

A hand reached towards me and pulled me up. I got to my feet.

'Thank you,' I mumbled to the person who had helped me up. Then I realised whose hand I was holding.

'Give us a bite . . .'

It was him. Sam. He smiled at me and then his face changed. Like he recognised me. He hurried off.

He knew. He knew me. He knew who I was. I was sure of it. All this time I had been trying to forget him, assuming that he'd never given me a second thought and here he was, recognising the face he had battered. Something came over me. It was coming from somewhere in the depths of my anger. I was by myself and I was not going to be popular with these men.

But something in me was different.

I knew how to stand my ground. I didn't understand my compulsion to follow him, but thrusting myself through the crowd, pushing and shouting, I did it anyway.

I rushed forward, firm yet planted, on my toes yet rock solid, like Shobu had taught me. It meant that the men bounced off me and carried on in the direction they wanted to go in.

I saw Sam in the crowd, looking back, seeing me, and then pushing forward again, rushing now, almost panicked.

Why was he afraid of me?

He had beaten me once. He could probably do it again, especially surrounded by men who would happily give him a helping hand.

What was I planning to do if I caught up with him?

The reality was, I didn't know. Part of me wanted to be sure that he recognised me. I also wanted him to know that I was no longer afraid of him. I needed to face him.

The movements around me felt more aggressive now. I was being carried along in the swarm of people running forward. I'd nearly reached the other side of the street. I could see him, entering a slip road into Queen's Square. I didn't know if it'd be as packed with people as here but all I had to do was push past the remaining men to find out.

I felt a tug on my hoodie and I was wrenched backwards. I jerked my body wildly, trying to free myself. Someone was pulling my hood. I threw my hips in a swivel and used a fist to break the grip on my clothes as the hood tightened around my neck, causing me to choke.

A man stood there, holding his hand in pain.

'You have no business being here,' he snarled.

I turned back to ensure I had eyes on Sam. People had stopped. They were forming a circle around us, sensing trouble.

'Leave me alone!' I shouted. 'Get the hell away from me!'

'You ain't welcome. Go home, scum!' he yelled.

People cheered in agreement. He ran towards me, head down like a battering ram, but I stepped to the side and he crashed into the circle around us. The chaos that followed allowed me to jump over the fallen body of the man, and run.

I felt people start to give chase but their friends yelled out for them to leave it, that I wasn't worth it.

I ran into the quiet of the square.

No one was here. It was deserted.

The buildings that lined the square insulated it from the crazy amount of sound coming from the riot.

I saw Sam step out from behind a tree and break into a run across the square. He kept looking back at me, which slowed him down. I was able to speed up. All those hill sprints in the park with Keir suddenly came in useful. I could feel the sun throbbing down on us. My feet were so hot in my trainers. My back was slick with sweat.

I'd nearly caught up with him and was about to grab for his T-shirt when he slowed and turned to face me, backing away. He had his hands up.

He looked terrified.

He was sweating, panting, his eyebrows raised in panic.

He was . . . not Sam.

I breathed out, hard. My entire body was on fire. It wasn't him. It wasn't bloody him. I'd been chasing the wrong person.

'Why are y-you after m-me?' he stammered.

'Sorry,' I said, getting closer to him and offering him a hand. He backed away some more. 'I thought you were someone else.'

'Yeah,' he said. 'Who's that?'

I felt the anger surge in me. 'None of your business.'

'Get out of here before I beat the shit out of you,' he said, suddenly emboldened, moving towards me now. He wasn't cowering any more.

My fists balled, ready to strike. I lifted them to attack position.

'Bruv,' I said. 'That would be a mistake.'

Who was I? What were these words I was saying? I could feel my feet, firm.

He swung for me so I pushed him back. Hard. He fell to the floor, struggling to breathe.

'Get up,' I said.

'Look, man, I don't want no trouble – just leave me alone, yeah,' he said. He stood up slowly.

He was afraid of me. I knew I had it in me to punch him till his face bled. Then, in the fear on his face, I saw myself.

All I'd wanted was the strength to stand up and walk away. Not to hit someone until his face bled. This was not why I had taken up boxing. It was not me. It was not what I was about.

I dropped my fists and flexed my fingers. 'Go on. Get out of here now.'

'Sunny!' My name rumbled across the square, loudly, coarsely.

I spun round.

Keir was running towards me.

'Keir!' I walked to meet him, a smile on my face.

'What are you doing? I saw you chasing some guy,' he said. 'Get the hell out of here.'

'How did you find me?' I asked.

Keir grabbed my wrist and pulled me close to him. I struggled, trying to wrench my hand free.

'Keir, let go.' The smile was gone from my face now.

'You need to get out of here,' Keir said. He said it so calmly and decisively, I stopped struggling. He slowly let me go. I noticed his forearm. 'Uncle Steve', in large calligraphy letters. He looked down at it.

'How did you find me?' I asked again, trying to calm my breaths.

He looked tired. There were bags under his bloodshot eyes. He was paler than usual. He'd let his crew cut and stubble grow out. He had darker hair than I remembered. There was a scar I didn't recognise on his cheek. It looked deep.

'You stick out. Brown guy dressed in black,' he said. 'They're all talking about you. Then I saw who it was.'

'I'm glad you found me.'

'What are you doing here?' he said.

'I came for you. To get you.'

'Why? I don't need you to *get me*. You need to leave.'

'Keir,' I said. I stopped. Looking at him, I suddenly didn't know what to say. I didn't know how to articulate what I was feeling.

'Sunny,' he said. 'I can't be seen with you. Not today. Look, you need to go.'

'What happened to us?' I asked.

'What do you mean, us?' he shouted. 'There is no "us". We were friends and now we're not. We're in different places. I'm where I need to be.'

'And me?' I asked, bowing my head slightly.

'You don't belong here.'

Without thinking, forgetting where we were, what had happened, I leant forward and placed a hand on his cheek. Only this moment mattered. He batted it away.

'You stay away from me, you dumb immigrant,' he snarled, backing away. 'It's your sort that's the reason my uncle is dead. You lot come over here and take it all, all our jobs and opportunities, and you use up all our resources, and then you complain that you ain't being treated fairly. That you want equality. You already took everything else. What the fuck more do you want, eh? You took my uncle. You took all those benefits. Who's paying for your dad's bed? My dad, that's who. He pays his taxes. My dad funded his own brother's death. And you want to act like it's all OK?'

'Why are you saying this, Keir? You don't believe this. This is your dad talking. Your brother. Your uncle. Not you.'

Keir pushed me.

'You don't talk about my family.'

I stepped forward and held my hand out to him.

'None of that matters, Keir. I just want to know that you're OK. Come with me. Let's talk. You remember when I first showed up at the club, all beaten up? And you asked what'd happened?' Keir nodded. 'Wanna know?' Keir stood still. I felt tears well in my eyes. 'People beat me up. Cos I'm not white. Two of them. They kicked me and punched me and beat on me till I was nearly unconscious. They called me racist words. And they left me.'

'I'm sorry that happened,' Keir said quietly.

'You're siding with people like them. The ones that don't think people like me are fully human.'

Keir spat on the ground. It landed near my feet. I stared at the globule of spit.

'My uncle's dead,' he said.

'You're not him. Come with me. Let's go . . .'

'Our friendship's dead too. It's been dead a while, but you can't take a hint. I'm with my family now. Family is all that matters.'

'How can you say that? I came here for you . . .' I said, feeling tears start to fall.

'Go home, Sunny,' he said. 'Go home.'

He turned and ran. I stood there, all alone.

I was stunned. I sat on the floor where Keir left me and stared at my trainers and wept. I was alone and he wanted nothing to do with me. I cried, my shoulders shaking with sadness.

I put my headphones in and listened to some music.

I closed my eyes and let the phantom of wind tickle at my facial hair. Everything was so fucked, I thought.

I cried again.

I don't know how much time had passed but I opened my eyes to see men running about all around me. It was chaos. I pulled the headphones off, letting Lauryn carry on singing. I jumped up. They were shouting and yelling as a thick line of police, all in riot gear now, pushed them back towards where I was sitting. I stood up. Two people threw a metal barrier and it clattered at the feet of some police. Someone launched some sort of missile and a shield was thrown up to defend the officer in its path.

I saw a man do a Nazi salute. A proper Heil Hitler. He was wearing a St George's Cross flag around his waist. The irony of that particular combination clearly lost on him.

Two men noticed me. One pointed. They were both red-faced with exertion. They ran towards me. One of them was grinning so wildly, it looked like his eyes might roll right out of his sockets. My body went on alert. I didn't know whether to run or defend myself. Both these men looked bigger than me. Also, two bouts of sparring didn't exactly make me an expert of anything. What was that Nelson Mandela quote that Shobu loved to throw at me so much?

'I did not enjoy the violence of boxing so much as the science of it. I was intrigued by how one moved one's body to protect oneself, how one used a strategy both to attack and retreat, how one paced oneself over a match.'

They reached me. One of them lunged, his hands outstretched to grab me. I realised what I needed to do – I needed to get the hell out. Keir was right. I did not belong here. I ducked and weaved my body away from the man. His heavy clumsiness meant he fell into the statue and on to the floor. I was away, running through the chaos. There were hundreds more of them. Everywhere. Gleaming white clothes and pink sweaty faces.

Running as quickly as I could, dodging people yelling at me as I ran, I reached the edge of the square, where everything seemed calmer. I could see a cafe. I ran to it, hoping to take a vantage point in the window and see if I could spot Keir. I was an idiot to give a shit, but I still cared if he was OK.

The cafe was closed.

'Oi!' I heard. I turned around. A policeman was pointing at me. He started to give chase.

I ran. Around the corner, back on to cobbled streets, running in the direction of the cycle path that led home.

I unzipped my hoodie to let some air on to my skin. I could hear the policeman running on the cobbles behind me. I was faster than ever. I ran until . . .

I tripped.

Catching my foot on the uneven paving, I crashed to the floor, feeling my ankle twist. I cried out as the muscles wrenched and pulled. I landed on my fists, which felt like they had been clenched for the last hour.

The policeman stood over me.

'Why were you running?'

'I was trying to get away from all the racists,' I said through tears. I was in so much pain. I couldn't move. I was on my fists. On the floor, one knee down to steady myself. And my leg with its twisted ankle was suspended, with my toes on the ground.

I breathed shallowly.

'You Antifa?'

'What?' I said. 'I'm a bloody teenager and I'm brown. Do I look like Antifa to you?'

'Enough of the language. You're coming with me,' the policeman said.

He pulled me up roughly and led me to a police van parked up the street.

I waited for thirty long minutes in the back of the van for help to show up. My phone ran out of battery from me scrolling mindlessly through Instagram. I was alone with my thoughts, waiting for someone to show up to take me home. Even though I was eighteen.

I told the officer I knew Detective Roberts and he backed off a little, didn't cuff me. Even said he'd radio him when I begged to speak to the detective. Then I texted Shobu from the van. I thought back on the confrontation with Keir while I waited. When I'd told him what had happened to me, for a second, I swore I'd seen sadness in his eyes. He knew what it had done to me. But he had pushed me away anyway and sided with his family. He must still care about me? I'd seen his face change when I'd told him my secret . . . He could be saved. He could be my friend again.

'I'll take it from here, officer,' I heard.

I looked up. It was Roberts. He was standing next to Shobu, outside the van. Shobu had her hands in her jacket pockets and her face was thunder. I heard Roberts take the officer to one side while Shobu leant into the van.

'You OK?' she asked.

'I twisted my ankle,' I said. 'I don't think it's too bad but I don't want to move it.'

'I can't believe you did this,' she said. I could hear the disappointment in her voice.

'I had to,' I said, staring at the floor, upset that I had let her down.

'I know . . .' she replied.

I tried to stand but my ankle was sore. I bit my lip so I didn't cry out in pain and I steadied myself on the side of the van. She reached out to me and grabbed my waist, taking my weight as I lowered myself to the ground.

'Easy,' Shobu said.

I felt my ankle twinge as she brought me up to standing position.

'That hurts,' I said, quietly.

'Trust me,' she said, putting my arm over her shoulders and taking my weight. She lifted. I lifted too. I was standing. I kept my bad ankle in the air.

'Try it,' she said.

I grunted and dropped my foot on to the ground. I could feel it throbbing. I could feel the muscle spasming. But it wasn't too bad.

'Can you walk?'

I nodded.

Detective Roberts tapped the officer on the shoulder and waved him off. He walked back to us and took my other shoulder.

'My car's over here,' he said. 'Are you OK, Sunny?'

'Just about,' I said. 'It's madness in there. Out of control.'

'We need to get us all out of here,' Roberts said. 'The riot police are doing their job. We don't need to be here.'

'I *told* you not to come,' Shobu said. 'It's amazing you only tripped. So much worse could have happened to you.'

'I should have listened. I'm sorry,' I told her.

They helped me to Roberts's car. Shobu got into the front seat, checking her phone. Once safely into the back, I looked out of the window and saw people being led into a police van, in handcuffs.

One of them was Keir. He had his head bowed and his body sagged, like he couldn't bear to stand any more. He shuffled forward.

Maybe he could feel my eyes on him because he looked round and saw me, sitting in the back seat of Roberts's car. I smiled. Just to let him know that I was still here for him if he needed me. He stared at me, blankly, then he was ushered into the van by an officer.

Roberts caught me looking. Saw my face falling when I got nothing back.

'You know him?' he asked.

I nodded.

'I used to,' I said, and let Roberts close the door on me.

*   *   *

We are trading blows thick and fast. Nothing can stop either of us. I punch him with all my might. I absorb his blows like they are rain on a tin roof. They clatter off me but do not penetrate underneath the skin. We are both so lost in the moment of hitting each other that the referee separates us and I realise the bell is still ringing, and has been for a while. I look out at the crowd. Everyone is applauding. I even catch Keir stifling a smile as he turns around and walks to his corner.

Round 8

'That's more like it,' Shobu says as I sit, panting, in my corner, hunched forward, elbows on knees, watching sweat drip off my chin on to the floor. 'Feel him weakening?'

'Yes,' I say.

'Me too. I think you can win this in the next two rounds. Now, listen to me very carefully. He is tired. He has been doing this all throughout the match. You? You're getting warmed up. I want you to get a couple of shots in quickly. Be the first one to land a few punches. Then sit back. Let him come to you. Let him work out some body blows on you. He'll want to look good after you stung him early. Hang back. Absorb the blows. Keep moving. Keep frustrating him. Let him tire himself out. He's nearly spent after that round. Next round is yours. Trust me.'

I stand up. Keir points at me, like he's saying, *Come on then, mate.* There is a look in his eyes that I haven't seen before. That makes me realise that maybe there is something left in the tank. He stands up taller and bangs his gloves together.

And he grins.

'You sure about that?' I ask Shobu.

'Have I ever steered you wrong?'

8.1

When Shobu and Roberts brought me home that night, to an empty house, I started crying. I was getting the milk out of the fridge, and I just froze there in the cold haze and felt a quiver that worked its way up from my chest into my eyes. I didn't try to stop myself. I let myself cry. I let them know I was crying. And this time, I felt like I wasn't ever going to stop. Shobu helped me into the kitchen and sat me down. Roberts fumbled in some cupboards and found a glass, pouring me some water.

Shobu put the kettle on.

The time it took to boil felt so long and made me sob harder and harder that when the click and bubble of the boil finished, I was louder than the appliance. Roberts said an awkward goodbye and left, leaving me with Shobu.

'It's my fault. I did this to him . . .'

'It's not your fault,' Shobu said, crying now too.

'It is, it *is* . . .' I sobbed. 'Everything's always my fault. I should have given that man the fucking samosa. Why didn't I do that? Why did I tell Madhu about the fucked up stuff Keir's dad said?'

'What?' Shobu asked.

'Keir was angry that I told a girl he liked, my friend Madhu, some stuff about his dad. Things weren't right between us after that, but I never had the chance to sort it out. I tried so hard, Shobu . . .'

'Darling,' Shobu said. 'That's just bad timing. You know, Steve lived in Keir's house for ten years, when Martin was in put in prison for GBH at a football match. Steve helped raise Keir and Joe. Whatever you think of Steve's opinions, Keir had a really close bond with his uncle. He was almost like a second dad . . .'

Dad. Now the floodgates were really open. Everything was on top of me. It kept coming. Dad dying. Not knowing how to grieve for him, for our relationship. How my cousin never texted me. How I felt isolated. How I wished I hadn't left London. How I was in danger of being kicked out of college cos I just didn't go any more. I laid it all out bare to Shobu and then ran to the toilet and hid, trying to calm down. I could hear sounds in the kitchen, and eventually the smell of onions and garlic. The house suddenly felt like my home again, and so I wiped my eyes and emerged from the bathroom, a bit wobbly but calmer now.

Shobu was making us food – a potato and pea curry – and heating up some frozen parathas. I sat in silence and watched her.

She put the plates in front of us and sat down, smiling.

'I haven't eaten this dish in years,' she said. 'My mum used to make it for me when I was feeling sick. It always made me feel better. Even now, the smell, it takes me back. I'll never get it to taste like hers did. But hey, you never tried her food so you won't know any better, will you?' I smiled. For a second. 'That's horrible, isn't it?' she said, laughing. 'When someone tries to cheer you up or calm you down by making you laugh.'

I nodded. My face stung. My eyes were sore. I was so tired. I suddenly felt like I hadn't slept in weeks. I hadn't slept well since the attack.

'I know I should feel sad about my dad dying,' I said. 'But, regardless of how hard he worked for us, I don't feel what a son's supposed to feel. He's silent. He's never been present in my life. You know, when some kids at school used to rag on me, do you know what he told me? "Don't cause a fuss. It'll settle down soon."'

'I get that,' Shobu said. 'Classic South Asian dad. Immigrate here. Get fed the myth that if you work hard, you will reap rewards no matter what hardships you encounter along the way. Racism, poverty, not having any opportunities cos you're not white. And then when you have kids, you raise them with this same mentality. And you almost don't want them to know the truth – that no matter what happens, we still have to eat shit.'

'I'm angry at Dad,' I said. 'He's the reason I got beaten up. He never taught me to stand up for myself.'

Shobu sighed and ate her food, nodding her head with each bite. Like she was having the meal of her life.

'That's unfair on your dad,' she said. 'It's not easy raising kids in this society. Whatever you do, someone will tell you you're not doing it the right way. Then they'll tell you that the racism is a figment of your imagination. Whatever he said and did, I'll bet he was thinking it was the best thing for you.'

I nodded. I understood what she meant. I had spent months now acting like my own attack had never happened.

'You know what's deep?' she said.

'What?'

'I am always angry. Always. I'm like the Hulk. All of the time in my head. Because there is all this shit going on. I see young people of colour like you up against a structurally racist society all the time. So many lose the resilience to move forward and just give up. The whole point of the boxing is to help you stay strong mentally. That's why I believe in it. And you lot.'

'Do you really believe this country is racist?'

'Sunny,' Shobu said, laughing. 'You got caught up in a march celebrating a racist today. He died because he broke the law, went to prison and then his sparkling, racist personality got him into the fight that got him killed. And yet, there were still thousands of people marching in his name, like he was the victim. Not the people he abused in the first place.'

'And Keir?' I said.

'Keir does not believe in any of that crap.'

'How do you know?'

'I know Keir. Remember I said I met him in a pupil referral unit and that he was in there for anger issues? They finally put him in there because he beat someone up who called his mate the N-word. And you know what Keir's family wanted? For him to go to a young offender's institute for it. Thought it would toughen him up a bit more. They were happy to see him banged up. Keir? Can you imagine? He listens to his dad too much. You know his dad wanted a different training partner for him. He wanted you gone. I pushed for you. That's why they wanted to meet you. But they're in his ears. And he listens. He does know the difference between right and wrong. He just sometimes forgets how to keep a handle on his temper. I think he's lost again, now.'

'Have you spoken to him since the sparring match?' I asked.

'No,' Shobu said. 'I need to though. It's time. And you – it's time for *you* to see your dad.'

8.2

I let Surinder take me to see my dad the next day. Shobu sat in the back seat with me. Mum sat in the front. There was no music this time but the car was filled with noise anyway. All three of them talked like they didn't have a care in the world, chatting about a film they all loved, laughing and quoting and singing the songs.

As we got closer, I felt the panic setting in again and everything in me wanted to beg for us to turn around.

We pulled into the driveway and Mum looked at me.

'It's time,' she whispered.

'I know,' I said.

She reached out and grabbed my hand. Shobu grabbed the other one. Surinder turned in the driver's seat to look.

'God, this is cheesy,' he said and we all laughed.

It was enough to make me to open the door and get out. Just enough.

I'd asked them all to wait in the car. If I was going to do this, I was going to do it for myself, on my own. I left them ranking the films of some Bollywood star I'd never heard of.

I turned back just before I went inside. Shobu was standing up by the car, holding Mum's fists. She was showing Mum how to jab and cross. I laughed. Shobu wanted to turn us all into fighters.

I entered the hospital.

8.3

Dad's room was still and quiet. All the lights were off. The curtains were half drawn, offering a gloomy twilight to everything. I could see his sudoku puzzle book on a table, next to a glass of half-drunk water. The radio was on, quietly, humming away with a one-day international. The rest of the room was anonymous. Just the puzzle book and the buzz of cricket. I could hear a sort-of purring sound.

He was asleep.

He looked worn, from what I could see. He still slept with his head wrapped in a grey shawl. He still slept on his side, facing to the right of the bed, like he had slept his entire life. One leg lay on top of the other perfectly. One hand clutched his head.

I could have traced this sleeping position with my eyes closed. This was how I remembered him. On the bed in our old flat in London, the one above the charity shop, tired from a day of work that mixed the physical labour of stacking and restacking shelves with bursts of customer chaos and busyness.

What did I feel for him?

I felt guilt. But the guilt was about feeling nothing for him. He was my dad in name only. He had been there for me financially, but I'd needed him emotionally. And that was surely much more important. I wanted to leave. He was asleep. I didn't want to disturb him. The half-drawn curtains were bothering me though. I tiptoed over to the window and pulled the curtains closed. The room was dark now. In the dark, I could still feel how clinical it was in here. There was a machine to help Dad breathe if he needed it. Also the vague smell of over-boiled vegetables and bleach was never out of reach.

I turned around and headed for the door, pausing to take in my dad's face, just in case this was the last time I saw him.

'Who is that?' he asked, softly, in Gujarati.

'No one,' I said.

I was so shocked to hear his voice that I couldn't move. I could hear it everywhere else in my memories. But hearing it here, now, suddenly felt so calming. Maybe it had just been too long.

'Sunny?' he asked, trying to sit up, talking in English now. 'Is that you?'

I heard him cough. That same shallow hack that had soundtracked the last few years of our lives before they'd finally taken him away. He shifted. I could see his slight frame in the dark, trying to sit up. I walked to the bed and helped him, grabbing him by his shoulders and sitting him upright.

He felt so light.

'Sunny,' he said. 'You feel different.'

'How?'

'You're strong.'

'Dad,' I whispered. 'You barely weigh anything any more.'

'They won't let me eat apna food. Only these bread sandwiches. Bread is mostly air.'

Dad had eaten the same dhal bhatt shaak rotli for his lunch for decades. Every single day, in a tiffin, the same meal cooked – through muscle memory – by Mum. For dinners, he had a wider palate. But lunch had to be the same.

'How are you?' I asked, feeling my chest swell with embarrassment. My breath quivered. I was going to cry. He was my dad. How could I have just left him to die?

'I am fine, Sunny, beta,' Dad said. 'Mummy tells me you are learning to box. Is this right?'

'Yes, Papa,' I said. I sat on the edge of the bed. It was higher than my legs could handle so I shuffled myself on till my feet were off the ground. I could feel Dad's legs shift under the covers to make way for me.

'Are you safe?'

'Yes, Papa.'

'You have the mind of a boxer. You are very determined.'

Am I? I thought. I was surprised to hear Dad offer an opinion on what sort of person he thought I was. Especially something I didn't quite believe about myself.

'You want something to drink? Nurse Paula makes a perfect cup of chai,' he said.

I smiled, picturing Surinder standing in the car park describing how good his own cuppa was to Mum and Shobu.

'Dad, I . . .'

'I like that you are the boxer now. If anyone calls you any names, like they did when you were younger, you can sort them out. You can be braver than I ever was.'

'Thanks, Dad,' I said, stroking his feet.

I had held so much anger at him for so long that here in the hospital I realised it *had* been a long time. Too long. I was tired of it.

'Tell me what you've been doing, beta?' he said.

'Studying, mostly,' I said.

'Where have you chosen to go to university?' he asked. 'Mummy has not mentioned anything.'

I considered what to tell him – what he wanted to hear, or the truth. It was tricky. Maybe this was the point I needed to start being honest with him.

'I'm not sure, Papa,' I said. 'I'm going to take a year. Figure stuff out. Figure myself out.'

Dad smiled. 'Good. Otherwise you will end up a shopkeeper like me. Unsure of what you want to do so you take whatever makes you money.'

He coughed. Took in some gulps of air.

I smiled. 'Thanks, Dad.'

'I lie here thinking about all my mistakes,' he said. 'All I have is time to think about when I could have been better.'

A sliver of tear landed on my cheek.

'Dad,' I said. 'It's OK.'

'I always loved you,' he said. I leant forward and cuddled him. 'My way of showing it was to push you to work harder.'

'Dad, it's fine.' I was shaking now, holding back the tears.

'I'm sorry,' he said. 'I wish I had been a better father to you.'

I held him tightly and we cried noiselessly, our chests juddering against each other.

'I think I would have liked to have been a boxer,' Dad said, softly.

I felt his body relax against mine; he'd fallen back asleep.

I gently laid him down on to the bed until he was comfortable, rolling him into that sleeping position I knew so well. I watched him breathe, in and out, for a few minutes before leaving.

'So you're the famous son,' a nurse said, out in the corridor. Her name badge read 'Paula'.

'And you're the one who makes a wonderful cup of chai.' I smiled at the nurse.

'Oh, your dad,' Paula said, with a grin. 'He's such a sweetie.'

'That's him,' I said, looking at the exit. I was ready to go. The air in the hospice was laden.

'He's been sleeping a lot,' Paula said. 'You know, it'll have made his month you coming in. Your mum comes every two days without fail, and his spirits lift every time. He talks about you a lot . . . You should—'

'I know,' I said, interrupting. I knew what she was trying to tell me. *Make the most of him. Don't regret not spending enough time. Put the effort in now. Or you will regret it for ever.* I knew.

I bowed my head, turned and walked to the door.

Outside, the air felt light and fresh. Everyone was back in the car. I walked over and opened the door, getting in behind Surinder, wedging my knees against the back of his chair that he insisted on keeping as far back as possible.

Each of them turned around to me expectantly. I didn't know what to say. What was there to say? That I was ready to forgive Dad? That it was still going to take time? But I was willing to give it a go? That I loved him? What did I want to tell them? What was the right reaction?

So I simply said nothing, just smiled. They could work it out for themselves. I felt the stains of dried tears on my cheeks and that was the realness I needed to remember that one moment of honesty with my father.

8.4

Shobu danced around me as I stood in the centre of the ring. I was tired and my gloves stank from wiping the sweat off my brow. She held paddles that she was flinging towards me in different strike positions. My objective was to meet each one with my fists. I was slower than I had been. My brain wasn't working quick enough to see each paddle before striking. And I felt heavy. Shobu stopped me.

'OK,' she said. 'You're too stiff. Shake your hands like this.'

We shook each hand and then each foot in a sequence that started with eight shakes of each, then four then two then one. And finally, she made me flap my arms like wings as she shouted out, 'Funky chicken!'

A month ago I would have cringed. But today, it made me smile. My shoulders felt looser. I threw them outwards, one-two. The paddles went up and I struck, one-two, and then three-four, hook and hook. Then one-two again, then three-four, and then a five-six slip and uppercut. Each one smacked against the paddles.

Shobu was screaming out encouragement, like, *Come on, Sunny. Yes, mate. Yes, Sunny. Do it, pal.*

I was in the zone, working faster and looser, feeling the power rise up from my legs, which danced between a skip and a root.

Shobu stopped and looked up and over my shoulder. I turned to see what was bothering her. The bell rang.

Keir was standing there, smiling, leaning on the ropes.

'Hey, Shobu,' he said, waving.

Wordlessly, Shobu nodded her head before turning her attention to flexing her fists, battered from the impact of training two to three fighters a day and absorbing every one of their blows.

'Shobu,' Keir said. 'How are you?'

Without looking up, Shobu pinched at her fingers and said, 'Fine, Keir, I'm just fine.' She looked at me and said, 'I'm going to the loo then we go again.'

I nodded at her as she shook her head, dropped the paddles to the floor and left the ring. I pulled at the Velcro of one of my gloves. Keir stepped into the ring, under the rope, and helped me pull it off. I shook my hand away from him.

'I'm fine,' I said.

'I know,' he replied, quietly. 'I'm just trying to help.'

I let him take off the other glove. He held them both. I could almost see the sweat from each one seeping into his white T-shirt as he clutched them under his arm. He looked different. Hunched. Smaller.

We stood in silence. Close. As close as we were the last time I saw him. I remembered touching his face. I remembered the chaos. I remember the hate in the air. The disgusting slurs being hurled around like they were chewing gum. Suddenly I was overcome with anger and I pushed past him and out of the ring. On the floor, I saw Shobu in the corner, checking her phone, like she was waiting for me to finish so we could continue. Our eyes met. She shook her head. I felt Keir following behind me.

'Can we talk?' he asked, softly. 'We need to talk.'

I turned and pulled my gloves out from under his arm and signalled to Shobu that I was ready.

'I'm training,' I said.

*   *   *

Keir was waiting for me outside the gym. I avoided eye contact and made a beeline for the gates to head home but he ran after me. We fell into a rhythm as we walked side by side, in silence until we reached the main road.

'I'm not looking for an explanation or an apology,' I said. 'All I wanted was to help you, to make things right between us.'

Keir stopped walking and pulled me back by grabbing my arm.

'You don't understand . . .'

'Then what do we need to say to each other?'

'I need a place to stay.'

He was a mess. Looking at him closely now, I could see his bloodshot eyes. His T-shirt had specks of blood on it. His usually crisp grey hoodie was grimy. He smelled salty.

'Your racist family kicked you out for fraternising with brown people, huh?' I said.

'Sunny,' he replied, looking out to the street. 'We really doing this? You *want* to do this?'

I gestured to my gloves. 'We can do it this way or . . .' I shook them at him.

'I'm not apologising for my family,' he said.

'I'm not asking you to,' I replied, and carried on walking down the road. I wanted to get home. 'It's not about your family, is it? It's about you. Who are you?'

Keir grabbed my hand so I stopped. 'You know me,' he said.

'No. I really don't. You disappeared weeks ago. Remember? Got the hump cos it turned out I wasn't a shit boxer. Then next time I see you, your bro is attacking me in your front garden because I've come to say sorry for my mate calling you out for being a racist and you tell me to eff off. Then, just when I think, oh yeah, I know him, that ain't him, you're at a racist rally . . .'

'It wasn't . . .' He paused. 'I didn't think it was going to end up that way. I thought we were marching for Uncle Steve. He's a victim of a miscarriage of justice. He paid the ultimate price. I didn't get to say goodbye.'

'Wow,' I said. 'Keir, you really are deluded, you know that? Leave me alone.'

I was nearly home by now.

'Sunny,' Keir called out. 'Please. I need a place to stay. I have nowhere else to go.'

I stopped and sighed.

8.5

It didn't feel right to have Keir in our home. I didn't want him here. I didn't know where we were. I didn't know who he was.

The first thing he did was take his shoes off. I watched him unlace them and then look to me for approval. I smiled. Some good still remained in him then.

'You want some food?' I said.

I watched as he went into my flat. He was looking at everything.

'You guys have literally no pictures on the wall,' he said.

I know, I thought. We weren't supposed to stay here for ever.

I went into the kitchen and put the kettle on. I heard Keir walking around. The light switch in the lounge went on and I ran to the room. He was staring at the hospital bed and the oxygen tank.

'That your dad's?' he asked, looking at me.

'You want some food?' I asked again.

'No,' he said, staring at the bed. 'I'm fine.'

I made myself a cup of tea while he waited awkwardly in the door of the kitchen.

We stood in silence.

'How's . . .' he started then stopped. He thought about it. I sipped at my tea. 'How you been?'

'Not great,' I said and sat down at the kitchen table, flicking through one of Mum's novels.

'Look,' he said. 'I don't owe you an explanation about my family. My family is my family. But I need you to know. I don't think like that.'

'Whatever, man.'

'What?' Keir said, indignantly. 'You don't believe me?'

'You feel the need to explain it, man,' I said. 'If there was no doubt, then you wouldn't need to explain it.'

'Those people, they took advantage. They turned the whole thing into a shitshow. It was meant to be a march for my uncle. Not all that other stuff.'

'You know what they were shouting?' I asked. 'They were calling us pakis. They were saying, "Immigrants, go home."'

Keir nodded, like he knew but had no idea what to say about it. 'I hear you, man, but you're not entirely innocent, are you? You were about to punch some guy out.'

My stomach flinched. 'Yeah, but I didn't, did I?' I said. 'I don't hate.'

'What do you mean?'

'Your family,' I said. 'They believe all this stuff?'

'Sunny,' Keir said, banging on the door frame. 'Stop asking me that! I ain't them. But they're still my blood. It's complicated.'

'Is it?' I said. 'You know, my dad showed himself to be OK with some really ignorant stuff. And what I did I do? I cut him off. And now he's lying in some hospice somewhere, and you know what? I didn't talk to him about it for years, I just hated him. Now he's dying and he's saying sorry and asking for forgiveness and it's so bloody hard.'

I gasped back the tears.

'And how does that make you feel?' Keir asked. 'He's still your dad. Isn't he?'

'Doesn't mean I have to agree with everything he says and thinks. I'm still my own person. I still have the power to tell him when he's wrong.'

'Exactly,' Keir said. 'I don't agree with Joe and my dad on a lot of things. What does that make me?'

'Someone who still needs to hold them to account. Do you tell them they're wrong?'

Keir immediately picked at something on his hoodie, avoiding my eyes.

There was a bang on the door. It made me jump and I banged my mug of tea down on the table a bit harder than I anticipated. I stood up and pushed past Keir into the hallway. I opened the door a fraction to see who it was.

Madhu was standing there, holding her phone and pointing at me.

'Where the hell you been?' she said, frowning.

I held my hands up.

'Madhu,' I said. 'I'm . . .'

'Sunny, bruv, where have you been? It's been a week and you're just leaving me to rot in college. What the hell, man? You OK? I heard a rumour that you went to that thousand-man paki bash? How was it? Did you get yourself bashed? Bruv, are you OK? I mean, I'd have come sooner but I texted you a million times like a normal person and you didn't reply. And now I'm standing here, babbling, and I'm, like, fam, are you even gonna let me in? Anyway, you really need to phone Amanda. She insisted I come over. She reckons she can save you from getting kicked out but you need to call her.'

I smiled and, in my hesitation, she pushed the door back.

Keir was standing there. In the hallway. I could see her face fall as she spotted him.

She pointed at Keir.

'Sunny, what the hell is this wasteman doing in your house? Did he remember that actually *some of my best friends are brown . . .*'

'Hey, Madhu,' Keir said. He stepped forward. 'If you must know, I was chucked out of my house. I have nowhere to go tonight. Know why I was chucked out of my home? Cos my dad said something messed up and I called him out on it. So be careful who you're calling names.'

'Calling names?' Madhu said, laughing. 'Mate, we haven't even started with the names I want to call you.'

'You watch your mouth,' Keir said. 'You're the real racist. You wouldn't go out with me cos I'm white.'

'Er, that's not true,' Madhu said. 'I can't be racist against white people. Which is a stone cold fact. Also, I said – clearly, I thought – that I wouldn't go out with you cos of your really actually racist family.' She looked at me. I could tell Madhu was so, so, *so* disappointed with me. 'You, Sunny. You need to work out who your mates are. It's him or me. Text me when you've decided.'

225

Madhu pointed her phone at me, turned and left.

I could feel Keir move closer to me. His closeness made the hairs on my arm, holding the door open still, rise.

'Madhu,' I called after her. I started to walk out but Keir grabbed my hand and stopped me.

'Leave her,' he said. 'She's a bitch anyway.'

I swung round and punched him in the cheek. Keir recoiled with the impact and put his hand to his face, gasping. He looked surprised then scared. He clenched his fist and lifted it. I put my guard up.

He shook his head.

'My dad was right,' he said. 'You pakis have no respect.'

'Get out. Get out. Right. Now.'

I was not going to let that word be in my home. Infecting my safe space.

He pushed me out of the way and walked past, picking up his shoes as he headed out of the door. I was shaking.

I closed the door on him. I held the handle for a second. *BANG.*

I felt a punch make the door shudder. I let go. I felt another one.

'Sunny, I hate you,' Keir shouted. 'You abandoned me. I hate you.'

He banged a few more times before I heard him shuffle away. I stood there for ten minutes trying to steady my breathing.

8.6

I watched Shobu closely as she wrapped me up for another sparring session, this time with a new boxer called Carly. She was serious. She was concentrating on something else, which meant she had to keep wrapping and unwrapping me to get it right.

'What's up, Shobu?' I asked.

She hesitated. She continued wrapping me then tapped my fists and I dropped them.

'Listen,' she said. 'These next three rounds are yours. They're only three minutes. All you have to do is keep moving and keep her moving. Keep anticipating and keep her guessing. Do you understand?'

'What's wrong?'

'Nothing,' she said. 'Look, I've been asked whether you want a spot at the next fight night. You know there are three early matches, one from our youth wing and two from our younger fighters training to become professional. Well, there's been a dropout and Chris, well, he wants to put you in.'

'I'm not ready.'

'Yes,' she said. 'Of course you are.' She paused. Like she was wrestling with something.

'What? Just say it,' I said.

'You've been challenged. By Keir. He has a new trainer. And he wants to fight you.'

I froze and looked at Shobu. She nodded. As if to say, *Yes, that's where we are*.

'Look,' she said. 'Don't worry about it right now. Focus on this session. Carly is fast and she likes using her hooks. Just keep close and she can't extend like that. OK? Close range shots and keep her moving.'

She pulled one glove over me. Then the other.

'But Keir and me . . . we have all this stuff going on between us. It wouldn't be healthy.'

'I think it would be. Exactly the right thing to do. Put it all in the ring. When punches are thrown, you both get to face each other in a constructive way.'

I thought about it as I sparred with Carly. Her hooks *were* fast. She smiled every time she used them. Like she knew this was her forte.

'I'll do it,' I said afterwards. 'I want to do it. I want to fight Keir.'

Shobu smiled as she pulled both my gloves off. 'Don't say yes because you're mad at him. That's how he'll destroy you. He's in your head before it even starts.'

'No,' I said. 'I want to, for me.' I paused. 'Also, tell your new mate Detective Roberts I'm ready to talk about the attack.'

Shobu hugged me.

8.7

'OK,' Detective Roberts said. 'Take me through that night.'

I had been nervous about talking to him but I had been feeling stronger, happier in myself. I was ready to take on my first proper fight. This was going to be my warm-up.

That said, I nearly cancelled on Roberts twice. I had been sick in the toilets waiting for him to collect me from the reception at the police station. Even now, thinking about what'd happened and who I had been then and who I was now, it felt like I was two completely different people. Perhaps the power they held over me was less now because it was like the attack had happened to a different person.

'I had been at college late, working on a paper,' I said. 'I remember, it was dark and empty and I was hungry but I

228

didn't want to eat while walking. I'd heard that's bad for you . . .'

I talked at Roberts for a good hour. I tried to remember everything. The detective had a kind face. He really listened. And the more I talked, the easier it became. My biggest fear walking into this tiny office had been that I would cry – that when I relived the moment I was hit, I wouldn't be able to cope with uncaging these memories. But it got easier and easier the more I talked. When I finished, at the point where Shanai introduced herself to me, Roberts smiled. He took a deep breath.

'Sunny,' he said. 'You're incredibly brave telling me that story. Thank you. Even though it's been months, the detail you have provided is still very useful and I am so glad you came forward. I reviewed the CCTV footage and I could see the edges of what happened, but you've now given me the full picture.'

'I want to see it,' I said.

'No,' Roberts replied, softly. 'Just as a friend, I'm telling you, you don't need to. No good will come of it. I promise you.'

I nodded slowly.

'I still want to see it,' I said.

Roberts waited for a few seconds for me to change my mind before opening up the laptop next to him and clicking around. I watched him. He puckered his mouth when he concentrated. He navigated the mouse like he had never seen a computer before. I almost wanted to laugh. When he had loaded up the video, he stood up and crossed over to my side of the table.

'Mind if I sit next to you?' he asked. I nodded approval.

His elbow brushed mine as he swivelled the laptop around to face us. The still, of the train station platform.

He pressed play.

I was instantly back there. Exactly where it happened, as it happened.

The platform was empty, so I sat down on a bench all the way up one end to wait. That way, I wouldn't have long to walk to get out of the station when I got off.

I'd just missed a train. Its lights glowed with a diminishing yellow as it disappeared in the direction of home. My brain was swimming with ways to attack my coursework. My feet felt like they'd been glued to my socks and trainers all day. All I wanted to do was take them off and rub my toes into the carpet before lying down and going to sleep. My stomach rumbled.

I took a samosa out of my bag and bit into it. It had gone soggy. I'd put it in the plastic container while it was still hot and closed the lid, cos I'd been in a rush. While the pastry wasn't very crunchy, it still tasted delicious. The lamb, the peas, the garam masala. Bristol Sweet Mart did not mess about. It was legendary for its bitings.

I heard some loud chatter to my left and stole a look. I didn't want to make eye contact with anyone. I didn't know this area too well and I didn't know who lived here.

Three guys were stumbling down the platform, clutching beer cans, yelling at each other at the tops of their voices.

The CCTV footage was silent. But I could still hear them yelling. I could hear the vacancy in their voices.

'And then, she basically let me kiss her cos I gave her a lift – what a stupid bitch . . .'

'Mate, that's nothing. There was this one girl who—'

'Shut up, you virgin.'

'Yeah whatever, mate . . .'

'I'm—'

'Virgin . . . virgin . . . virgin . . .'

I put my hood up and tried to make myself as small as possible. I carried on eating.

'Here, I'm starving – can I have a bite?'

I looked up to see one of the guys standing in front of me. He was pointing at my samosa.

'What is that shit anyway?'

'Stinks like curry, dunnit . . .'

'Stop it,' I said. 'I don't need to see any more.'

Roberts hammered on the space bar and nodded.

'Wise choice,' he said. He paused. 'Sunny, what were you doing at the Steve Radley march?'

I flinched.

'It was a march for racism,' I said, correcting him.

'It was a march for Steve Radley,' Roberts replied.

This made me angry. I stood up, feeling my chair clatter to the floor behind me.

Roberts stood up too.

'Sunny . . .' he said, then paused, like he was choosing his words carefully. 'The approved march was for Steve Radley. Obviously the press and—'

'You know I was there,' I said. 'You saw the state of me. You know what it was like. You know what actually happened, Detective. How can you just act like it wasn't a march in the name of racism?'

'Because,' Roberts said. 'That would require a full investigation. One the police force isn't . . .' He paused. 'OK, enough tangenting. Tell me what you can remember about Sam. I'm going to load up some mugshots. It would benefit the investigation if I knew who I was looking for at least. I need you to help me. Can you help me, just a bit more? That way, I can best help you.'

I shook my head.

'Sorry, Detective Roberts,' I said. 'It took me everything to be here. Because I've told no one the things I told you. And I told you, because I trust you. But you can't even acknowledge the one thing that would make me believe that we can get justice for what happened to me. So what's the point?'

I left the room.

Roberts caught up with me in the car park.

'Sunny,' he said. 'Sometimes you have to accept that the things that are in play are above your head. Which feels hard because you're coming from a position where you've been the victim of a horrible crime. Look, I should not be sharing this information with you, in fact, I could lose my job over it, but I feel like I owe it to you – this Sam, if he's who I think he is, and I can't be sure as we didn't do the mugshots, but if it's him, he has an important mum. Once I work out the best way to bring him to justice, I will. Please believe me. I want nothing more.'

'How do you know?' I asked. 'About his mum.'

'Because I've had run-ins with him before. Look, I'm going to have to verify it's him . . .'

This stopped me in my tracks. I looked at Roberts, not sure whether to trust him.

'If you've had run-ins with him before, why isn't he locked up?' I asked.

'I know. I know,' Roberts said. 'Sam's done some heinous stuff but has always managed to evade us. But you, your story, it's enough to put him away.'

232

'Who is he?' I asked. 'Who is his mum?'

Roberts smiled. 'I definitely can't tell you that. All I can ask is that you come in, you look at some mugshots, you tell me the truth. I am only interested in the truth. And that's all you have to do. And then, we figure out what happens next.'

'OK,' I said, and followed Roberts back into the station.

8.8

I turned up at Madhu's house around dinner time. I could see her family all sitting down in the front room to eat. They were all laughing but sort of distracted by the Bollywood videos on the TV screen. I sat on some grass across the road from them and waited. I didn't want to interrupt their meal. My phone had run out of juice so all I could do was watch the street and try not to appear too suspicious. Random bloke sitting there, staring at a house. Random brown bloke no less. It'd give the nosey neighbours a thrill.

I was holding a letter from college. I knew what it said before I even opened it. I was on academic suspension. They weren't going to let me take my exams. I could resit the year or, now I was eighteen, drop out, but either way, I wasn't going to be taking my A levels. I had a meeting with the principal and Amanda next week. But until then, I wasn't allowed on campus.

I didn't even know if I'd bother going to the meeting. My future felt rootless. I didn't know what the point of university was, because I didn't know what I wanted to do.

Watching Madhu through the window and the ease with which she sat with her parents, laughed with her sister and told her dad something, the way they all sat and ate a meal together, it made me jealous.

I loved being with my mum but I wished we could have had mealtimes like this when Dad had been at home.

I wondered about Mum. Was this how she imagined her life would turn out? Her sisters were all back in London. My cousins too. All Dad's family was either in Leicester or Baroda. Had they wanted me to be on my own? Had they wanted me to have siblings? Why hadn't we had easy family mealtimes like Madhu's? Why had we uprooted ourselves to Bristol, only to put Dad in a hospice? I remembered asking Mum about it, upset that I had to stay.

'Do you know how hard it is to earn money to keep us going, and to pay for the hospice and to pay for you to go to university? And then to keep moving? I think we stay and we try it. Maybe we stay after Daddy passes and maybe we go home. But what we need right now is consistency. A home.'

'This isn't my home,' I'd shouted at her. 'I'm always alone here now. You're always working. Dad is somewhere else. Dying. It's not a home. I feel like I live in a hotel. It smells like dog and fags. It's just horrible. I hate it here. I hate it.'

I cried, remembering the shame of that moment. I cried, remembering that I made my mum cry. I cried thinking about how much of a hard time I'd given her in that moment. The only other time I had made her cry was when, at primary school, I'd said I wished my name was Thomas, not Sunil. I'd hated the name Sunil; everyone made fun of it. I'd wanted to be adopted by white parents. I hadn't wanted her to drop me off at school any more. The two times I had made her cry were both about rejecting her as a parent, and rejecting our version of a family.

234

I watched Madhu and thought, *This is what I want.* I want to sit with my mum and my dad and talk about my day and be annoyed at whatever the American president did and discuss the dance moves in those particular Bollywood numbers and let Dad drone on about cricket. But I could never have that. Surely that was OK? I could feel my shoulders tensing, stopping me from bursting into big tears. I felt a dog next to me, sniffing around me, and I jumped. As I turned around to shoo the dog away, I caught the face of its owner. She smiled sympathetically, and I saw what she could see – a teenager, sitting on the grass, crying into the night air. I bet she thought I had a broken heart.

She would be right. My heart *was* broken. It was broken for my mum, who was working too many jobs to count, just to keep things afloat. For my dad, either fighting to stay alive or fighting to die, depending on how you looked at it. Keir, lost to an ideology that made me less than human. For Madhu, who had been my fierce, loyal friend and I'd thrown it back in her face by not giving up Keir for good.

I sobbed for an hour, till I felt the damp of the grass penetrate my clothes. I stood up. They were all clearing away the dinner table except for Madhu's dad, who was watching the news.

I walked across the road and took a deep breath before knocking at my best friend's front door.

8.9

I sat in the lounge with Madhu while the others continued to clear up. When Madhu had opened the door, she'd been smiling. As soon as she'd seen me, her face had fallen and she'd quietly said, 'Come in.'

We sat in silence. Madhu was still, staring at me, watching for me to speak. I shifted uncomfortably and searched in my head for the right things to say. Nothing was coming to me. Everything seemed blank.

'Well?' she said. 'Why are you here?'

'I wanted to see you.'

'Why?' she asked. 'Is this a conversation where you apologise and then things are awkward for a bit and then we move past it, or is this a conversation where you come to double down on your bullshit, and we have a screaming match, meaning you're storming out of my house and my family is all making fun of us behind our backs? Which is it gonna be?'

'I think it might be some of both,' I said.

Madhu leant forward, her chin resting in her hand.

'Interesting,' she said. 'Explain.'

I looked around the room, at family pictures, at some holiday brochures, at the line of birthday cards for Madhu's sister and then back at her. She raised her eyebrows expectantly.

'OK, so look, I did what friends do. I know I'm hardly the expert when it comes to friendships, but I'm aware the one unbreakable rule is that you back your friends and if they do stuff you don't agree with, you pull them up on it. So I did what I thought was the right thing with Keir. I should have done right by you too though . . . I'm sorry,' I said, watching Madhu roll her eyes.

'Bruv, it's simple. My man's a racist, innit. Punch him in the face and move on,' she said. 'It's not hard.'

'It is,' I said.

'Why? Cos you think you can save him? Why do you even want to save him? What do you think you could say that would change his mind?'

'I'm not sure any more. Maybe it's not about saving him, but it's about not pushing him closer towards all that hate. My uncle made fun of gay people all the time till my mum got pissed off and told him about me.'

Madhu interrupted. 'But that's the point. You shouldn't have to know someone who is gay or brown or a woman in order to treat us like humans all the time. It's like when some dad has a daughter and he's, like, oh yeah, now I'm a feminist. I'm, like, sorry you had to have a daughter to teach you how to treat women like people.'

'I guess.'

'How exactly was I right in this? You said it was somewhere between the two.'

'I'm just trying to explain to you why I was like I was. I realised that you were right. He's got some issues. And I don't think I can help him, not in the way I thought I could, anyway.'

'Why do you think that?' she said. 'Cos he's a racist?'

I didn't know how to answer Madhu. She needed everything to be so black and white. She was so quick to cancel people and she didn't believe in redemption or challenging your friends in order to help them change. She only really believed in what she believed in and everyone else was a problem. It was part of what made her so compelling to be around. She was funny and she was certain.

'Whether he is or not, I just know I can't help him any more. It's damaging me too much. It's damaged us.'

237

'Exactly – this is why I don't believe you should debate a racist. Because the debate becomes about your right to exist. And that is not up for debate.'

'I think,' I said, closing my eyes, 'I think he'll be OK but our friendship is collateral damage. And that makes me sad.' I welled up. 'I liked him.'

Madhu put her hand on mine.

'I'm sorry about that,' she said. 'It sucks when your friends disappoint you. Like, I was disappointed in you but I'm glad you came. And you're right – however you handled it, whether it was the right thing or not, you believed it at the time to be the right thing, and I respect that. I don't like it, but I respect it.'

Madhu's mum popped her head into the room and asked if either of us wanted dessert. I nodded and Madhu nodded. She stood up. I rose too and kept holding her hand.

'There's one more thing,' I said. 'He's challenged me to a proper fight.'

Madhu laughed.

'So you're gonna literally punch it out over your issues?' I nodded. 'That's so male. You're such a male.'

She laughed again.

'At least I get to punch a racist, like you said,' I replied, smiling. I threw up my paws to mime it. 'Right in the face.'

'True. I would like to see that. Just, don't expect to kiss and make up at the end of it.'

'Will you be there? I need some people in my corner.'

'Like a trainer?' she said.

'Yes, a Madhu pep talk will be exactly what I need,' I replied. I imitated her. *Why you letting him hit you? Stop being an idiot. Thump the twat.*' We laughed, hugged and, for those few seconds of abandon, everything seemed OK.

* * *

Keir runs towards me. I can see his left fist vibrating, telling me he's gonna throw an uppercut. He wants to put me on the ground as soon as possible and show me who's boss.

I remember what Shobu said and keep him moving. He throws an uppercut that I step out of and aim a few hooks to his head. He recoils as sweat spatters off him.

At least I landed the first punch. I go to continue the strikes but there is something in his eyes. It looks like worry. I hesitate.

He throws another uppercut. It connects with my eye. Powerful and rooted from low down as he struggles to regain his balance.

It throws me back on to the floor.

Round 9

'I can't open my eye,' I say to Shobu. I can feel the tightness in my chest. I'm panicking. My breathing is rapid, my heart is thumping. Keir is sitting on the stool, staring at me and smiling. My eye feels cold as Shobu splashes water in it.

'They won't let you carry on if you can't open it,' she says, calmly.

I focus all my energy into my eye. I'm thinking about it opening like a flower. I'm breathing in: in for four, out for eight; in for four, out for eight. But the breathing is shallow. The air cool against the back of my teeth. My face is stained with salt and sweat. The referee has taken an interest in us. He's walking over. Slowly, I'm opening my eye. Everything around me is blurry and stings with salt and blood.

'He OK?' the referee asks Shobu.

'Talk to me,' I say, staring at the referee, panting. 'Not her. Me. Ask me if I'm OK. To my face. I'm right here.'

'Are you OK?'

'Yes,' I say. 'Fine. Ring the bell.'

The referee smirks and turns around.

'Don't get cocky,' Shobu says.

'I'm not,' I say, turning to her. 'I'm angry with my opponent. And he's going to know about it. Put all your energy into the ring, you told me. Fight him in here, not out there, you said. But for god's sake, please just let me knock some shit out of him.'

Shobu puts a hand on my shoulder.

'You're gonna lose, thinking like that, Sunny. Remember your training.'

9.1

I met Shobu at the basketball court behind the gym. It was early and so, while the sun sprayed peppercorns of light through the trees and kids arrived jubilantly at the school on the other side of the court, Shobu got me working on the tractor tyre. I had two minutes to take the tyre to the other side of the court and back. It was hard work. There was stagnant water splashing out of it. I grimaced and pushed, while Shobu shouted motivational lines at me:

'One fight, one round, one punch, one fighter.

'Your biggest enemy is yourself.

'Keep your problems out of the ring.

'You want to fight your best friend? Your best friend let you down? He is no longer your friend. He is in your way.'

I was heaving with sweat, gasping with thirst.

I got to the end.

'Two minutes and four seconds,' Shobu said. 'Go again.'

Without hesitation, feeling the burn up and down my legs and sides, I pulled the tyre up.

'You're slower than before. Move.

'You wanna win? You gotta get out of your head. You get in his. He let you down? So what? That's on him. Think he feels guilty? Think he cares? Think he likes pakis pining after him?'

I stopped, letting the tyre drop. I was halfway down the court. I put my hands on my hips, panting, my mouth agape.

'The hell, Shobu? What's that about?'

'You do this until you do it in two minutes. You're behind.'

I kept going.

The next attempt was three minutes.

The one after that was two and a half minutes.

I held my hand up as I crouched, squatting and trying to recover my breath.

Shobu threw me a water bottle.

'You have ten seconds,' she said.

I squirted water into my mouth and clumped over to the tyre.

'Go,' she said.

We sparred in the martial arts studio. It had blinds you could draw across for specific lessons where they wanted privacy. Shobu closed the blinds and held her paddles up.

This time, she came towards me. She flapped the paddles forward quickly and pushed into me with her chest.

She was moving quicker. This was a more simulated match, where I didn't have time to think. I had to strike the paddles or slip them and if not, they slapped against my shoulders and sides.

It was disorientating to start with. Shobu's face had changed. She was concentrating, strategising, trying to find her way in, trying to highlight my weaknesses.

After the first round, she dropped the pads and squirted water into my mouth.

'You don't return to your guard position quick enough with the uppercuts,' she said. 'Your feet are all over the place.'

'It's hard,' I replied. 'It's a lot to remember at once.'

'True,' she said, picking the paddles up again. 'Or you could just defend yourself faster.'

'And my feet?'

'You know where they need to be – you don't need me to tell you, Sunny. Make sure they're there. Or you go down.'

I shadow-boxed around the ring.

Shobu was checking her phone. When the bell rang, she put it away and pulled a wire from one post and ran it over to the diagonal one, clipping it on. She did the same with the two remaining diagonals, so the two wires formed an X across the ring. She showed me what I had to do. I needed to duck and weave, either side of the rope, land a jab on the right and a cross on the left.

She made me run the drill ten times till I could feel my legs going all jelly-ish and weird. I was mentally drained. Too empty to even think about Keir. My body was running on fumes. I felt strangely elated with achievement.

At the end of the session, she massaged my thighs.

'OK,' she said. 'Tomorrow. Seven-thirty a.m.'

When I arrived the next morning, there was no one else in the gym apart from Shobu. It didn't usually open till 8 a.m. She was waiting for me in the centre of the ring. She was wearing her boxing gear. I had seen photos of her dotted around the gym, all gloved up in her Team GB kit. But never in person. When I arrived, she was wrapping her hands with white wraps. She crouched in the middle and wrapped her fingers slowly and deliberately. It was almost like she was meditating.

I stood there and watched her, having wrapped myself in front of the mirror before leaving. I was hypnotised by the power she exuded as she pulled her wrap taut and sealed it.

She stood up and started pulling on her gloves. She noticed me.

'Skipping,' she said. 'Two rounds. Go.'

As I skipped I watched her shadow-box in the mirror. I kept tripping over the rope because I was bewitched by the way she moved. Slowly and gracefully, punching with clarity and power. Her movements were like water, rippling and ebbing and flowing. I watched her feet. She was on her toes when she needed to be, planted when she landed punches. She was fast too.

After two rounds of skipping, I pulled myself up on to the ring.

'Right,' she said. 'Glove up – we have twenty minutes till someone else comes. Let's go for it.'

Nervously I put my gloves on.

The bell rang and she ushered for me to come to her. She threw some punches, so quick, it was all I could do to dodge them by bouncing backwards. The ferocity with which they came meant that I was immediately on my back foot. She had me on the ropes. She put her gloves on my shoulders and pushed me. I feel deep into the ropes and stumbled.

'Hit me,' she said.

'You're too good.'

'Sunny, I'm a former professional boxer. This is like me thirty per cent on, OK? If you can beat me at thirty per cent, you can beat Keir. Hit me.'

I put my fists up and approached her. I threw punches, but without hitting back she dodged and moved around, always avoiding me, keeping me on my toes, keeping herself away from me. She was winning without having to throw a single punch.

I gritted my teeth. She stood up straight. As she did, I, frustrated, threw a hook at her unprotected head. She dodged backwards. With the follow through, I was pulled to my right. She pushed me over.

'Hit me,' she replied.

I drew myself to my fight position. As I was dropping my chin and raising my guard, she punched me across the face. It wasn't hard but it was hard enough to send me to the floor.

I started to get up, and again, she punched me across the face.

'Stop it,' I shouted.

'Hit me then,' she replied.

I sprung up and pushed her. As she fell backwards, I drove an uppercut into her chin.

'Shit, you OK?' I asked as she rubbed at it.

'Right, OK,' she replied. 'Sunny showed up to fight, finally.'

'Was that too hard?'

'Sunny,' she said, shooting me a look. 'Seriously, you can't hurt me. But you should still try to.'

The bell rang.

Shobu and I were leaving the gym. We were saying goodbye.

'You going to college now?' she asked.

I shook my head.

'Don't tell me . . .' she said, her face falling. 'Sunny, you have to go to college.'

'I . . .' I started to say but knew the answer would be a lie, so I just shook my head.

'I'll tell your mum,' she said. And I believed her.

9.2

My phone rang in the middle of the night. I squinted, trying to note the time and the caller. It was about 2 a.m. It was Keir. I fumbled the phone and answered it.

'Hello?' I asked, tentatively.

'Can you hear me?' he asked. 'Listen, I don't know who said what to Chris but if I find out you're the reason I'm kicked out of the gym, then I will end you. Do you understand? I know where you live, Sunny. You can't get me kicked out of the gym! For what? What did I do? I'm their big hope. Me. Not you. And you come along and now you think you can get rid of me? No chance. I'm going to end you on fight night. Because I grew up here. And now I'm not welcome? You're lucky Chris still believes in me cos he found me a new sick trainer even if I have to go to a gym on the other side of town.'

He hung up.

9.3

It was the last day of term and I was heading into college to face the music. I'd thought about Shobu's face at the gym. I didn't want her to be disappointed in me. Not showing up was not the same as not wanting to go.

So, I went.

I sat outside the principal's office, waiting, massaging my aching knuckles. Amanda walked in, saw me and smiled.

'You OK?' she asked. I nodded as she approached and plonked herself down on the chair next to me.

'I'm fine,' I said.

'I have been so worried,' she told me.

I nodded and we fell into silence.

The principal, Ms Jafari, held her hands on the desk and looked over her glasses at me. I stared at my hands, mirroring hers, but in my lap. I shook my leg, furiously. I was desperate to get out of here.

'What do you have to say?' she asked.

I didn't have anything to say. I gave what I thought was a light shrug and waited for her to tell me off. All I needed was to get that bit over with and then I could get on with what I planned to say. I was going to ask to come back but I needed her to tell me what the college thought I had done wrong so I could show I was sorry.

'Can I speak?' Amanda said, standing up. 'This young man has shown a lot of triumph in the face of adversity. His father lies dying in a hospice. He goes through a racist attack. And still we are fixated on his attendance. What about our attendance for him? We failed him.'

How did she know about the attack? Madhu. It must have been. Everyone else owned my story. Not me. I didn't even get to choose who to tell.

Ms Jafari nodded. 'It's a passionate plea, Amanda, and we know things are hard for Sunny at home. But the question remains. Do you have anything to say, Sunny?'

'I don't know, miss,' I said. 'I really don't know what to say . . .'

'In which case, I do,' Ms Jafari said. 'We can't let you take

249

exams this year. It'd be silly for you to even consider it. You've missed a term. You'll fail. We'll fail.'

I nodded.

Ms Jafari continued to consider me over the top of her glasses. Eventually, she sighed and said, 'OK, Sunny. Why don't I see you on the first day of enrolment next term, and we can work it out then?'

I realised she was dangling a carrot. I hadn't spent a lot of time thinking about my future recently. I didn't know whether to take it. I wasn't sure what I wanted.

Shobu worked me hard the next day. As college had finished for the summer, we could go all day. I wanted to ask her about Keir but she didn't give me any space to be in my thoughts. Every single thing we did was about being in the moment, working through the movements, building my strength, speed and strategy.

As I rehydrated and she unwrapped my wrists, I looked at her and said, 'What do I need to study so I can be like you?'

9.4

At home, I found Mum waiting outside the flat, in Surinder's car. She motioned for me to get in. I wanted to go for a shower. My face stung with salt residue, my armpits ached from sweat, I had a sore knuckle I wanted to hold in the icebox for a few minutes. Mostly I just wanted to fall into bed. The fight was two days away. I didn't want to save it all for the ring. What was going on with me and Keir was bigger than the ring. What was between us was about society and who got to be considered human and who didn't.

'Where are we going?' I asked.

'To see Dad,' Mum replied. Surinder smiled at me in the rear-view mirror.

'Is he OK?' I asked.

'You don't know what day it is?' Mum asked.

I shook my head. It took me a second. I looked up the date on my phone. I had been too wrapped up in my own business to remember.

It was Dad's birthday.

Dad was propped up in bed, watching a home improvement show on the television. He smiled at us both and Mum asked what he was watching.

'I will be dead soon,' he said in English. 'It is cruel to watch these programmes on how to make my house better.'

'Stop that,' Mum replied in Gujarati.

'Will you both go back to London?' he asked. 'After—'

He stopped himself saying it. I knew and I smiled, looking at Mum, who nodded at me to answer.

'Bristol is starting to feel like home,' I said.

Dad smiled. 'This is nice to hear.'

Mum turned the television off. She separated the compartments of a tiffin on the tray table and moved it closer to Dad.

'Rus, khichdi and kadhi, lovely. Your favourites.'

Dad smiled.

'Thank you,' he replied. He looked at me. 'My son the boxer, how are you?'

I nodded that I was fine.

'Your son has his big match coming up,' Mum said. 'On Saturday.'

'Acha?' Dad replied. 'Will it be on television?'

I laughed and shook my head. Dad coughed and Mum wiped his mouth with a tissue.

'You are strong, my darling,' he said. 'Can I give you some advice?'

'Yes,' I mumbled.

'When you get in that ring on Saturday, you must not worry about me or your mummy or anyone else. You just worry about winning the fight.'

'Yes, Papa,' I said.

Mum presented him with a birthday cake and lit the candles. We sang Dad 'Happy Birthday' in English and then the Hindi Bollywood version, replacing the name Sunitha with Dad's.

I sat on the edge of his bed, laughing as Dad cheated while we played cards. It was the most human moment I had spent with him. It was the most we'd felt like a family my entire life.

As we left, well after visiting hours, Dad wished me luck, flexing a fist at me. As he smiled, his teeth caught on his dry bottom lip and I wanted to cry.

9.5

'I am going to come to your fight,' Mum said. 'Surinder has offered to buy me a ticket. I will sit with him.'

'Mum,' I said. 'I don't want you to feel you have to do that.'

I stirred some porridge. Mum hated the stuff but it had become my breakfast of choice in the training phase.

'Why? I want to support my son.'

'You can support me from here,' I said. 'It'll be tough for you to watch.'

'Why? Are you going to beat him to a pulp?'

'No,' I replied. 'I just need to be focused.'

'You will need us all around you. To help you.'

'OK,' I said.

I stopped. Mum smiled. 'I will invite Madhu too. And anyone else special in your life?'

I shook my head.

'I like you like this,' she added. 'Whatever that sport has done, you seem much more confident than you were before. Shobu has done good things with you; it is very nice.'

She paused.

'I did not think boxing was for you. But look at my boy, so very much his own self now.'

I hugged her and she held me tight.

It was the day before the fight. I had no training today. Only a three mile run and a technique class to help me stay loose. I decided to run to the police station, as I had to see Detective Roberts for something he'd asked me to come in to look at. Then I'd run on to the gym.

The run, in a circle around Bristol, was peaceful. It seemed like everyone was still asleep. Or at work, more likely. It was a Friday. There was a slight breeze, which made up for the mugginess of the last few days. I dodged a couple of cyclists and dogs, and looked out at my city as I ran alongside the M32 into town. I ran through the shopping centre, past students and buskers, crossing over to the main road and then into the police station. It felt very different to the last time I'd been into town. People moved for me this time.

9.6

Roberts met me in the lobby and led me up to a meeting room on the second floor. There was another officer waiting inside, who smiled at me and shuffled some papers before gesturing for me to sit down.

'This is Reena,' Roberts said. 'She's going to go through some photos with you. You've identified Sam but we need to try to find out who else was with him. Things are moving along.'

I sat down and Reena smiled at me.

'OK,' she said, placing a piece of paper with nine faces on it in front of me. 'Recognise anyone?'

I cast my mind back to that night. Since talking to Roberts and nailing Sam in my statement and then going back in to identify his mugshot, I'd spent every evening before going to bed doing the opposite of what my body had been trying to do since the fight. I'd been attempting to put details back in for the other two – on their faces, on the way they moved, on the things they wore. The only blank for me was the man who'd jumped me from behind. I had not had a good look at him. I'd seen the man who'd walked off. He needed to go down as well. He was complicit in an assault by witnessing it and walking away from it instead of trying to break it up.

I didn't recognise anyone on the sheet. Reena flipped over another sheet. Again, I didn't see anyone I recognised. A third one and I stopped.

There he was.

His eyebrows pursed. Bearded. Angry small eyes. Close crop of hair. That was him. The man who'd known what had been happening was wrong but had done nothing. The man who'd walked away.

I pointed.

'Him,' I said. 'That's one of them.'

'Who is he?' Reena asked.

I explained the story and she nodded, making some notes. She asked me to initial next to the photo of the man I recognised. It was strange how clearly I could see him. I hadn't got a close look at him but there he was, staring at me, and I knew exactly who he was and what he had done.

We went through the rest of the sheets and I apologised repeatedly, saying I didn't know who else had been there. I couldn't remember. I hadn't got a look at the third guy. Reena was patient with my frustration. Roberts watched everything, standing up and leaning on the door.

Finally Reena ran out of sheets to show me. She packed away her things and left the room. Roberts sat down.

'Thank you,' he said. 'You've been brilliant. I can't imagine how hard this is for you.'

'Can you nail them?'

'We're going to try our hardest. Are you OK?'

'I will be,' I said. And I meant it.

9.7

'Your father said he will come with us too. Me, him and Madhu, we are all going to come to your boxing match tomorrow,' Mum told me. She was on the phone with him in the hospice and I was heading to the gym for my technique class before the match.

'OK,' I said. 'Thank you. If you are sure . . . but . . .'

'But what?'

'I can't stop you,' I replied.

'So much enthusiasm,' Mum said, laughing. 'I hope you are more enthusiastic about your chances of winning.'

I allowed myself a smile. We said goodbye and I hung up the phone. I carried on walking along the main road, my hands in my pockets, holding my phone and earbuds together. I could hear the bass drum of some grime playing out of a car, and the hubbub of people congregating in front of a pub. I was crossing a road near the gym when I heard someone shouting.

I looked up. It was Joe, Keir's brother.

'Oi, Sunny, you shit skin, go the fuck home,' he shouted. 'I knew you'd be here eventually . . .'

I stopped in the middle of the zebra crossing, staring at him. A car beeped its horn, annoyed, and screeched around me. I bunched my fists and kept them firmly in my pocket.

Joe repeated himself. Louder. I carried on walking across the road. He moved towards me to meet me on the pavement.

'I'd go home now,' he said. 'My bro is going to kick the shit out of you and then immigration will have to deport you in a body bag.'

'Whatever, man,' I said and kept walking. 'That doesn't even make sense.'

Joe walked alongside me, repeating his threats. He kept calling me shit skin. It didn't rile me.

'He wanted to go easy on you. Do just enough to beat you. But I told him he has to crush you. Or swarms of your lot will keep on coming. Time to send a message.'

I stopped and looked at him, smiling. I let him get close enough to me that we could go for each other if we wanted. I waited. He waited.

'Nah,' I said. 'You're not worth it.'

This seemed to anger Joe. He grabbed my arm. I pulled it out of his grasp and carried on walking.

He pushed me in the back and I turned around.

'Hit me,' he said. 'Go on. You know you want to.'

I smiled, realising what was happening. I'd spotted one of his friends standing in the doorway of a disused shop – the guy from the night I'd turned up at their house – filming everything on his phone.

'I said you're not worth it. And I meant it.'

I walked off.

As I arrived at the gym, I got a text through. It was from my cousin. He said that Mum had invited him to come and watch my match tomorrow. He already had plans but wanted to come to the next one.

Give me more notice next time, Spook! Then I can cheer you on to the Olympics. Miss you, innit. Visit soon.

It made me smile. Even the use of the nickname that had given me such anxiety growing up. I replied with a thank you and told him I missed him too.

The gym was empty. It was rest day for everyone fighting in the big night tomorrow and classes didn't start for another hour. Shobu was in the ring, practising on pads with Hari.

I stopped. My heart did a little murmur of warmth on seeing him. He was drilling and Shobu was correcting his stance. He wasn't planting his feet, meaning he was off balance. They repeated the shot a bunch of times before noticing I was also in the room.

'Hey,' Hari said.

Shobu shouted, 'Wrap up. You're gonna go a few rounds with this guy.'

'What?' I said. 'With Hari Ramsaroop?'

I was, like, *Say what now?* Embarrassed. Happy. I didn't know.

'Go easy on me, bruv,' Hari said. 'I have a fight next week.'

I couldn't help myself. My grin was broader than Broadway, as the song sorta went.

I wrapped myself up and tried to slow my breathing. I was gonna spar with Hari. This was too much. I didn't feel like I deserved to be in the ring in the first place, let alone be boxing someone as good as him, but I wasn't going to pass up the opportunity.

Hari jumped around and shadow-boxed while Shobu came over to check on me.

'You OK?' she asked. 'With this . . .' She gestured behind her.

'I don't deserve this,' I said.

'Then I haven't taught you anything,' she said, smiling. 'Hari is really fast. And he is hard to catch. But what do we think about fast people?'

'Sometimes they forget to plant?'

'Exactly.'

'OK,' Shobu said, loudly, as I entered the ring. 'We're just tagging each other. Body shots only. I don't want either of you knocking each other out just before big fights. Stick to the rules, and go.'

Hari held his gloves out for me to bump them. I did and his face changed. He went from smiling and inviting to serious and concentrating. I tried to mirror him and do the same. He bopped me on the shoulder. My guard wasn't even up.

'Concentrate,' he said.

I threw my fists up.

Shobu shouted instructions to us from the side. Telling us both where to move and how to move. I was still so star-struck that I allowed Hari a few more taps. The last one was quick and hard and it shook me into remembering that we were in a combat situation, so I used his snapback time to hit him on the side.

He smiled and nodded.

'Yes, bruv,' he said. 'That's more like it.'

Shobu shouted at me to move around more. Keep my guard up. Strike. Hari kept coming and coming. I was only able to get him back on a counterstrike.

We kept dancing around each other and landing punches. It was the happiest I had been for a while.

As soon as Shobu told us to stop and rest, I burst into a grin.

'Hari,' I said. 'Thank you.'

'Bruv, I'm you,' he replied. I saw something in his eyes. This hint of a memory of something painful. He banged his glove against mine and smiled, finally. 'Stay loose. You're too stiff. You need to be loose.'

'Wise words,' Shobu said. 'Very wise words.'

Hari and I sat on the side of the ring and I ungloved so I could squirt some water in my mouth.

After a pause, he said, 'Wanna go again?'

I nodded, grinning.

*　　*　　*

I ran home, buoyed by my sparring session, and the gift Shobu had got me. She'd had some boxing shorts made with my name on the waistband in gold. Hari wished me luck for the match and he and Shobu disappeared for dinner.

At home, I was surprised to find the lights on and music playing. Confused, I walked into the kitchen to find Mum sitting with Madhu, drawing on some cardboard. They both sang away to the song and looked up when I cleared my throat.

'Hey,' Madhu said.

'Beta,' Mum replied. 'We need to feed you up before tomorrow. I saw a poster for your fight at the bus stop. When it said your name, I got excited.'

'What . . . what is going on?' I asked. 'What is all this?'

'Your cheer squad is getting ready to make the entire crowd scream your name,' Madhu said.

Mum smiled. 'I love this girl. She said you might need some support in the room. Because some of these racist benchods have been giving you a hard time. She suggested we make some placards for you. So you know you are supported.'

'Mum,' I said but my voice quivered. 'I don't know what to . . .'

I ran into my room so they wouldn't see me cry. I lay on my bed and gulped in big sobs. All these people being so nice to me, it was too much. They wanted good things for me. I deserved good things. I deserved to win. I sat up, trying to compose myself, ready to rejoin them and maybe make some food for them. I had to eat something protein based, but maybe I could make samosas for my cheer squad. I noticed an answerphone message on my phone. I didn't remember it ringing but I hadn't really paid attention. I was too excited and nervous about the fight to care about messages.

The first few seconds of the message were quiet, except for breathing. Then I heard my name, quietly.

'Sunny . . .' Then clearly, 'Sunny.' It was Keir. 'Tomorrow, I am going to knock the shit out of you. And when I'm done, I want you to know you ain't welcome at that gym any more, around those fighters, near me or my family. Do you understand? If I see you in Bristol, that beatdown is coming. I'd say goodbye to your loved ones now. You are dead. You hear me?'

I hung up the phone. I couldn't listen to the rest of the message. Sitting here, with my best friend and my mum next door, doing everything they could to make me feel supported, I suddenly felt alone and heavy again. I flopped back on to my bed and tried to steady my breathing.

Keir is tiring. I can feel a slowness in his punches now. He already gave it his best. Shobu was right. I speed up. I can take him in this round or knock him about so that he's not at his best in the last one. My movements are wild and erratic and I send him backwards and backwards and backwards. We're nearly in his corner. I can hear his coaches screaming at him to wake up, to take me, to pull himself together. One of them refers to me as the jihadi. 'Kill the jihadi.' I don't pause. I do a three hit combination, quick and deadly. Keir rolls with the punches so I land a couple of blows to his face and I see his eyes close shut, for just a second.

When he opens them, his guard is slightly dropped, so I draw power up through the canvas and land a punch on his chin that sends him to the floor.

This wakes him up.

Keir stands to his feet as the bell rings. His coaches call him in.

I look around me. Shobu is ushering me towards her. I walk up to the referee instead.

'What's the problem?' he asks me. 'Get back to your corner.'

'Did you hear that?' I say, watching Shobu throw up her hands, like, *What's wrong?*

'What?' the referee says.

'One of their coaches called me a jihadi. Can you tell them to shut up with the slurs?'

'I didn't hear them. Get back to your corner.'

'So what if you didn't hear them?' I shout, annoyed. 'It's your job. And I'm telling you. Isn't that enough?'

'Get back to your corner.'

'Fine,' I say. 'Allow racism. On your watch.'

'Want me to penalise you?' the referee says, towering over me.

'Whatever,' I say and push past him. I hear Keir and his team jeer behind me. A swell from the crowd follows.

Back in my corner, I sit down. Shobu squirts water into my mouth.

'What the hell was that?'

'Nothing,' I say, keeping my eyes on Keir.

Round 10

When the bell rings, Keir springs up, ready to go. I stay seated.

It's the last round. Time for things to end. Time for this all to be over. Time for that knot in my stomach to get stretched out. Time for life inside and outside this ring to collide. We respect these rules for a reason. They keep the chaos out. But I can feel the outside world creeping in.

I stay in my seat. I remember waking up this morning. I remember going for a walk around the canal. I remember watching the only YouTube video of Shobu fighting on my phone at home. I remember eating khichdi, which Mum only usually made when I was unwell, because I thought it'd be perfect good. I remember walking here. I remember sitting in the changing rooms, waiting for Shobu to arrive, sweating in my hoodie and tracksuit bottoms. I remember getting out my shorts and changing from my tracksuit bottoms but leaving the hoodie on. I remember not choosing the kicks Keir gifted me but deciding to stick with my old favourites, my shit beaten-up hand-me-down Nikes from my cousin. I remember wanting to be sick. I remember Shobu forcing me to meditate. We did those four-eight-four breaths. In for four, out for eight, four times. I steadied myself. First my feet, then my legs, then my pelvis, then my torso, all the way up my spine to my nose. I rolled my body down, breathing slowly, imagining every single bone folding in a roll on top of each other. I remember seeing Keir arrive and staring at me. I remember the slow walk to the ring from the changing room as they played a song Surinder had selected for me. It was Panjabi MC. But the Jay-Z remix, so as soon as the song kicked up it announced that the Roc was in the building. And here I was. A rock. The crowd laughed at that. I remember shaking the referee's hand as I entered and bouncing up and down in the ring, feeling my nerves falter, seeing everyone around me.

I remember finally taking off my hoodie and feeling the clamminess in the air oozing slick all over my body. I remember Shobu slipping the gloves on to my hands. I remember realising that I couldn't see where Dad and Madhu and Mum and Surinder were sitting. Which was good. I remember Keir walking out to 'Ante Up' by M.O.P. I remember the lights making me feel hot, and the quivering core of cold I felt around my heart. I remember being brought to the middle to touch gloves with Keir and hearing the ground rules from the referee. I remember Keir avoiding eye contact with me. I remember feeling like everything was moving too quickly and my brain was struggling to keep up.

Does any of this even matter? Shobu kept saying to save it for the ring. *And here we are. Is this what we were saving it for? Could some things be hashed out here only? Or is there a problem still being ignored? Or swept under the carpet? Or whitewashed? So does any of this stuff truly matter?*

I remember my brain not having time to process the questions.

Cos the bell rang.

'You coming?' the referee shouts. 'Shah, come on. Last round.'

I shake my head. He walks over.

'What's the problem?' he barks at me.

'You need to keep the racism out of the ring,' I say. 'I will not fight if you don't do your job.'

The referee crouches down and hisses in my face, 'I said, I didn't hear it. I can't do anything if I don't hear it.'

Shobu tuts.

'You could believe Sunny for a start,' she says.

The referee stands up and looks around.

'OK,' he says. 'OK. Come on.'

I bait him out for as long a pause as I dare and then I stand up.

'There's banter and there's unacceptable shit,' I say, as I walk past him.

I'm mad as hell. Like Shobu said a while back, *'I am always angry. Always. I'm like the Hulk. All of the time in my head. Because there is all this shit going on . . .'*

There is all this shit going on. And it never ends. I lost a part of myself at that train station. I fought to be seen as human again. And I am angry. But everything since that event, at the train station, has led me here, and I have never felt more myself.

The trick is accepting that's how I feel. And that is OK. Because I have every right to be damn angry.

Keir is waiting for me.

He makes an explosion noise as I approach. I side-eye the referee but he chooses to ignore it.

The bell rings. People cheer. But it all fades into silence as I remember this is the last round. I have to win. Either on points or by knocking him out. There is no option to fail. All roads have led us here.

We punch at each other.

Everything slows to this tessellated second where I can feel everything in me vibrating. Pulling me towards Keir like we are magnets.

Pulse. Pulse. Pulse.

Our bodies move in perfect balletic slow motion as we careen towards each other at great speed. It can only end one way.

We're the only ones in the room.

I don't recognise him. The anger in his eyes. That isn't my friend Keir. The tensed shoulders. That isn't my friend Keir either. That cheap shot of an explosion noise. That is definitely not my friend. And yet, here we are. Together. Friends no more. Trading blows like this is for keeps not for sport.

My jab catches his chin again. His guard is low. I follow it through with a cross. From the sprung floor through to my toes to my calf to my knee to my hip . . . all the way up my core to my shoulder to my arm to my fist to my knuckle. Everything goes into the punch.

Dad getting cancer ... us moving city ... having to start again ... being beaten up for being brown ... making a new friend ... losing that friend to an ideology that wants me dead ... being treated like I'm subhuman.

When life knocks you down, you *can* learn to fight back.

So I put everything into that cross.

Everything.

Every atom of me is in that cross. Every damn thing. Everything I have.

And when it lands on Keir's mouth, spraying blood across the ring, and he falls backwards against the ropes, I remember to snap my fist back into a guard position. Strong. Ready to strike again. Ready to block.

He is stunned from the force of my punch and his eyes widen as he steadies himself up to standing. I let him.

He comes at me again and we link arms till we're chest to chest, pushing against each other, trying to free ourselves so we can trade blows. The magnets. Connected as he pushes me out into the centre of the ring.

'Paaaaaaaki,' Keir sings in my ear. 'Come on, paki ... What you gonna doooo, paaaaki?'

He knows the effect that word has on me. He's taunting me. Thinking he'll knock my concentration.

But I am calm this time.

I remember Shobu once saying to me, early on, during that first day when she was showing me around, that the trick to fighting is knowing when to fight and when not to fight.

And in that second, I realise something. The trick to fighting is knowing when to fight and when not to fight.

I remember that feeling on the train platform. It isn't about defending myself or fighting back. It is about getting up and walking away.

What am I doing?

Why I am here?

Who am I fighting and why?

What am I doing this for? I think.

More importantly, who?

I know what I have to do.

I push myself off Keir and step back, ripping the Velcro from one of my gloves. He weaves towards me with his gloves up. I drop my glove to the floor. I pull the Velcro off the other one and I drop that to the floor as well.

I hold my hands up. There is a shift in the crowd as it quietens awkwardly. People are listening, I can hear them. But they're all whispering, asking each other what is happening. The referee moves so he is in between me and Keir.

'What's the problem? Can't take a beatdown?' Keir screams.

I turn and walk away from him. He will not dehumanise me. I am a fighter. I am a person. I am a boxer. I am a human being. I do not fight for the right to be recognised as such.

Shobu enters the ring and runs to me as I grab a rope and step out of the ring.

Keir is screaming at me. The referee grabs my hand. I wrench it out of his grasp.

'Where are you going?' he shouts.

I look at him. And in that moment, he's not the referee. He's unsure. He seems smaller. He seems quieter. Worried.

'You didn't do your job,' I tell him.

Keir runs over. 'Get your arse back in here,' he shouts. 'Finish this fight.'

Stand up. Walk away.

I look at him and then I step down on to the ground.

It's all I've ever wanted. To stand up and walk away.

'No, Keir,' I turn and say. 'No way.'

It's not my fault.

It was never my fault.

I head to the changing room by myself. I can hear him shouting at me to come back and face him. I keep my eyes forward. I can hear Shobu calling my name, Keir shouting swear words, the referee yelling, but none of it matters. I'm gone. I'm done now. I don't have to fight. As I pass the crowd, I allow myself a smile. I feel alive. I feel more myself than I have felt in a long time. I feel happy.

Recovery

I'm running away the aches in my knees, flexing my fists open and shut. My knuckles are bruised. My face is sore. I should be resting. But this is the first time I've been by myself in days so I'm running for as long as I can manage.

I don't have earbuds in so I can hear the twinkle of birds and the rustle of trees and the *tuk-tuk* of cycle wheels. I'm by myself and I feel good.

Madhu tried to show me the piece they wrote about me in the local paper, about the brave teenager who stood up to racism. But I didn't need to read it to know why I did what I did. Shobu and Hari found me in the changing room after the fight and I told them both what had happened. They gave me big hugs and told me how brave I was and how proud they were of me. I tried to tell them I didn't do this out of bravery. I did this because I had to. I took a stand.

'You did the right thing,' Shobu said.

And I think, *Of course I did.* I have never been more sure of anything in my life.

Surinder drove me, Mum and Dad back to the hospice. They were all in tears, but I was calm the whole time, smiling.

When Mum took Dad inside, Surinder asked what I was smiling about.

'I feel like myself,' I said, quietly, and he didn't ask me anything else. He knew.

I got a text from Keir days later that said: **SORRY**. That's all it said. I didn't need to reply. I had the closure I needed.

Mostly I just ate. The two days after the fight, I ate samosas, dhal, bhatt, shaak, rotli, pizza, KFC – everything I hadn't been allowed to have. Until Shobu intervened with a protein shake one morning.

I hobbled around my area. I sat on a bench and watched the world go by. Summer was starting and I needed to find a job. Just to tide me over till term started again. I'd do my final year. And I'd do it well.

Sam won't be prosecuted, Roberts phoned me to say. Blocked by his boss. He was so apologetic. I almost didn't care. Everything had lifted. I did what I needed to do. I stood up and I walked away.

I'm going to see Dad this afternoon. When I get home from my run, Madhu is going to bring over a recipe for kadhi, Dad's favourite. Mum can't make it very well, according to Dad. We're going to cook the kadhi, steam some rice and take it over for him in the hospice. I'm going to give him some magazines too.

I'm no longer afraid. And I love my family – the one I'm related to and the one I've found here in this new city.

Maybe in the future, I can finish out a match.

Until then, I'm hopeful.

And training starts again the day after tomorrow.

Acknowledgements

Thank you to my editor Emma Goldhawk for being the Shobu to my Sunny, and to my publicist Emily Thomas for being the Madhu to my Sunny. Thank you to everyone at Hodder Children's Books and Hachette. Writing for teenagers and young adults has been a dream. I love doing school visits. If you want a school visit, get in touch.

This book started life as an actual incident that happened late at night on a train, to me. Having taken up boxing since, I've learned more about myself, my body, my confidence, my ability to take up space and my own resilience. I owe a debt of gratitude to everyone at Empire Fighting Chance in Bristol, who welcomed me with open arms.

Thank you to Anne-Marie Bullock, the BBC Radio 4 producer for commissioning my one-on-one series that led to fascinating conversations with writer Hayley Campbell, promoter and ex-boxer Kieran Farrell, and criminologist Dr Deborah Jump. These conversations ended up forming the themes of the book and the journey that Sunny goes through. Thank you to Thomas Page McBee for his book *Amateur*, which details his training for his first ever boxing match. I read it while editing this and it gave me pause to think about the mentality of those who choose to fight. Thank you to my editors at *Observer Magazine*, Shahesta Shaitly and Harriet

Green, who encouraged me to write a four-part column about learning to box during my short tenure as a columnist. It clarified, for me, what I wanted this book to be.

Thank you to writer and boxer Robert Kazandjian for his support in ensuring the language used around boxing was sensitive to the sport and accurate as well.

Thank you to librarians, in schools, prisons and in public libraries, who do the work of putting books into our hands when we need them the most. Thank you to booksellers for doing the same. You are all the MVPs of this industry.

Thank you to my agent Julia Kingsford for being the heavyweight champion of the world.

I once asked a writer I admired for some advice. He said, 'Don't ask for permission.' He then took my book to sign and said, 'I never know what to write so I just imagine what Jean-Claude Van Damme would write.' He signed my book: 'Stay tough . . . next time we fight.' Thanks to him, I have never asked for permission. And I'm ready if he ever wants a match.

Racism is bad, folks. Really bad. It's 2019 and I shouldn't have to be telling you this. But in the times we live in, it sadly bears repeating.

Discussion Points

- *'I couldn't take the train. I knew that. The thought made my lungs feel like they were filled with hot air.'*
  Sunny experiences an extremely traumatic event that impacts on his everyday life. We can see it in his fear of taking the train – can you identify any other moments when Sunny displays symptoms of trauma?

- If you or someone you know was racially abused, what would you do? Would you call the police? If not, why not?

- *'Why had they called me a Paki?'*
  Sunny is surprised by his attackers' use of racist slurs to verbally abuse him. Why do you think this is?

- One of Sunny's reasons for beginning to box is so that he can dominate his own space. What does owning your space mean to you?

- *'Sunil, we've totally misjudged you.'*
  Martin and Joe project stereotypes onto Sunny. Why is racial stereotyping and labelling wrong?

- What are the reasons for the breakdown of Keir and Sunny's friendship?

- *It was my fault.'*
  Sunny repeatedly blames himself for the situation he finds himself in, as opposed to blaming others and allowing them to be accountable. Why do you think he does that?

- Is there a moment in the story that, if things had happened differently, might have prevented Keir becoming radicalised? How much do you think Keir is to blame for what happens to him?